CW01656451

THE WRONG VICTIMS

The Wrong Victims

Graham H Miller

OFFICIAL
WOOTENSHIRE
LICENCE

Published by Graham H Miller Cyf

ISBN 978-1-9161307-5-3

Typesetting services by BOOKOW.COM

ACKNOWLEDGMENTS

Thank you to Rosie Cranie-Higgs for her valuable insights as a check reader, Dane from eBook Launch for the cover design and to Melanie Underwood for her skills as an editor.

Chapter One

Eileen dragged the heavy cart behind her. She should have known better than to drink on a work night, but her friends had all been out and she was easily led. Now she had a hangover. At least her job as a chambermaid didn't need her to think too hard. She could clean a room in less time than most of these new, Eastern European teenagers. And when she'd done her allocated floor of rooms, she would go home. If they wanted to hang about on other floors gossiping, let them. She wasn't helping.

She came to the final room of the corridor. She knocked and called out, 'Housekeeping!' No reply. She waited a few seconds, head cocked to listen. No sound. She tried the handle – the room was locked. There was no "do not disturb" sign. She called out and knocked one more time. Silence. She hesitated for a second. She'd had more than enough experience of walking into a room to find a naked man casually walking out of the shower or playing with himself. As she always went through this routine before entering a room, she knew it was intentional. But this time, there was nothing – no shower, just silence.

Deciding the room was empty, with one swipe of the pass key she opened the door, leaving the cart in the corridor and dragging the hoover behind her.

She stopped and sniffed. There was a strange smell. A bit metallic, maybe coppery. Had there been an electrical fire? And it was cold. She shivered. But she was used to guests doing weird things with the air conditioning.

She was in the narrow corridor with the bathroom on her left. Beyond that the room opened up to its full size. She could see the desk, chair and a slice of the foot of the bed. She couldn't smell any sort of smoke, so there wasn't an electrical fire or illegal cooking by a guest.

The curtains were drawn and only the main light was on, giving the room an odd timeless feeling – it could've been any time of day or night. She glanced into the bathroom to see how bad the job was going to be. Pleasantly surprised, she saw it was clean and tidy, all the towels in the bath.

Shrugging, she continued into the room. There was a man sat up on the bed, leaning against the headboard. As she stepped forward, he turned to face her and his eyes opened.

'Sorry,' she stammered.

Something was very wrong. He was deathly pale and there was a deep red cut around his neck. He was dead. And looking at her even though there was no life in his eyes. He was dead and he had turned to look at her.

Her brain struggled to make sense of the facts and failed.

He was obviously dead, his skin was like marble and there was a chill in the room. Yet, equally obviously he had turned to her and opened his eyes.

She had no idea what to do, so she carefully shuffled one step further into the room abandoning her hoover in the hallway.

Then, the dead-not-dead man moved a hand across the coverlet, as if trying to reach her. The very last vestiges of control that she had melted away as his body overbalanced and fell towards her. But only his body.

His head stayed where it was, hovering against the wall. His eyes remained open, and stared emptily into hers. Her bladder let go. The warm rush down her legs was the only real thing left that made any sense at all.

Eileen stood stock still, transfixed by the scene. The body had come to a halt, lying across the bed, the arm brushing the floor. He was a headless corpse, endlessly searching for his keys under the bed.

Her brain shut down all higher thought. Nothing made sense any more. She didn't scream, she didn't run. She turned, tripped over the hoover, and walked, like a zombie, out of the room. She carefully shut the door, making sure it clicked locked and walked back up the corridor to reception. When her manager found her, she was sat in a chair with a pool of vomit between her feet. She wouldn't say anything except to mumble the room number over and over again.

Within minutes, the manager had been to the room, seen the situation with his own eyes and was back in reception. He'd also had the presence of mind to lock the door and had managed to keep his distress to a quiet series of profanities muttered under his breath. After so long in the hotel trade, the last thing he wanted to do was scare the guests.

He reached for the phone with a trembling hand.

Chapter Two

Emma Angel stood in the foyer of the police station, suddenly unsure of her ground. The sergeant behind the desk was similarly unsettled. He took one look at her, nodded in greeting then went off to make a phone call.

She hadn't had a warrant card since that evening several weeks ago when the raid on the warehouse had gone so disastrously wrong. Aside from one long morning of interviews with Professional Standards, she hadn't been on police property or even had contact with her department. Now she'd been instructed to return to work.

She was met by the impeccably groomed DS Maxine Jones who nodded curtly at the sergeant and beckoned DC Angel to follow her into the station. DC Angel bristled a bit at being escorted into her own station but there was nothing she could do about it now.

Soon they were seated in an anonymous meeting room with coffees from the machine.

DS Jones smiled and slid a clear envelope across the table to DC Angel. 'First of all, Emma, thank you for your patience in all this. I know these things take time, and I can appreciate how worrying it must be. So I wanted to return these to you first to set your mind at rest.'

DC Angel shook out the envelope, retrieved her warrant card and slipped it into her pocket then put her security pass around her neck. She wouldn't admit to herself how much happier, more complete, it made her.

'Now that's out of the way,' DS Jones said, 'I can update you on the investigation. We've completed out the preliminary enquiries and all the evidence we've gathered corroborates your statement.'

'The two bodyguards?'

DS Jones looked down at a file. 'Yes, Trevor Swain and Kim Lawson. They're both going down the "no comment" route. It doesn't matter, Billy King's blood is all over Lawson's clothes and the knife, which only has his prints. Likewise, we recovered a short wooden truncheon which had only Swain's prints and DCI Haines' blood and hair. There's little doubt they acted together, so we're preparing charges of murder and attempted murder against both of them.' She stopped being official and looked up at DC Angel with warmth and respect. 'I have to say, Emma, there's no doubt that you saved DCI Haines' life. I'm not sure I'd have rushed in against two huge guys like that with no backup.'

'I didn't really think,' Emma said, flustered. Michelle Jones with her oriental looks and sleek black hair had always been unreadable to her. She wasn't used to being complimented by her. 'I could see that he was in trouble and rushed in. To be honest I got lucky. I should've hung back and called it in. But if I'd done that, well, I doubt Haines would still be with us.'

'Well, we're all glad you didn't. The last thing we need is a police funeral.'

'So, my behaviour on the day?' Emma asked. 'The injuries that I inflicted on those two bodyguards?'

'Entirely justified. They were both armed, and there was a clear danger both to other officers and the general public.' She stopped, as if considering whether to confide in DC Angel. 'In fact, I shouldn't say this but a file has been prepared for the chief constable. I expect you'll be getting a commendation out of this.'

Not knowing how to reply to this, DC Angel just nodded, her head spinning. She had been scared in that alleyway and didn't feel like she deserved anything. She rubbed one hand over the other, feeling the nearly invisible scars where she'd grazed her knuckles.

Without thinking, she rubbed the back of her head and down to her ear where she'd also been injured. Although everything was healed, it was a nervous tic that she couldn't shake.

'So, what happens now?'

'Now? You go straight back to work. Obviously there have been a lot of changes in CID so you'll need to get used to the new team. And if you have any problems settling back into routine work or any issues relating to the traumatic event you've been through, counselling is always available, totally confidential.'

'Changes? Who will I recognise?' Emma was concerned again. As well as tackling the bodyguards, she had also arranged for her entire team to be investigated by Professional Standards. What had happened? Would she still be welcome?

'Well, Haines is still off on medical leave, and obviously we've arrested Hargreaves so he's suspended. Aside from that, the whole team is also suspended with the one exception of DS Andrew Stonor who's been demoted to detective constable.'

'Andy's been demoted, why?'

'It's not for me to comment on another officer's case.'

'Oh, come on, if it wasn't for me you'd still be sniffing around the edges of the case.' Emma sat back and thought through what had happened that night. 'In fact, if it wasn't for me, both King and Haines would be dead, and Glen Hargreaves would've walked straight through the cordon and set Garoza up as the big name in Bradwick. You'd have been back to square one, except far worse off.'

Maxine nodded slowly. 'Well, as you told me, the whole department was corrupt. All skimming money and hiding it in accounts all over the place. Forensic accountants are still chasing it down. It appears that Stonor never actually took a penny. At least, if he did, we can't find any proof. But on the other hand, he was very good at looking the other way. He can't have been that deeply embedded in the department for so long and not have some idea what was going on. So we've issued him a reprimand on his record and put him down to detective constable for not reporting crimes being committed.' She paused and leant forward, as if unsure whether or not to continue. 'There were high-level discussions about Bradwick CID. One side favoured moving everyone out and installing a whole new team. But I, along with others, argued that some continuity was essential. So that's why you're not being reassigned and why Andy Stonor's still got a job.'

Emma sat back and thought. That was a lot of pressure on her shoulders. She'd been in CID for all of five minutes and now she was expected to carry the torch and help the new people understand the territory of Bradwick? On the other hand, amid the chaos, she still had a job and approval from her bosses. Sometimes that was all you could hope for.

* * *

There was no way to avoid it. DC Angel was led into her own department. Except it didn't feel like it. She had a weird nod from DS Andy Stonor, who was now DC Stonor. And there was a crowd of strangers in the office.

'So,' DS Maxine Jones was still talking, 'let's start at the top. This is the new boss of the department, Detective Inspector Kevin Slater.'

'Morning, boss,' Emma said, holding out her hand to shake. Slater was a short man in his late fifties or even early sixties. He had short grey hair. He looked neat and precise.

'And,' DS Jones led Emma over to the open area, 'this is Detective Sergeant Susan Berman.'

'You can call me Suse, everyone else does.' She shook Emma's hand in a firm grip. Emma took an instant dislike to her. Suse? Not Sue, or Susie or Susan, but something halfway in between. It was almost like she was going out of her way to be difficult.

Suse was taller and larger than Emma with a stocky body and a short, unflattering hairstyle. Unfortunately she had rather a large square face as well. Even though it was the era of political correctness, hashtag me too and sensitivity training, Emma had no doubt that Suse would've put up with a lot of whispers about female rugby players and lesbians all the way through from school into the police locker room. No amount of rainbow flags and diversity workshops could change the fundamental male officer mindset.

'And this is the other sergeant, Brian Chisholm.'

Emma tried to hide her surprise as the other man shook her hand. He was obviously, like DI Slater, older. She knew the pension age had crept up to sixty but he must be close to that. His hair was full grey, cropped close to hide where it was thinning. He had a big red nose, lined with veins from excessive drinking. He wasn't particularly tall, but he was quite overweight. Whatever his age, he didn't look like he'd be able to pass the current fitness tests.

As if reading her thoughts, DS Jones continued, 'DS Chisholm has worked in nearly every department across the force. His experience will really help the team at this difficult time.'

Emma dutifully shook his hand and wondered why he had moved around so much without progressing beyond the rank of sergeant.

'You know Andy Stonor, of course,' DS Jones said, and Andy dutifully waved. 'Which only leaves our newest recruit, Detective Constable Nicholas Dent.'

He ambled over to shake her hand. Whether it was because Emma had just met DS Chisholm or not, he looked about twelve. He was tall and lanky with a shock of ginger hair and had a round face that looked still unformed.

Emma went to sit at her desk, log into the computer and see what had been happening in Bradwick while she'd been gone. As she suspected, violence and drug offences were both up. A month ago they'd disrupted a large smuggling operation, and a different network had also been inadvertently disrupted when its head was killed. Reading between the lines of the reports it was now a free for all on the streets of Bradwick.

She resolved to check in with Lukas, her friend and paid informer. He'd know what was actually happening on the streets. She also thought around the structure of her new team. Slater and Chisholm were both easy to understand. Officers at the end of their careers who'd been enticed to come back in for a final six months. Whatever favours or inducements had been offered, they'd be there for the short term to ensure that CID was on an even keel before permanent replacements could be found.

She looked carefully over the top of her screen at Chisholm. Detective Sergeant Brian Chisholm. She rolled the name around her mind, trying see if it sounded familiar. Was he once Inspector Chisholm? Had there been a fall from grace?

She made a mental note to ask DCI Rob Haines if there was any history there. As soon as she'd had the thought, she felt the deep loss like a punch to the gut. She had spent the past few weeks under investigation by Professional Standards, so contact with any member of her team had been forbidden.

She had desperately wanted to find out how he was doing and had relied on the rumour mill. She had found out that he was out of hospital and back home, but that was all she knew. Several times, in a moment of weakness she had brought up Rob Haines' number on her phone but had stopped before she hit the call button.

Her entire team had been under investigation and had all been interviewed separately about the events that led up to the drug raid. If she'd been in contact with someone else also under suspicion then her job would've been on the line. She knew that in this day and age there was no way to get in touch with her old boss without leaving a trace. Any contact between them could add up to a whole heap of trouble.

Until today, she'd managed, more or less, to put him out of her mind. She couldn't help looking over at Rob Haines' office. But the person behind the desk was DI Kev Slater instead. Now she was out from under the cloud of suspicion, she would go round to Haines' house after work and find out what had happened. And get the unofficial information on her new team.

This resolution was tinged with nerves. She had been instrumental in the collapse of the police raid and the Professional Standards operation. She knew, in her heart, that if she hadn't got involved, then she would've lined up with the rest of her squad, stab vest on and ready to charge in. If that had happened, then DCI Haines would be dead and Bradwick's drug scene would be controlled by a drug baron working with a corrupt police officer.

The problem was how could she explain to her boss and friend that while she had saved his life, she'd also betrayed him and his secrets and ultimately led to his being under investigation. It would be a very delicate conversation – Rob Haines highly valued loyalty in his officers and although she wasn't going to run from a difficult situation, she still wasn't looking forward to it. Hopefully, Rob Haines would see that she'd acted in his best interests.

She was also curious as to what had become of him. Last time she'd seen him, he was being loaded into an ambulance. But in her experience, mild concussion was usually an overnight stay in hospital for observation followed by a return to work. She knew that following injuries to sports stars, concussion was treated more seriously but she still couldn't see how he'd swung weeks and weeks off work.

In anyone else she would've suspected a ruse to escape the investigation but this was Rob Haines. He had old-school values – work hard, play hard and go down with the team. He was the last person she'd expect to skive and dodge the consequences of his actions. Despite her misgivings she would have to go and see him and see what was up.

Emma took furtive glances at the rest of her team. There was something about the other sergeant, Suse, that set her on edge. She carried herself in a way that was just beyond assertive, almost aggressive. Emma understood that you had to stand your ground in the police, but something about the other woman unsettled her. She was just a bit too confrontational.

Her musings were disturbed when the phone rang.

She picked it up and was soon talking to a constable.

'We've got a body for you at the motel on the services. The one on the junction with the A361?'

'Yes,' Emma said. She could picture it, one step down from a motorway services with a big chain motel, petrol station and café that was also a chain. 'What's the deal? People die in hotels. Call the pathologist and the coroner and get it checked out. If he's absolutely certain that it's murder, then call us out.'

'Oh no. The pathologist is on his way. But trust me, this is not a natural death. You need to be out here.'

'You can't just say that. I need details before I leave my desk.'

'I'd really rather not say. But this is a murder case. And CID need to be here.'

'All right then.' Emma shook her head. Bloody overdramatic uniform PCs. He'd obviously watched too many police dramas on TV and thought that this approach would fast-track him into CID.

'I'm off out,' she called across to Suse, who was her nearest superior.

'What's up?'

'Some uniform over at the motel on the main road services. Has a body, he's certain it's murder.'

'God! Can't he wait for the pathologist, then make a decision? Why do CID have to be in so soon?'

'He was insistent but wouldn't say why over the phone.'

'Right. If he's pissing you about, get his name and number and I'll get our boss to have a word with his boss.' She stopped to make sure that Emma was listening. 'Have you been out there? It's pretty much a full on turf war. We can't be out and about holding a uniform's hand just because he found a body.'

Chapter Three

Soon Emma was parked up outside the motel. Even at lunchtime on a sunny day it was a depressing place. The traffic from the main road droned in the background and she could see across the car park to the petrol station, with the café set off to the right. She walked towards the motel and joined a group of people standing outside reception. She glanced in – it had a slightly worn dark carpet, small lobby, and white chipboard reception desk.

She was greeted by the uniform, who was strangely subdued, even worried. All thoughts that he was somehow winding up CID evaporated.

'Good that you're here. I've summoned everyone else – the coroner and scene of crimes. But you should have a look first. There's the manager over there, he'll sort you out. It's room one two seven, end of one of the ground floor corridors.'

Emma's disquiet increased when the manager gave her a passkey and directions but refused to accompany her to the room. She went through the reception and suddenly understood why everyone was stood outside. Someone, presumably the chambermaid who'd found the body and then wet herself, had sat down in the only chair and then thrown up on the carpet. Given that reception was a small room with a glass front and one door into the rest of the hotel, the smell was intolerable on a hot day. She went through into the motel, which was now strangely quiet. It was the period between checkout and in so it should've been busy with the sound of hoovers as the rooms were turned around. But she'd seen all the other chambermaids outside.

What had she walked into? Finally she got to the room and slid the passkey through the lock. At first, it was just a normal room, bathroom off to the left making a narrow corridor. But when she got into the room and looked at the bed, she had a shock.

A head was fixed to the wall, looking at her.

She blinked, and then forced herself to examine the rest of the room. The body was lying across the bed, one arm hanging down to the floor. There was some sort of bracket screwed into the wall to support the head. And the air conditioning had been turned on to full cold. The head was at the height it would have been if the man had been sat on the bed, bent at the waist and leaning against the wall. And the feet were in the right place too – that was obviously the position he had fallen from.

She nodded slowly to herself. There was no point in trying to explain this over the phone. And no doubt whatsoever that it was anything but a murder.

She didn't dare move, for fear of contaminating evidence, so she stayed stock still and let her eyes roam over all the details. Not much blood on the bed or wall, so he was killed elsewhere and brought here. There was a bright red and white poster on the small desk below the television. That stood out, as the only other belongings in the room were the usual – an open overnight bag, a jacket over the chair and a laptop on the desk, half under the poster.

Not theft then, she thought. And she could smell blood, and death in the air. She stepped back into her footsteps and looked into the bathroom. The smell was stronger there and she could see small flecks of reddish brown here and there.

She carefully backed out of the room and removed her gloves and overshoes after locking the door. First job would be to find out if the victim was the occupant. If so, then he was most likely killed in the bathroom and dragged to the bed.

She walked back down the corridor to be met by the pathologist and the scenes of crimes.

'Watch yourselves, lads,' she said. 'It's a bit of a weird one. Proper spooky.'

They all looked at her funny, but nodded and muttered thanks.

'So, you've seen him then,' the manager asked. Emma nodded. 'Eileen, the chambermaid, said that he turned to look at her, but he can't have done, can he?'

'No, he's definitely dead. No doubt about that.' She looked at the group of chambermaids who were chatting and smoking, a bit off to one side. 'Is Eileen here? Can we interview her?'

'No, I'm sorry, she was obviously in a state. I called her a taxi to take her home and get cleaned up if nothing else. I'll give you her details. But there would've been no point anyway. She hasn't said a word except to give us the room number.'

'Okay. Well if you give us her details, we can take it from there. Can we also have the details of who had room one two seven last night?'

Emma and the manager went back through the reception and into his office where he gave her all the information she needed.

Chapter Four

Emma stood outside the neat front door of the detached house in a nice suburb of Bradwick. She'd last been here several weeks before, when she had started a train of events that had torn Rob Haines' world apart. And had turned her own professional life on its head. Now she was back to atone for her sins.

She knocked on the door.

Jem Haines, all dark curls and effortless chic opened it, nervously at first, then flung it wide. 'It's Emma Angel isn't it? From Rob's work? Is everything all right?'

'Yes, yes, it's all fine,' Emma said. 'It's just a social visit.' She had to explain. It was the curse of the police officer – her arrival anywhere usually heralded bad news. 'I wanted to see how he is.' She caught something flicker across the other woman's face but couldn't identify the emotion. 'It's just that Professional Standards have been investigating and while that was ongoing, I've not been allowed to contact any of my colleagues. But I went back to work today, so here I am.' She stopped again, aware that she'd been talking away but something was wrong.

'Not to worry, you're here now, do come on in,' Jem said. She went back into the house, calling out, 'Rob! You've got a visitor.'

Emma was shown into a living room where Rob was sat on a sofa. He paused a black and white film as she came in. He looked up for a moment, and focused on Emma and his wife. Something flickered across his face, but Emma couldn't read it. Was it fear, or frustration or incomprehension?

Somehow though, Jem picked it up. With false brightness she repeated, 'Rob, look, it's Emma Angel from your team, from CID.'

Emma didn't know what was going on but was distracted when she properly saw Rob. She was shocked by his appearance but tried not to show it. His hair was no longer curly – instead he had a fuzz of even dark hair right across his scalp. He was wearing a baggy dark grey T-shirt and tracksuit trousers. He was even wearing slippers. He'd lost weight but in a way that made him look gaunt instead of healthier. All the time she'd known him, he'd been in the office, with shirt and tie. Now she was unsure how to deal with him looking so different.

'Oh yeah,' Haines said, catching her staring. 'The hair. They kept shaving bits here and there to see how the cut above my ear was healing and to stick electrodes on and look inside my head. As soon as I got out of the hospital, I had it all shaved off, nice and even. It'll grow back.' He ran his fingers over it, lingering above his right ear where a cut was almost totally healed.

Emma nodded. 'I was just saying to Jem that we've all been under investigation so I wasn't allowed to contact anyone from CID so that's why I haven't been round earlier. How are you? Did they keep you long in hospital?'

'Nearly a week all told. Apparently I had swelling on the brain and they wanted to keep me under observation until it sorted itself out. But I'm home and fighting fit now!' Emma could tell forced jollity when she heard it.

'So, you're recovered?' DC Angel asked, sitting on the sofa. 'Will we see you back at the office? What have you been doing with your time?'

'He's been cluttering up the place, watching old films and shouting at the TV,' Jem said, coming back in. 'The kettle's on and I can rustle up some biscuits. What do you want to drink?'

'Milky tea, one sugar,' DC Angel said automatically.

The silence stretched out, only punctuated by the sounds of Jem making tea that floated in from the kitchen. Finally Haines said blankly, 'I can't come back to work.' He paused and Emma was about to ask him to explain when he continued. 'I'm trapped. The hospital say that I've got retrograde amnesia. It means I can't remember anything for several days before the attack and my memories start again the next day, lying in a hospital bed.

'Professional Standards can't interview me while I'm on medical leave as the doctors will say that my memory is unreliable.' He stopped and looked a bit uncomfortable. 'But I can remember most of it, going back years, all that's still up here.' He tapped the side of his head. 'The problem is that if they declare that I'm fit to return to work, I'll be suspended from duty before the doctor's ink is dry on the form.'

The mood was broken as Jem came back into the room with a tray of drinks and a plate of biscuits.

'You said you couldn't recall the days before the attack, sir,' Emma said carefully, sipping her tea even though it was too hot. 'But you remember everything before that?'

'Oh yes. I remember that very well. Some days it seems that the further back I go, the clearer the memories are. Me and Billy King. Hargreaves and Patterson.' He stopped and stared into space.

'But those last few days?' DC Angel prompted.

'Nope.' He shook his head. 'I remember we had a third victim who survived and you went to interview her in the hospital. Then I met with Billy and he gave me the information to set up that big raid on the industrial estate outside Bradwick. After that, nothing until I woke up in hospital.' He stopped and frowned. 'You know that I was working with Billy King, don't you? Information from him in return for protection from me? And of course, we'd split whatever we could skim off the raids on other dealers. All fairly done, cash to me and the team, product to him.'

Even Rob Haines sensed the mood in the room. Emma and Jem looked at each other nervously.

'I've done it again, haven't I?' Rob asked. 'The doctors say it will get better, but I don't have any filter. I just think something and I say it. That's the real reason I'm not going back to work. I know that Professional Services will crucify me. If they catch me on a bad day and ask the right question, then I'll just tell them everything. I'll ride out the medical leave as long as it takes for the Police Federation to work out a deal.' He looked downbeat. 'I've come to accept that the best outcome for me will probably involve leaving with my pension and honour intact and not having to answer any questions.'

DC Angel felt the ground being cut out from under her. She hadn't known what to expect when she went round to see her former boss, but it wasn't this. All those events from weeks earlier crowded back in on her. Patterson, Dark Car Man, Hargreaves and Garoza all jostled for space in her head, but she couldn't say anything for fear of blundering in. Haines was unaware of everything that had happened.

She looked at Jem for help and she responded by subtly shaking her head and warning with her eyes.

'What? What are you two doing? All those sideways looks, I'm bloody sick of it.' Haines was already shouting. 'Weeks I've had! Stupid woman won't even let me have a paper to read. My daughters turned up but as soon as it was clear I wasn't about to die, they scurried off back to university. Fuck this! Now you're keeping secrets from me in my own home.' He threw the TV remote across the room with a flick of his wrist and it exploded against the opposite wall. All three of them watched the batteries roll across the floor, one disappearing under the TV.

Emma instinctively tensed up and prepared to defend herself before logic kicked in. Could she really use her self-defence skills against her former boss? In front of his own wife?

Luckily it never came to anything – Jem moved to sit beside Rob. Instantly the tension drained out of him.

'Hey. The doctor said you're not to get upset.' She leant into him and he put an arm around her. 'Don't let it worry you, we'll see what the doctor says next week.' She stroked his arm.

'Yeah, sorry,' Rob said softly. 'I know you're not stupid, didn't mean it. It's just so frustrating, all of it.'

It was an intimate moment but Emma didn't feel that she was intruding.

'I wouldn't get upset if I knew what was going on. I can't be having these secrets.' Rob had calmed down now, his anger come and gone like a flash flood.

Emma looked between Jem and Rob. Jem gave a slight nod. Something was needed.

'Sir, I know you said that you didn't remember anything about the raid. But what do you know? Have you seen the news?'

'I've been trying to avoid the news but you know what it's like. I've heard bits and pieces and my fed rep told me a few things.' He paused, obviously trying to remember. 'I saw obituaries for both Billy and Reg Patterson. That was a shock.'

'But no details?' Emma asked.

'No, the press reports don't go into detail, especially when court cases are pending. And my fed rep knows but he's not saying.'

As gently as she could, Emma went through what had happened in the alley before she'd triggered the raid.

He sat back and rubbed his chin, obviously trying to take it in. 'So, the two bodyguards were actually trying to kill me and Billy?' Emma nodded and Rob continued. 'So, I've got you to thank then. You must have saved my life.'

'I wouldn't say that.' Emma shook her head. 'We were in a situation. I'd have done the same for any officer.'

'And Hargreaves? I do remember that I'd had doubts about him in the last few weeks.' He stopped and tried to gather his thoughts. 'I don't mean the last few weeks I've been stuck here. I mean the weeks before. Before everything happened. I was keeping an eye on him – he was always having meetings, disappearing and not telling me where he was going.'

Emma nodded. 'I haven't been given the whole story. But he was seen leaving the operation before it started, with Pietr Garoza. Hargreaves was arrested with five thousand pounds in cash and Garoza had two kilos of cocaine on him.'

Rob struggled to understand all this information. 'So... Hargreaves? He must have planned it? Paid off the bodyguards? I mean he was always slated to take over.'

'Looks like he wanted to start with a blank page. A whole new plan working with Garoza and you and King permanently out of the way.' She silently prayed that Rob wouldn't ask too much about how Hargreaves had been caught. She wasn't sure she could dissemble well enough to explain how Professional Standards had been there at just the right time to catch Hargreaves.

'Wow.' Haines was wide eyed with wonder as he tried to figure out everything. 'You know, I think that might help. With the memory, you know. I wasn't sure what I remembered about Glen Hargreaves. Whenever I thought of him, I had an uneasy feeling, but I didn't know why.' There was another pause. Then Rob said, as it occurred to him. 'What happened with those murders? Two girls and one who survived? Who took that over?'

'Well, I think they closed the case, while I was off. I've had a look but the CPS won't action it.' She didn't want to say too much – as little as possible was her basic rule when lying. But she also couldn't resist point scoring. 'I think it was the Dark Car Man in the end. But he killed himself before we could bring charges. And with no one else involved, the case is closed.' She held her breath. He knew that Reg was dead and she now prayed that Rob wouldn't connect the dots.

More confusion clouded Rob's face. After a second he gave up. 'There was something. Dark Car Man. I know you were looking for him and I was annoyed with you about it. But it's gone now. Like trying to grab fog.'

Emma caught a look from Jem. She looked back at Rob. He was looking tired and distracted. He had retreated into an interior world as he processed everything that he had just been told.

'Listen, boss, I just popped round to see how you were. I ought to, you know, get myself off home. Don't worry too much about the memories, they'll come back when they're ready.' And hopefully, I'll be ready as well, she thought.

Jem picked up the thread. 'And the doctors said there's no point in trying to force yourself to remember. You'll just tire yourself out. It's probably time you had a rest, anyway.'

'Yeah, yeah,' he said distractedly. 'It was lovely of you to drop by though, Emma. For all the doctors say, I think I needed to see some of the old guard. Next time though, come over for a couple of hours. We can watch a film or something.'

'I'd like that,' Emma said. Jem led her to the door. When they were alone, Emma said to her, 'Was that okay? I don't know how much he knew or what I should say?'

'No, no, that was fine,' Jem said. 'I'm sorry about the outburst. He's either been like that or just sits there saying nothing. I'm out of my mind with worry but the doctors say it's all normal and will get better with time.' She paused, as if deciding what to say next. 'Listen, do come back. He meant it. And he's been more interested today than since, well, you know, since it happened. Could you put up with watching a classic war film from the sixties? Or maybe James Bond?'

'Actually that might be nice. Be a bit less confrontational than just sitting there talking. I could do with finding out what he knows about the people I'm working with now too.'

'I would really appreciate it and that would really help him as well.'

Emma went down the road and got back into her car. What had become of her former boss, Rob Haines? And what had she just agreed to?

Chapter Five

The next morning DI Slater called a case conference in CID. He wheeled a whiteboard into the centre of the open area and they all clustered around, some sat on chairs, others perching on desks or leaning against pillars.

'So, DC Angel went out to view a crime scene yesterday,' Kev Slater said. 'She's given me a preliminary report and now it's up to me to decide, with input from you, if this is a case we should take or if we should kick it up the chain.'

To Emma's surprise it was DS Berman – Suse – who spoke first.

'I think we should view this as a transaction,' she said. 'What will we have to put into it and what can we get back out? I understand that there is a lot of evidence and we're getting a clear idea of identity?' She looked questioningly at Emma.

'Yes. The room was occupied by Oliver Fairthorpe. We're chasing up next of kin and the mortuary are trying to make the body viewable. But we've seen his driving license photo and it's him. All his belongings are in the room, including his credit cards and other identifying documents. Everything points to him staying there alone. Going through his effects, he was an independent financial advisor, covering all of the south west and part of Wales. He was down here on business, a one night stopover before a morning meeting in Exeter.'

DI Slater nodded to himself. 'So there'll be plenty of motive then. First of all money – he was handling lots of other people's savings.

We could look into his business and reputation to see if he has any skeletons in his closets. And, he was staying away from home a lot, so the hot second favourite for any murder comes in.'

'Aye, sex,' DS Chisholm said. 'But I thought he was the only one in the room? So not playing away?'

'Not this time, maybe,' Suse said. 'But a lifestyle like that, he could have any number of girlfriends squirrelled away up and down the country. It was obviously a personal attack, someone really hated him, to not only kill him but to do it in that way.'

'Do we actually know how he died?' Emma asked.

'Not yet,' Kev Slater said. 'Pathology and scene of crimes are still working.' There was a pause and he looked around the group. 'Nicholas, you've been quiet. What's your take on it?'

'Well, it doesn't really matter what's been done with the body, does it?' He shrugged. 'It's a murder so we process it. Motive, means and opportunity. Collect evidence, interview suspects, work it till we solve it. It doesn't matter if he's stabbed and left for dead or if someone makes an effort to stage it like this one.'

Slater shook his head. 'I wish it were that simple. This could be a millstone around our necks. First of all, the crime scene is a hotel room so all the evidence will have to be weighed against the multiple previous occupants. Secondly, the victim's lifestyle. He will have had hundreds of clients, scattered over a wide area. We'd need to liaise with Devon and Cornwall and Gwent Police and maybe other forces depending on how far north or east he went as well. He could have stayed in maybe over a hundred hotels over the past year.' He paused for effect, nodding slightly at Suse Berman. 'And after we've invested all that effort, we're not guaranteed a result. Murders like this can easily go unsolved.'

'Can I ask you, sir, what your role is here?' Emma asked.

'What do you mean? I'm here as the team lead, your superior officer. What are you getting at?' Slater obviously didn't like being challenged.

'Well, I'm not being funny, sir, but I take it you're not here for the long haul. Are you trying to re-establish the team or wind it up?'

He studied her carefully, considering whether he should answer. But then he saw that everyone else in the room was watching the exchange. 'Right, well, no point in beating around the bush. It's no secret that this CID lost its way under DCI Haines. A clean sweep was needed, but Bradwick needs a CID and will do for the future.' He nodded. 'I was going to retire, but I was asked to come back for six months to set this team on the right track. To pick new officers and make sure that past mistakes are not repeated.' He stared pointedly at Andy Stonor and Emma. She suddenly knew that Slater was one of the voices that had campaigned for a clean sweep – a whole new team. 'Why do you ask, DC Angel?'

'Well, our job is to do cases like this. If you want to rebuild this team, then you can't do it by taking the tricky cases away from us. We can't spend our whole time here mopping up attacks and arresting drug dealers. I know the outcome wasn't what we wanted but the last big raid we launched got a significant amount of drugs off the streets, arrested a lot of dealers and closed off a potential import route.' Emma could see that there were nods around the room.

'So, let me ask you a similar question then, DC Angel,' Slater responded. 'Why do you want to do it?'

'For the same reason I come into work every day. I don't want to do it because the outcome might or might not be good for us, but because Fairthorpe's family deserve to know. He came onto our patch, expecting to get a night's sleep before moving on and doing a day's work. But instead he was murdered. That's not right, and it's not right that the killer might get away with it. Our job is to do everything we can to find them.' Emma stopped talking and waited. Had she just dealt her career another blow? Was she too insubordinate? On the other hand, she couldn't sit here and listening to the rest of the team discuss a brutal killing as if it were a series of columns on a spreadsheet.

DI Kev Slater took his time weighing up the arguments. Eventually he said, 'Right then. We'll take it. But the onus is on you now to make it stick. DC Angel is right – this team needs a win. And, just because we've got a murder that's going to be high profile, don't let your other work slide. I know the team is a bit understaffed, but that's the new reality. We have to do more with less. Don't let me down.'

There were mutters and sideways glances at each other. Emma wondered about her colleagues – were they just here for an easy ride? If so, would they resent her for taking on a complex case? Whether they did or not, she knew she couldn't let cases like this slide through, get taken over by a team from Bristol. If the team wasn't taking the hard jobs then they would lose heart. She might be a DC, the lowest rank in the room, but she knew that it would gut the team if they just kept arresting drug dealers and dealing with street violence. They needed to prove themselves, and now she just needed to get them to see that as well.

* * *

All of CID had been gathered by Kev Slater in the hastily assembled incident room. Emma had spent her lunch hour eating a canteen sandwich at her desk and going through the preliminary on Oliver Fairthorpe. As suspected, his business as an independent financial advisor had hundreds of clients, spread over a wide area. The first job was to sort through them into active and historical clients.

She was glad to be drawn away from her monitor for a while. When she'd been down to the canteen, the rumours of the strange murder and beheading were already swirling around. Usually the pathologist would type up her report and it would be circulated to the team. This time however, she had come up to the station to give a briefing directly to the officers. The pathologist, Dani Price, had grown up on the other side of the estuary and still had an accent from the Welsh Valleys.

When everyone had settled, she addressed the room. 'Right, we have a strange one. I know that the rumours will spread like wildfire so I wanted to come in now and talk to you before I submit my report. I've had a chat with the scene of crime team and they've briefed me.

If I deal with this now, I can take questions and stop the rumours spreading. Or at least try and stop the outright lies from being passed around. Now, DC Emma Angel was first on scene. Could you give us your first impressions?'

'Yes. The body had been staged so that they appeared to be sitting up in bed, leaning against the back wall. Somehow the head was fixed to the wall. When the chambermaid came in, she disturbed something as the body fell off the bed.' She stopped and looked a bit awkward. 'We have a report from the woman who made the discovery that the deceased, Oliver Fairthorpe, turned to look at her, opened his eyes and then keeled over the side of the bed. Obviously, the body was posed to be angled towards the door and her brain just filled in the gaps when it fell over.'

'Actually, she might be right on that,' Dani Price said. Everyone was focused on her now. She picked up a tablet, and fiddled with it before it connected to an overhead projector.

'That's where the budget went then!'

'Ah, be quiet, this comes from the SOCO budget. Here's a plan of the room.' A 3D model appeared on the screen. 'Now, this is just like tens of thousands of rooms up and down the country. A rectangular box with an en suite fitted into one corner. This gives us a narrow corridor into the main room. So far, so normal. But, this one had been modified. Whoever our killer is, he likes a bit of DIY.' The screen changed to show a small brass ring with a screw thread attached. 'We found over half a dozen of these brass screw eyes fixed all over the room. They are small, about ten millimetres across. They were used as guides for fishing line to make tripwires. Fishing line is perfect for the job, it's next to invisible yet it has a very high breaking strain.' The picture changed back to the hotel room, now with bright red straight lines all over it. 'These are where the tripwires went. That narrow corridor is where it starts. Our witness had no choice but to hit that wire.' She indicated a red line across the narrow corridor. 'That pulled all the way round to here and moved the head towards her. Shorter wires were attached to the eyelids to make them open.

Finally, this one was attached to Fairthorpe's finger and pulled him sideways off the bed.'

'So, basically, the body was just a human puppet?' Nicholas Dent asked.

'In essence, yes.' Dani paused to judge the mood of her audience. 'This guy is very organised and obviously calculating.' She clicked her thumb and a different picture came up on the screen. 'These hooks were custom made from wire and sharpened to a point. Look at that winding on the wire where it forms the loop, it's perfectly regular and neatly done. And he worked out the mechanics of it all. And as well as this fine work, here's something else that's a bit bigger scale.' Another click and a new picture showed on the screen, this time of a shelf bracket modified with a steel spike sticking straight up. 'This was made by our killer and transported to the scene. It was attached to the wall and the head mounted on it. This is how the head was able to swivel and how it was left behind when the body toppled over. Our killer certainly takes a lot of care with things. No one reported hearing power tools, so likely all the fixings were done by hand. And it would've taken some figuring out to get it all to work properly.' She stopped and took a deep breath. Emma had the chills – she could hear that Dani was almost idolising this killer and she understood why. There was something so methodical about the work that he would've have made a good surgeon rather than a killer. Dani ran her fingers through her hair and some of her professional demeanour dropped away. 'Someone went to a lot of trouble to do this. I've given you the how. Now you ask me some questions and see if you can get to the why.' She twisted her hair back into a ponytail.

'How was he killed?' This was Suse, straight to the point.

'Exsanguination. And he had taser burns on his chest, left hand side. I don't want to tread on scene of crimes' toes, but they're taking apart the bath drain and I've heard they're finding a lot of blood.'

'So,' Suse said, thinking while she spoke. 'You can get a taser off the Internet that looks just like a mobile phone. Someone knocks on his door, Fairthorpe opens it up to this guy who's holding a phone, he wouldn't have seen a threat. Bang with the taser, push him back and into the bathroom, and what? Where was he cut?'

'We think there's a hint of an extra cut in the neck. It might be hesitation or it might be that he was stabbed there. The killer already knew that he was planning to decapitate his victim. In the absence of other sites, and the lack of blood in the body, we have to assume that's what happened.' She paused and looked at her notes. 'We have three closely grouped taser sites on the chest so he probably kept tasing him while he got him into the bath.'

This was one part of the job that Emma hoped she never got used to. The dispassionate discussion of someone's last moments. Those moments would've been filled with fear and pain, and yet here they were, calmly working out what had happened.

Emma was weirdly detached from the presentation. She'd got used to how callous murderers could be. She'd seen bodies dumped where they fell and she'd seen shallow graves and more elaborate ways of hiding bodies. Some killers tried to hide their crimes by burning or destroying the remains with acid.

But this was a whole new level – the killer hadn't even attempted to hide the body or to get away with the crime. Instead there was a theatricality to the whole operation. It wasn't that he wanted to get caught, but he was showing off, trying to impress. He wanted Fairthorpe to be found.

'How long are we talking about to set it all up?' Suse asked. 'Can we work back to a time of death?'

Dani Price wrapped a loose strand of hair around her finger. 'DIY is not my area of expertise.' A ripple of laughter broke the tension. 'But not long, about an hour maybe? Bodies are difficult to move around on your own. We know he was killed in the bathroom and presumably that's where the messy work was done. He had to be dragged in and then reassembled on the bed. That's a lot of work, so allow an hour all in if there was one assailant and he's relatively fit and strong. As to the time of death, the room was kept cold so that would delay rigor mortis. Ten years ago I'd have said that meant he was an expert, but now it just means he has access to the Internet. Even so, he didn't have much time as the small muscles, like those in the eyelids, stiffen up first. So, our killer was either very lucky or very organised.' She looked around the room to make sure someone was taking notes. 'Everything else was planned, so the chance is that he watched the hotel to see what time the chambermaids went through. Or he might have simply added a bit of leeway onto the checkout time. But he had a relatively small window to kill Fairthorpe, set everything up properly and get out. Too late and he'd be interrupted by the chambermaid. Too early and rigor would have set in and stopped everything from working. I'd say he was killed between eight and nine in the morning and all set and ready to go at around half nine to ten. With a ten o'clock checkout time that would work.'

There was a pause as the room absorbed all this detail. 'Was he beheaded in the bathroom?' Suse asked. 'Was that after he was killed?'

'Yes. All the blood is in the bathroom so that makes sense. It's hard to behead someone so it's doubtful that was the cause of death but we might never know. It would be easier to stab him in the neck, if you hit the carotid or jugular he'd bleed out in a few minutes. Then it looks like he used a saw to remove the head. I suppose that he wanted to keep the mess out of the way so he could stage the scene and make it look normal. But that's only guesswork.'

Another shiver went down Emma's spine. The killer was not only posing the body like a puppet, but he was dressing the set so that it looked like a normal hotel room.

DI Slater caught the look on Emma's face. 'Emma, you look like you're bothered, what's up?'

'I was just thinking that most of the murders we deal with, the whole point is getting rid of somebody, and then once you've done that, the next objective is to destroy the evidence and try to get away from the scene without being caught.'

DI Slater nodded. 'That pretty much fits with what I've seen.'

'But this guy, he could have had the job done in the first few minutes. Victim opens door, taser him, push him back and then into the bathroom. Knife in the neck and it's game over. He could have been away inside five minutes. He could've used the "do not disturb" sign to buy himself even more time.' Emma started warming to her subject. 'It's the bit after all that has happened that's interesting. He forced him into the bathroom, beheaded him and then dragged him back to the bed.'

'On top of all that,' Dani Price added, 'he redressed him as well. We found blood stained clothing in the bathroom. He must've gone through the overnight bag and found a change of clothes.'

'We all know how hard it is getting a drunk friend undressed and into bed,' Emma said to another ripple of laughter. 'It must be important to our killer, this whole theatrical side to things.'

'Has anyone checked online?' DC Dent asked.

'What do you mean?' DI Slater asked.

'Well, this kind of thing,' Dent said, eyes down, obviously uncomfortable in the spotlight. 'It's like the most extreme YouTube video ever.'

'It wouldn't be allowed surely?'

'No, but we could check the dark web.' DI Slater frowned, so Nick continued. 'There are very few verified incidences of genuine snuff videos, so I have my doubts, but it's worth checking. If someone uploaded a video of our mannequin corpse then they'd become an Internet legend overnight. And it'd give us somewhere to start looking.'

'Listen, I know this is going to hit the press and I know they'll come up with some gruesome name for the killer.' Kev Slater was serious now, talking with the authority of their boss. 'All that in mind, if I read the phrase "mannequin corpse" anywhere in the news either print or online, I will find who leaked it. I know this is a gruesome, macabre murder, but our central focus here must be Oliver Fairthorpe. He had a family, a sister, parents. He didn't deserve this. We need to ignore all the speculation and strange elements around this and focus on our core job. Someone, somewhere wanted Fairthorpe dead and they chose to do that on our patch. So, we need to look into his past and find that person. Most murders are motivated by either sex or money. Now, Fairthorpe was a financial advisor so that's where we start. Did he swindle someone out of their life savings, are there upset grandchildren, investors who lost everything? That's what we need to know.

'But don't ignore the other side of things. He travelled a lot, his patch was most of the south west so he was often staying in cheap hotels. Could he have been having an affair? Or more than one? It's certainly the kind of lifestyle that would fit with that. I'm not saying his wife should be under suspicion, but it needs looking into widely – anyone he was having an affair with could have a husband or boyfriend who took offence.' Kev stopped and looked down at his papers. 'Other evidence – Emma, it says here that a poster was recovered from the scene and you were actioned to look into that. Any update?'

'Yes, sir. It's a poster from a missing person case about fifteen years ago. A boy called Calum Frost.' She paused and looked around the room and was met with several nods. 'The wife claims she's never seen it before.'

'When I worked in fraud, you'd be amazed at what people did to bury the paper trail,' Kev answered. 'They'd buy things and return them, start multiple companies and loan money between them, all sorts of things. This is similar. All this set-dressing, theatrical stuff is exactly that. Do any of you know what the most important thing is in a magic trick?' He looked around the stunned room. They were mostly working out how he'd jumped from accounting to stage magic. 'It's misdirection. That's what all of this is. It's designed to make us look the other way. So what if there's a poster about a child who went missing over fifteen years ago? He, our killer, wants us to follow that trail down the rabbit hole. I've said it before and I'll say it again, let's get back to basics. Take the victim's life apart and you'll find his killer.'

Chapter Six

It was gone six when Emma pushed back from her desk and rubbed her eyes. Most of the rest of the day had been spent filling out forms and making requests for other forces and departments to start the investigation into the life and work of Oliver Fairthorpe. Hopefully over the next few days they'd generate a list of clients who could be interviewed to build up a picture of his life. His wife was due to come in to be interviewed and to identify the body. Emma shuddered at the thought.

'Remember when we interviewed Gregory Watts?' Andy Stonor had come to stand over her desk.

'Yes?' Gregory Watts was the one who got away. He'd preyed on schoolgirls, waiting till they were sixteen before moving them into his house and getting them pregnant. By the letter of the law he was doing nothing wrong, but Emma knew better. His interest in school girls made her skin crawl.

'I promised to take you out to the pub. Remember?'

Emma cast her mind back. They'd had a conversation about how well she fit into the team, and the pub had been vaguely mentioned. But that had been back when they were a team. And groups drinks after work was a world away from a one on one with a colleague. 'Something was said about the pub, I think. But now is really not a good time. It's been a very long day.'

'I know. It has been harrowing.' He paused for effect. 'But I really need to talk to you.' He looked around. 'Away from the office.'

Emma groaned inwardly. Even if there was any attraction between her and Andy – which there wasn't – having any personal involvement with a colleague in the same office was a recipe for trouble.

'No,' Andy said, obviously reading her expression. 'Not that. I want to talk about work, and what happened, when, well, you know.'

Emma had many misgivings but she could see that one evening in a pub would be far better than not hearing what he had to say. If he didn't get his say then he might try to have the conversation in the station. Or she might find out through the grapevine or something could happen without her knowing about it in advance.

Emma pushed her way into the pub with some trepidation. Just to make sure that Andy Stonor got the message, she'd come straight from work without straightening her hair or checking her make-up.

The pub he'd chosen was a brash, modern bar with lots of slot machines and a huge area dotted with tables. The light and noise levels were high and she relaxed a bit. It was the last place you'd choose for an intimate evening. One drink, she thought. Have one drink, let him say his piece then get the hell out.

Soon she was sat opposite him with a bottle of beer in her hand. Their corner was quiet but she didn't feel isolated. She had no idea what the usually taciturn Andy Stonor wanted so she resolved to keep quiet and let him talk.

'I know we haven't always seen eye to eye,' he said. 'But now that we're the only two who've survived, questions are going to be asked, fingers are going to be pointed.' Emma realised where he was going with this. Because she knew the truth she hadn't thought that the rest of the force would be trying to work out what had happened. 'Professional Standards turned up too quickly and they knew just what had been going on in the team before they were told,' he said. 'I don't know what they asked you, but when they interviewed me, they were laser focused. That raid wasn't a fishing expedition – they knew exactly what they were going after. If you combine that with the gossip swirling around the station, then it's obvious that it was an inside job. Someone inside our CID team was a spy. Someone was passing info back to PS while pretending that they knew nothing.'

Emma sat back and kept quiet. She rubbed her ear and smoothed the hair over the back of her head. With the thumb of one hand she rubbed across the knuckles on the other, checking for scars. She had made the decision in the small hours after an emotionally charged day. She hadn't expected the repercussions of that decision to still be haunting her now. And she certainly wasn't going to be tricked into making an admission of guilt.

'A lot of people thought it was me,' Andy said with nod. 'With my background and the fact that I kept my job.'

'Wait a minute, what do you mean about your background?' Emma was jerked back to the conversation by Andy's odd statement.

'Oh, you really aren't local are you? I'm third, maybe even fourth generation in the job. My family, the Stonors, are police through and through. Even if they're not front line, I've got cousins, aunts, uncles who work somewhere in the sector – answering the nine nine nine phones or doing admin jobs, working in forensic labs.' He shrugged. 'It's what we do. Obviously not every single one of us, but enough. So when Rob started up his little scheme, well, he didn't actually start it, but when he took over from Patterson, I just couldn't join them. If I'd been caught being bent, I'd have lost my family. There'd have been whole branches who would never have talked to me again. No invites to the usual round of weddings and funerals. Christmas would've been miserable.'

'But you did look the other way.' Emma said this as a statement of fact, not a question.

Andy rubbed his face and looked uncomfortable. 'I suppose I did. And I'd rather that didn't come out either. I've walked a very narrow path for so long. In my family there are two cardinal sins – not supporting your colleagues and being bent. I had to choose between the two.'

Emma nodded to herself. 'So, that's why you always seemed a bit off with me.'

'What's that supposed to mean?' Andy bristled.

'Well, you were always very buttoned up.' Why had she started down this path? She'd been caught up in her own thoughts and had just spoken without thinking. 'Terse. Abrupt. Almost rude.' She smiled and hoped it would be enough to take the edge off her comments.

'All right, all right, that's enough!' He smiled and held his hands up in mock surrender. 'I was so stressed these last few years, trying to juggle it all. And even when I'm okay, I'm not usually one of the lively, chatty ones so I suppose I did come across like you said.'

A silence fell between them. Andy was screwing up his courage to get around to what he'd actually come here to say. Despite his confession, Emma had no idea where he was going with the conversation, so there was nothing she could say to help him. He nervously sipped his pint.

'Anyway, I wanted to thank you, really, Emma.'

'Me? What for?' Emma took a sip of her beer bottle to cover her confusion.

'Because I know. I know that you're the one who talked to Professional Standards. It's obvious really, you were the new recruit and an outsider. You'd be the one they'd try to turn. You did what I didn't have the guts to do. What I should have done on day one. As soon as I found out.'

'Well, you might be grateful, but I suspect you're the only one. I can't have this being spread all over the station.' A cold ball of fear settled into her stomach. Until this moment she hadn't realised how tense she'd been, constantly living with this secret that she didn't want people to discover.

'No, I can see that. I was actually wondering if I could take the credit for this one. Subtly I mean. Just a few whispers in the right ears, here and there. Not definite but stoke the rumours.'

'Why would you want to do that?' Emma was confused now.

'Well, as you said, I already have a reputation of being quite dour, quite uptight. With my family history as well, if people see me as being a stickler for the rules, I probably won't even get to hear about any other schemes that are being planned. And it's best for me to not even know about other bent coppers, the other scams that are being run.'

Emma sat back and thought while she toyed with her nearly empty bottle. Andy was taking a cowardly approach, but also a pragmatic one. She knew the risks of being ostracised by your colleagues. And she certainly wouldn't be able to build her own career if people didn't trust her. She nodded decisively. 'I think that'd work,' she said. 'You can't be the only person who's worked out that I'm the most likely person to be the mole.'

'How do you think you're going to play it?' Andy asked.

'Play what?'

'Well, if someone just straight out asks you or makes an accusation.'

Emma had to think for a minute. At the time she was working with Professional Standards, she had made decisions based on what was in front of her at the time. She hadn't had the luxury of being able to plan ahead. But what Andy had just said rang true. Someone, somewhere would eventually pin her down. Really, it was either her or Andy Stonor who'd be in the frame.

And the question they'd really be asking, the one that they wanted to ask but wouldn't was this – can we trust Emma Angel? She would have to get the answer right or she'd be finished in this force.

'You see,' Andy said. 'You can't do that rabbit-in-the-headlights thing if someone corners you. I know what the office gossip is like and that will show that you are guilty. You need to get your story straight.'

'You're right, it's fairly obvious.' She thought quickly, put herself back in the frame of mind she was in when she started in CID. 'I was the new girl in the team and everyone else had been there forever. No one trusted me so I had no inside information to pass over.' She shrugged to show that she had been helpless. 'Professional Standards did approach me but I had nothing to offer them.'

'Well, anyone but me would have believed it,' Andy said with a smile.

Emma smiled – it wasn't perfect but was the best that she could hope for.

'What do you think you would've done?' Andy asked. 'I mean you must've known what was going on – we all knew that Rob's induction was more than the standard approach.'

'I don't really know how it would've panned out,' Emma said. 'I mean it went the way it did and I'm quite grateful that Professional Standards approached me because it gave me independent backup. But without them? I don't know.'

Andy studied her over the rim of his pint glass. 'But if it had been a normal raid. Would you have stayed for the division of the spoils at the end? Or would you have kept clean?' Emma couldn't think of an answer. The past was the past and she didn't want to waste time on what ifs. 'It's a simple question,' Andy pressed.

Emma took a deep breath. She had reached the end of her tether. 'It's anything but simple. I know you've heard the rumours of what happened and probably pieced it together from the questions you were asked in interview, but you weren't there.' Andy sat back a little from the table, surprised that she'd gone on the offensive. 'I don't know if you've forgotten or you never knew but it was me who found the body of Reg Patterson once he'd blown his brains out.' She paused briefly for breath, but ploughed on again before Andy could interrupt. 'And I know, it's the job, it's what we're trained for. But it doesn't mean that it was easy. And then, before I'd had a chance to draw breath, I found myself in that alleyway. I saw Billy King get killed and Rob Haines nearly died.' She paused as she faced up to the truth. 'In fact, I was lucky that I wasn't the third body in that alley.'

She couldn't really cope with any more revelations, so she leapt up from the table, the chair nearly overbalancing behind her. She didn't think about anything except getting out of the pub. It might have been brash, modern and noisy, but in her head she was back in the quiet of that old alleyway.

Chapter Seven

Emma Angel arrived in the office the next morning feeling decidedly the worse for wear. After running out of the pub she'd gone straight home to a bottle of wine. She supposed she should feel grateful to Andy for making life easier for her, even if it was the coward's way out for him. And she was frustrated by his attempt to pigeonhole her.

She sat down with a strong, black coffee and checked her computer for the day's actions. She hadn't got far through the list before DI Kev Slater appeared by her desk.

'I've been looking over the reports. We need to get a handle on these drug related crimes,' he said, coming straight to the point. 'The big raid on the industrial estate was a good start, but it has left a power vacuum in the town. Take Suse with you over to hospital records and see if we can get some data. We need to build a clearer picture of the current situation on the ground.'

'What about the murder, sir?' Emma asked. 'First twenty-four hours and all that?'

'We've drafted in some help to go through all the guests at the motel that we can trace. They need to be interviewed and put on the system. Likewise we've got the technical people to go through his laptop and have a look through his phone. See if we can build up a picture of his clients. Likewise, his wife needs interviewing but the FLO can handle that.' He paused for effect. 'So, until all the interviews are completed and written up on the system, there's not a lot we can do. So I need you to be getting on top of the drug trade.'

'Right then, boss.'

Suse came over and joined the meeting. 'What data do you want from the hospital, boss?'

'Usual things. Admissions for personal violence, any drug overdoses and any incidental problems related to drug use.'

'What kind of thing?' Suse asked.

'You've seen the town centre when there's a new legal high comes out. Young people stumbling around like zombies, falling into plate glass windows, wandering into traffic and getting run over. You get the idea. Plus the usual revenge beatings and fights over turf.'

'Some days I think we should just let them get on with it,' Suse said, half to herself. DI Slater looked at her quizzically so she continued. 'Well, people that choose to do drugs, they're just a drain on the system.'

Emma was horrified. Was Suse suggesting that they let her friends like Lukas just die because it would save money and effort? Lukas was her only friend who'd known her while growing up. She thought of him, and his friends, as people that had a problem and needed to be cared for. She hadn't really examined her relationship with him too deeply – she didn't look for evidence of drug use and he didn't tell her. Now she'd signed him up as an informant, she had a bit more leeway.

Faced with this opinion, she thought that her safest course of action was to keep quiet and see what everyone else thought.

'Well, that might be a private opinion,' DI Slater said, 'but I wouldn't say it in public. Everyone in Bradwick should be our clients, whether they're upstanding citizens or drug addicts. That's the official view and you'd be wise to remember that.'

Message received, thought Emma. She'd have to play her cards close to her chest. It did mean though that information from Lukas would be vital and no one else would have anything similar.

There was nothing either of them could say, so they went out to the hospital. The rest of the morning was spent in endless meetings with administrators looking over spreadsheets and PowerPoint presentations.

Tension between her and Suse simmered over the morning. The sergeant obviously felt it too because she spoke out over some disappointing sandwiches in the cafeteria.

'I saw your expression this morning when I was saying that it'd help us if some of the addicts got on with killing each other off,' Suse said.

'Well, it was quite harsh,' Emma said. She was unwilling to give too much ground to her superior. And she certainly didn't want this woman knowing about her friends. 'They are still people after all. Someone, somewhere still cares about them.'

'I thought you might be one of those bleeding heart liberal types,' Suse replied evenly. 'Take it from one who knows, you'll just burn yourself out in no time.'

'What's the solution then?' Emma asked. 'Put it all into a spreadsheet so you can work it all out as profit and loss? Effort expended versus advantage gained?'

Suse missed the sarcasm and smiled warmly. 'Nice to hear that you were listening yesterday. It's all about how much energy you put in to get a reward. I'm in this for the long haul. I want to keep on getting promotions and move up the ranks before I get too old and left behind. And you don't get there by caring for people and trying to do the right thing. You get there by looking at the data and picking the cases that will look the best and progress your career.'

'So, if you were in charge, you wouldn't have picked up the motel murder case then?'

'God no!' Suse shook her head. 'I know they all look glamorous and there might be a special on Channel 5 in the future, but about half of these complex cases become a graveyard for people's careers. Cold cases that stay open forever and can't be closed.'

'But what about the families? Don't they deserve to know?' Emma was horrified at how cold Suse was being about it all.

Suse shrugged. 'For sure they need closure. But I don't think I've got anything special. I'd rather someone else took on the cases. I've really got my eye further up the tree. I'd rather be the one making the decisions, allocating the budget and sorting out the logistics.' She looked smug. 'That way I can help tens or hundreds of families to get the justice you think they deserve.'

Emma took a deep breath. She could now see where the bosses she struggled under came from. It was quite chilling to see a young woman deliberately setting her sights on senior management to play the same PR driven, numbers game that made all their lives harder in the rank and file.

'What about all these cases we've just read about?' Emma asked, changing tack.

'What about them?' Suse asked.

'Well, when you read about someone being beaten and having internal bleeding, or getting his fingers broken, what do you think?' Suse shrugged, not getting the question. 'You don't wonder if there's someone, somewhere worried about them? If they've got families at home struggling to get and visit them?'

'I could do, but I don't see what good it would do. We're here to do a job and that job is to catch criminals. If those people choose to do drugs, worse than that, if they choose to get involved in dealing those drugs, then they must know what they're doing. It's not really a surprise if they get beaten up or overdose. Not to us, and certainly not to them.'

Emma opened her mouth and then shut it again. She could tell that she was poles apart from Suse on outlook. She was able to empathise with people, to see how they were a product of upbringing and circumstance, not just individuals who'd chosen a life of crime. 'Well, I think we'll just have to agree to disagree,' Emma said finally. But then she couldn't resist having another dig. 'But when it's all said and done, we're still working the murder case.'

Suse sighed. 'Yeah, we are. So we'd better work together and make sure that it's one of the good ones. One that looks good on the statistics.'

Emma leant back from the table and considered her options. She could try to bring Suse on side. She knew that there was definite value in chasing down the whole Callum Frost angle. But on the other hand, she still didn't wholly trust Suse. She resolved to have an initial look at the old missing child case. Maybe she'd ask Rob Haines for his take – he would've been on the ground at the time.

If it looked like it'd help them catch the killer, then she'd find out if she could rely on Suse to help out. If she had a weak case she'd need all the allies she could get. And her sergeant would probably do it, if only out of a sense of self-interest.

'Thanks,' Emma nodded. 'We don't have to see eye to eye, but at the moment we both want the same thing which is to catch the killer.'

Suse nodded as well. 'Maybe you're not the head-in-the-clouds liberal that I thought you were. That almost sounds like pragmatism creeping in.' This time however, there was a gentler edge to her voice.

'Well, I'll do whatever it takes to catch this guy.'

An awkward silence fell between the two women. Emma was frustrated, as two women on the same team they ought to be supporting each other. But she couldn't bring herself to agree with Suse's outlook. Emma needed to get away from the hospital, the police station, and all the talk of spreadsheets and targets.

'Listen, Suse. I've got a source, he's quite...' she paused. 'He knows a few of the dealers and he's been useful in the past.'

'Is he official? On the books as a CHIS?'

Emma could never bring herself to use the official acronym "Confidential Human Intelligence Source". Lukas was her friend, a complex person, and not a "source". Nevertheless, she nodded. 'Yes, I put him on the books just before it all kicked off a few weeks ago.'

'What are you thinking?'

'Well, we've got all the data from here. Why don't I go round and see my source and see if I could flesh out the numbers a bit? Give Slater the whole picture.'

Suse looked unimpressed. 'So, you want me to finish up here and go back to the station while you go off and have tea and biscuits with your mate?'

Emma considered telling her that the chance of biscuits was close to zero unless she brought some with her, but decided not to. 'You said we should work together.' She sighed. 'When you get back, put all the files together into an email. Send it over to me and I'll write up the report for Slater.'

Suse looked a lot happier at the thought of not having to write up the day's work. 'That's a good idea. You can add in what you learn this afternoon.' She paused. 'But, send it over to me first, so I can check it through before it goes any further.'

And take credit? Emma wondered. But she didn't really care about that. If super-ambitious Suse wanted to take her credit then that was a fair trade in return for an afternoon away from the station.

Chapter Eight

Of course, Lukas Mills wasn't someone who you could just drop round to visit. He was itinerant – not exactly homeless, but then again, not someone who had one fixed address.

She started with the address she'd last known him to live – a house in a rundown terrace in one of the more interesting ends of Bradwick. A nervous looking woman with dirty blonde hair opened the door a crack, looking suspicious.

'Is Lukas here?' Emma asked.

'Who's asking?'

'Just a friend. Haven't seen him for a bit. He was living here.'

'Yeah, he was. Not any more.'

The woman's attitude was starting to grate on Emma. 'I figured that much out. I'd like to find him.'

'You tried his phone?'

'Of course. He's not answering. Sent him a text.'

There was an awkward silence. Emma had way more experience with waiting for answers than this woman.

'You could try the pub,' she said when the silence had stretched too long. Emma raised her eyebrows. 'Down the road, the Wheatsheaf. Might be in there.'

Emma didn't have time to say thanks before the door was shut. She got increasingly frustrated over the next hour or so, tracking him between pubs, where she was viewed with distrust, and houses that may or may not have been squats but where drugs were certainly being consumed.

Eventually, when she was on the point of giving up, her phone chirruped with a reply to her text. Cryptically it was just an address but it did come from Lukas' mobile.

She wondered what he was playing at, but followed it to the nicer end of Bradwick. She had to park and walk the last part as it was in a touristy area of winding streets that led to the sea.

Finally she found the cottage and was led inside by Lukas. Soon she was settled onto a couch in a living room. To her surprise, it was very nice, and even quite clean. There was a bay window that showed a view out over the sea.

'Well, you are a hard man to find. I feel like I've walked all over Bradwick looking for you. And here you are – this is a bit of a step up for you. No wonder none of your old friends knew where you were.'

'Yeah, yeah, new girlfriend, down here on holiday. Rich parents have this place as a holiday flat, so...' he shrugged and looked around at his surroundings. 'I'll get you a tea.' Emma watched him move around the space. He still had his long blond hair and was still thin but she thought he'd filled out a bit. If she wasn't mistaken, he wasn't quite as wasted as he usually was.

The living room was open plan with the kitchen so Emma could keep talking to Lukas while he fixed the tea. 'So how have you been keeping?'

'Like you see, I'm good, landed on my feet.' There was something evasive about his manner though.

'What are you doing here? What I've heard this afternoon, you haven't been around your usual haunts for a good ten days. Who are you hiding from?'

'Well, with your job, you must've seen the stats. It's a battlefield out there.'

'I've been out of the loop for a bit. Formal investigation into the raid at the industrial estate means this is my first week back at work. We've just been collating stats from the hospitals and everything.'

'Well, with King out of the picture and your lot lifting a whole load of gear from the Birmingham gang, it's turned into a free-for-all. Any little thug who can pay a few fourteen-year-olds reckons he's the next boss. Until someone stabs him, that is.' He shook his head. 'And the market is all over the place. Some stuff not available. Weird pills and legal highs coming in then disappearing. You never know if you're going to get the good stuff or something cut with some godawful crap.'

'So, this is your solution is it?' Emma looked around the flat.

Lukas shrugged, apparently unembarrassed. 'Listen, Kelly likes a bit of rough for a holiday romance, and I could do with cleaning up for a while. I've done it before, it's no problem. I'd rather this than wondering if some school kid's going to stick a knife in me to prove a point. And like I said, I'd like to get out of my head, but it's just too much of a gamble right now.'

Emma shook her head. 'And where is the mysterious Kelly right now?' She wasn't sure she could deal with a posh, possibly jealous girlfriend.

'She's gone up to Weston with a few friends from London. Apparently there's a posh hotel there so they can drink cocktails on a balcony and watch people on the beach. Didn't seem like my kind of scene.'

Emma could see that he was doing his best to look at home in the chic holiday cottage, but she couldn't imagine him sipping cocktails or shopping in upmarket boutiques. Finally he came through with two mugs of tea and a pack of biscuits under his arm. Emma laughed.

'What's so funny? I've got you a tea and a few biscuits.'

Emma picked up the mug – it had fresh milk in it. 'I owe my sergeant an apology. She reckoned that I'd be having tea and biscuits instead of working hard. I never thought it'd actually happen, though.'

'Like I said, I landed on my feet.'

'Yeah, but really, Lukas, who are you hiding from?'

'I ain't giving you no names, but I did get in a spot of bother. Got some gear, paid the guy. He goes out and gets stabbed, just stuck in the leg, not killed or nothing. But he loses his money. Now his boss reckons somehow I've got to pay twice.'

'That can't be right?'

'They're talking bollocks about how maybe I was working with the guy who shanked his dealer. Got my money back. At this stage it's not really business any more. It's not about buying cheap and selling expensive, making a profit. This is more like extortion or a protection racket. Get some thugs to scare people and collect up the money. At the moment it's down to who has the most bodies to throw at a problem.' He looked around at the comfy sofas and pastel colours. 'So I'm hiding up. When we can figure out who's won, then I'll make amends if they need making.'

Emma privately thought to herself that when she found out how it all ended, she'd see if she could put in a word to make sure Lukas came out all right.

'I know you're hiding out here, but is there anything I can take back to my bosses?'

Lukas shrugged, as always moving with a natural, fluid grace. Emma deliberately shut down that part of her that found him attractive. She couldn't go there. 'I think they need to go back to basics. While you've been gone, the police haven't done any more than nibble around the edges of the problem. And while you've had a power vacuum, the same thing has happened to the dealers I know as well. First thing you need to do is clamp down at the train stations and make some inroads into the County Lines.' He paused to see if she was listening. 'You know I said earlier that it wasn't about commerce? Well that's the local boys. County Lines are from the cities. They want to sell product and take money back to their handlers. Any violence they do is usually to other rival gangs, not locals. What you really need is to set up the same system that was running before.' Reading Emma's expression, he quickly moved on. 'No, not backhanders and missing product. No, you need to get a network of informers and fast. Find out whose house is being cuckooed and what the new phone numbers are. You need the inside information on the County Lines before they get established. Once you can get a bit of control over the outsiders, then you'll have half the battle won.'

'And you won't mind telling me who I should be arresting? Well, I was going to say your friends. But you know, I'll be rounding up dealers and trying to reduce the drug trade overall.'

'Don't get too many ideas about how effective you'll really be, babe. What I want is a nice peaceful town, not too many knives and not too many idiots trying to prove how hard they are. No matter what you do I'll always be able to get a bit of blow or some charlie to liven up a weekend.'

Emma nodded then sipped her tea. She could see his logic. In fact, she had long ago understood that it was shared by most of the residents of Bradwick, from the great and the good of Spalley Road all the way down to the lowest residents of Coopers End. All anyone really wanted was to go about their business without fear of being mugged or stabbed. If they had a bit of money left at the end of the week and could get married and settle down, then they'd be happy. Especially if no one looked too closely at how they spent that money.

It did leave her with one problem though. How to reactivate Haines' network of informants without offering them the same incentives as before?

'King Kabs are still going, you know,' Lukas said. He'd always had that knack of knowing what she was thinking. 'Might be worth making enquiries, seeing who's running the show now Billy's no longer on the scene.'

Emma nearly asked if they were still offering extra services alongside taxi fares, but she knew the answer. She was also on Lukas' wavelength and had definitely picked up the inference in his words. She would definitely have to see how the land lay over at King Kabs.

Lukas was restless, his leg jiggling up and down as he waited. Finally he asked, 'What can you tell me about the raid out at that abandoned industrial estate? The one that got you suspended? I keep hearing things, and I know we ain't got Billy King no more, and the head of one of the big city gangs was arrested.'

Emma picked up her cup and swirled the dregs around. There was no getting away from it. 'Okay, but don't go spreading it around.'

She briefly filled him in on that evening, deliberately downplaying the emotion, and mainly focusing on what had happened to Haines and King.

Lukas nodded slowly. 'That makes sense. And are you okay? I know if I had to see someone killed in front of me, I'd be proper messed up. And I know you train and all that, but it's still dangerous if you go up against someone in a fight. Anything can happen. That's why I'm hiding out here.'

Emma shook her head. How could she explain the emotions swirling around her head? She had saved her boss and failed him at the same time. She hadn't prevented his life-changing injury but she had stopped the life-ending one. On top of which she'd seen death close up too many times for it to just slide off.

Lukas seemed to understand her need to not reply. He stood up and moved towards the balcony that opened off the back of the house. 'Fancy a cigarette?'

'I gave up.'

'I know. Right when you left home. Always tickled me that did. Most folk start smoking when they leave home, not quit.'

'Yes, then.'

Fair play to Lukas, he had landed on his feet. There was a lovely balcony looking out over the sea. Emma leant on the railing with her cigarette, taking shallow breaths as she wasn't used to smoking. But the shared experience, and the waves crashing onto the beach, helped to calm her down.

She had managed not to cry, but it was a close run thing. She was fine, always fine, right up to the point where someone cared for her. All it had taken was Lukas asking her if she was okay. How was she coping? Just like every other officer, work hard and drink hard.

'Thanks for that,' she said, flicking the end into the scrub off the balcony. 'No, I'm not coping particularly well, as you asked. I feel like I saved my team and that I betrayed them at the same time. I feel like I'm superhuman because I beat those thugs but also I feel incredibly vulnerable because I nearly failed. If one bit of luck hadn't gone my way, I wouldn't be here. Add in a big dollop of survivor's guilt and generally feeling like a fish out of water because everything's changed and that's about how I'm feeling. But each day is better than the last, so, you know. Getting there.'

Lukas nodded. 'Wait here.' He went back into the kitchen. 'I don't want to make your day worse or set your recovery back, but have you seen the paper today?'

'No, after the debacle of the raid I've been trying to avoid the press. Well, there's one journalist who's got hold of my number and she'd love to do a feature on me.'

'And you're not keen?' There was a mischievous glint in Lukas' eye. He knew full well why she'd be more retiring than most.

'Apart from the obvious, I know what they'd do. I'd be reduced to the most humiliating single phrase to make it simple for the readers to understand. I'd be "pint sized hero" or "blonde bombshell" or something else. And then, do you know what would happen?'

'Go on then, what would happen after that?'

'There would be press cuttings everywhere. In my locker, on my desk, you name it. And with technology now, it'd never be forgotten. The police can be unforgiving if you get in the press.'

'But you did a good thing. Saved Rob Haines' life.'

She turned around to lean on the railing, with her back to the beach. 'Yeah, but that's what we're meant to do. At the end of the day, I saw crimes being committed and a fellow officer being put in danger so I acted. I got lucky because they were untrained and underestimated me. And I got one kick that just landed right.'

'You can say that again,' Lukas said, tapping the paper.

'It's not going to be good news, is it?' Emma asked.

'No, but I thought you'd rather hear it from a friend first. Get prepared, like.' He passed the paper across, folded to a story on an inside page.

There was a large photo of Trevor Swain, the man who'd hit Rob Haines over the head and nearly killed him. The headline was short and to the point – "Police Brutality?" – at least there was a question mark. She skim-read the article about damage to the ligaments in his knee, the surgery he'd had and the long process of recovery. Finally, she got to the point – the fact that he was suing the police for compensation due to his injury plus loss of earnings.

'You've read this?' she asked.

'Yeah. Was that you then?'

'That was me. They conveniently don't mention that he was about to kill a man. He was lining up to take a kick at Rob Haines' head when he was lying on the ground. I kicked out the leg he was standing on.'

Lukas picked up the paper and scanned it. 'That accounts for the damage. It says here he's had surgery, and is now lined up for six months of physiotherapy and rehabilitation. And even after all of that he might never walk properly again. His career as a security consultant is over.'

'He was a second-rate bouncer and bodyguard before this happened. And he doesn't have a career. All that medical work will be done while he's on remand in prison, waiting for his trial to start.'

She turned around to look over the sea again. During her enforced time off, she had found it hard to sleep without the routine of going to work. In the small hours of the morning she had gone back over the events in that alley, scrutinising her decisions and seeing if she could have done anything differently.

She had been up against two armed men. Logic dictated that she had to put one out of the fight before tackling the other one. If she'd gone easy on Swain, then she'd have been at risk of him attacking her from behind while she dealt with Lawson. Even if she'd put him onto the ground but not seriously injured, he would still have been able to strike out at her legs while she was facing a man with a knife. That was a potentially lethal situation.

She sighed, this hadn't been why she joined the police. She genuinely wanted to help people not put them in hospital with life changing injuries.

'You okay, babe?'

'Yeah. I do feel kind of bad that I wrecked his leg. But I just can't see that I had any choice.'

'You didn't. It was those two goons who made the choices. They went there with weapons, they made many choices stretching back years that threatening and beating up people was how they wanted to make their living. It was bound to come to a bad end sooner or later. It's just your bad luck that you were the one to do it.'

'Yeah. I know you're right. Logically it all stacks up. Doesn't stop me feeling bad.'

'Well, if it's any consolation, those two guys are washed up anyway.'

'What do you mean?' Emma turned back around to study Lukas.

'If you pay some guys to act as your bodyguards and hired muscle, there's one thing you need more than anything. Loyalty. This isn't a world where you can go to human resources and complain that they're in breach of their contract.'

'And those two sold out to a higher bidder.'

'Exactly. I mean, literally stabbing someone in the back is bad, as is attacking a man lying on the ground, but that is worse. Even when they get out of prison, no one will go near them.'

'Strangely, that is good to know.'

'So, what do you reckon the score will be with the legal crap?'

She paused, unsure of whether she should disclose confidential details. But Lukas was safe – he'd never betrayed a confidence. 'The physical evidence is so stacked against him, I might not even have to take the stand. He's definitely going down for murder.'

Lukas nodded and tapped the paper. 'So he won't have a leg to stand on.' He creased up at his joke and Emma joined in with the laughter. It really was a ridiculous case, done for publicity and not much else. It certainly had no chance of success but she supposed she should go and check in with the police legal service, just in case.

'What do you mean, murder?' Lukas asked. 'I thought he didn't kill Haines.'

'Doesn't matter,' Emma said, shaking her head. 'He was working with Lawson, who killed Billy King, so he can be got on joint enterprise. Both of them will face trial for murder and attempted murder as they were together.' She frowned at the article again. 'This makes no sense at all. Every time I was called in to meet with my bosses about what happened, I asked them if I was in trouble for excessive force.'

'And?'

'They said it was fine. Clear danger to public, police officer already attacked, two on one and they had weapons.'

'That doesn't make sense,' Lukas said, picking up the paper. He frowned as he read it carefully, word for word. 'Yeah, thought so. It's all fluff. I wondered how come he managed to get in the paper while on remand. He didn't. They might have a photo of him, but this is all the lawyer.' He nodded as he kept reading. 'Very smart. No mention of the offences Swain's charged with. Just trying to generate some sympathy and a bit of money at the same time. It's all the lawyer talking and not really saying anything.'

'That's a relief, but I'll keep an eye on it.' She shook her head. 'It's bad enough that we're being asked to do more with less, go out single-crewed and stuff, but now we've got to deal with idiot lawyers.' She picked up the paper. 'His name is Bishop, I'll make a note. I know that defendants have to have representation but some solicitors are better than others.'

They wandered companionably back into the living room.

'I know you said it was okay but I'd better make myself scarce before Kelly comes back. And I've got a report that I promised to write back at the office.'

'So, you'll be all right?' Lukas asked when they were at the door.

'You know, I think I will.' It was clear now – the legal case was completely frivolous given how serious the fight at the industrial estate had been. Time in Lukas' company was just what she'd needed as an antidote to office politics. She knew however that this respite was short lived – she had made promises to Suse and to return to the station.

* * *

After her break with Lukas, Emma had to go straight back to the station. She spent a frustrating afternoon at her desk. She had statistics to collate on overdoses and violence. Although the individual incidents were dramatic, the numbers themselves were very boring. It was a case of copying and formatting and then comparing and looking for patterns.

When she compared the most recent numbers from those she'd worked on when she'd first started, it made sobering reading. Lukas was right – in her absence Bradwick had turned into a battleground. Gone were the days of stability under Haines' regime. When she'd finished compiling the report, she typed "Conclusions and recommendations" in bold and stared at it. She had to find a tactful way to frame Lukas' suggestion that the good parts of Haines' network be revived without the illegal activities. She knew how conservative the police could be so she knew it would be a hard sell. As an organisation they were far more likely to distance themselves from anything that had the taint of corruption. On the other hand, it made perfect sense – the criminals and dealers would like nothing more than to get the incomers from County Lines out of their town. She started typing, using as many current management phrases as she could. She talked of cultivating CHIS from all strata of society. While she was crafting the report, she kept in mind that Suse would see the report and pass it on to the inspector. She also had to take care with the wording so that if Suse wanted to take the credit she'd have a hard job editing out Emma's involvement. She wished it wasn't necessary, but there it was. In an ideal world they'd be working together to advance in the police, but that wasn't going to happen any time soon.

When the report was all packaged up and sent across to Suse she called up the Companies House website. Lukas' basic idea of restarting the information network intrigued her. It was worth finding out who was running King Kabs now, to see if the idea had any merit.

Unsurprisingly, following their deaths, both Billy King and Sean Astbury had been removed as directors. Presumably the accountants and solicitors dealt with that after their deaths. But there was a third name, Thomas Quinn, who had also resigned his position as director. There was one new name on the list – Marnie King.

She cast her mind back to the barbecue earlier in the summer and recalled the image of a large woman, in every sense of the word. She had colourful clothes, lots of jewellery and long dark curly hair. A big personality, but she hadn't struck Emma as an astute business woman. Maybe appearances were deceptive.

Emma had never learned about the nuts and bolts of how the relationship between Billy King and Rob Haines had worked. Did Billy have an open door policy with his drivers, collate the information and pass it on to Rob? Or were individual drivers assigned out to members of CID as informants? There was obviously a close relationship between Rob and Billy, but with Rob's mental health still obviously quite shaky, asking him about a recently deceased friend was hardly a good idea.

The other side of the equation was Marnie King. Had she been put onto the paperwork in name only to let accountants run the company? Or was she more hands on? And if she was, how involved was she with the illegal side of the business? Emma would have to think hard about the correct approach to take. She couldn't contact a grieving widow and ask about how her dead husband had paid corrupt officers.

Chapter Nine

Rob Haines was slowly getting used to the rhythm of not going to work, waking later and watching reruns of classic TV from the past fifty years. He kept meaning to look The Sweeney up on Wikipedia and see how many episodes there were. He was sure that they were starting to repeat.

He knew that he was annoying Jem. She was constantly popping out, to work, to shop, to have coffee with friends. He knew that he should move forward, find a way out of the maze, work out what life held for him.

As fictional detectives rushed across the screen with bad haircuts and wide ties, he went back over the details as he understood them. He had done this too many times before but it was like worrying at a sore tooth. Like pieces on a chessboard, Rob Haines kept on rearranging the facts of his case and his recovery in his mind. He'd pressed the doctors about his memory loss and they thought that some of it might slowly return. But it was as certain as it could be that there would always be a gap in the events surrounding the head injury.

What this did mean, however, was that he was able to remember what had happened over most of his career. Stretching back years, and even decades, he was very clear on the toxic triangle that had existed between himself, Billy King and Reg Patterson. He could even recall that he had been preparing to hand over to Glen Hargreaves.

Now that King and Patterson were both dead and Hargreaves had been arrested, all the focus was on him, the last man standing. The deaths and the arrest had all happened in the big blank spot in his memory so he couldn't be called to testify. He had to hope that he could wait it out and that the authorities would focus on Hargreaves and let him off the hook.

Hiding behind his medical history wasn't his style. He was more of a kick the door in and arrest the bad guys policeman. But after talking with his police fed rep, he had submitted a brief medical statement which said that he had a "traumatic brain injury leading to memory loss and personality changes".

As a car chase unfolded on the TV screen, vehicles that were now classics sliding recklessly around south London streets, Rob Haines decided to be honest with himself. He hated this. He hated being painted as some sort of cripple who wasn't quite himself and couldn't remember what had happened. He knew that if, or rather when, it got out around the station there'd be a mixture of disbelief and sympathy. He wasn't sure which was worse.

But what was the alternative? If he confessed that he knew everything that had happened up to a week before the raid, he would be faced with two unpalatable choices. Either do a series of embarrassing "no comment" interviews which would all but confirm his guilt in the face of the evidence. Or, he could sell all his colleagues down the river and spill everything in the hope that he'd be allowed to keep his pension. And, despite calling in some favours, he still didn't know how much actual concrete evidence they had.

The truth of it was, however much it rankled, being seen as incapacitated by his head injury was his best course. He knew that there would be very little political will to prosecute or investigate him while he was on sick leave. All he had to do now was to find a way to negotiate that into a permanent exit from the force. A permanent exit that preserved his reputation and pension rights.

He was restless, he needed to do something. Reaching for the phone he called one the contacts who'd still talk to him.

'Rob, what's up?'

'I'm feeling a bit at a loose end. Any good gossip? Anything I should know?'

'Well, there is a juicy case floating around the station. Did you hear about the body at the motel?'

'No, haven't seen that one.' Rob didn't want to admit that he had got out of the habit of reading the news.

'Well, they didn't make much of it in the press.' The contact paused for effect. 'But the word is that the body was beheaded. And staged. Like something of out of one of those American serial killer films, from what I heard. Proper spooky.'

'Thanks for that, I could do with a distraction. I'll look it up on the news.' And I'll ask Emma Angel, if she ever comes back. 'And I'll see if my contacts in technical can fill me in a bit more.' He needed a good strong case to work on, to make himself feel more like he used to. And this was perfect.

Once he'd hung up, he used his phone and soon got the basic facts right. The press reports hinted that something wasn't right, but didn't go into the gruesome details.

The front door banged open and Jem came into the hall. He switched off the phone and dropped it on the sofa. 'Hi, Rob, I'm back.'

'Hi.'

She came into the lounge and squinted at the TV. 'That's Dennis Waterman, so I'm going to say Sweeney? Or Minder?'

'Right first time,' Rob said. 'But I think that I've seen it before.'

'Well, that'll happen when you spend all day at home sat on the sofa.' She stopped and studied him closely. 'I suppose there's no chance that you've been out today?'

He shook his head. 'You know I haven't. Just can't take the risk. You know that.'

'I do understand, but I also know that you've got to get out there at some point. I don't know what you're waiting for. Even a walk around the block would be a start.'

'It might get better,' Rob said in a quiet voice. 'The brain is incredibly flexible. No one really knows.'

'Rob, what did the doctors actually say?' Jem's voice was firm but insistent.

'Some things might get better. The brain heals itself. I've had fewer outbursts, I can feel myself becoming more normal, I feel more like more me.'

'Robert Haines, don't you mess me around. You know what we're talking about. Your problem. What did they say about that, the last time you asked?'

'They said it was very rare but if that's what it is, then it probably won't heal.'

Jem sighed. 'So, what are you waiting for?'

'I don't know.' Rob got off the sofa and moved towards the kitchen. 'I just don't feel like the time is right.' He paused to see if the conversation was over. Receiving no response, he said, 'I'll put the kettle on, you want anything?'

The awkward mood was broken when the doorbell went.

* * *

Once again, Emma stood on the doorstep of the Haines' house. This time however she'd phoned ahead and knew what would be waiting for her. She was still apprehensive but her first week back had made her realise just how much she missed her ex-boss at work. She had a list of questions that she needed answers to.

'Emma, come on in,' Jem said, breaking into her reverie.

Soon she was sat on the sofa with a cup of tea and a classic James Bond film was just starting on the television.

'The Spy Who Loved Me,' Rob said from his armchair. 'Classic stuff, mid-seventies, Roger Moore and a Lotus Esprit.'

'Do you mind if we talk while we watch this?'

'No, I've seen it before. Just don't talk over the good bits. What do you want to talk about?'

'I was wondering if you could give me some idea of who's who in CID now?' Rob gave her a completely dead stare, shocked that she'd just come straight out with it. She heard what she'd just said and how tactless it was. 'I mean, if you don't mind. What with you being replaced and all.' Rob continued glaring at her. 'No, forget what I said. I was being silly. Thoughtless.'

There was a tense silence, broken when Rob laughed. 'Oh dear God, I haven't had that much fun in ages. Listen, I've had a bang on the head and my career's probably down the tubes but that doesn't mean I'm holding onto a grudge or anything.' He paused and got a bit more serious. 'Also, I still want to help you. Who have they put into CID now? I know they've booted most of us out.'

'Thank you,' Emma said sullenly. She hated the feeling of being tricked, but it was nice to see Rob in a good mood. She couldn't remember the last time that she'd seen him laugh. Certainly not since he'd had his head injury and in the weeks before that he'd been under a lot of stress.

In the background, Roger Moore was riding across the desert on a camel in full Arab clothes. Her childhood had meant that she'd missed out on the simple pleasures like watching James Bond films on a Sunday afternoon. She did feel weird however that she was doing it with her ex-boss who was now a friend of sorts. 'What about starting at the top with our new inspector, Kevin Slater?'

Rob laughed again, more of a chuckle this time. 'I know of Slater and he's anything but new. He's been around the force longer than I have and that's saying something. I'd have thought he'd be retired by now.' He stopped to think. 'Although I can see that. Old hand, persuaded to delay retirement for six months, set the ship back on an even keel. How is he to work for?'

Emma stopped to think. She thought of her interest in the Callum Frost case and his inability to see anything beyond his own theory. 'He is a bit stuck in his ways. Inflexible. Doesn't seem very imaginative.'

'Yeah, that figures. Most of his life was spent working in fraud and white collar crime. Give him a computer, Internet connection and a load of spreadsheets and he's your man. But finding criminals in the real world?' He shook his head.

Emma considered correcting him and pointing out the real harm that financial crime did. But she knew what he meant – Slater would never be the one who was kicking in doors and organising raids. He'd be in the back office cataloguing the evidence and making a watertight case. 'I think that attitude has bled over into his work,' Emma agreed. 'He likes everything tied up. Because our latest case involves a financial advisor, he's convinced that it's about the money.'

'Is that the beheaded body in the hotel?' Rob asked innocently.

'I see your network hasn't completely dried up while you've been off, sir.'

'Of course not. I like to keep my ear to the ground. And that is a very unusual case. Not the sort of thing that the likes of Slater would be able to deal with. What's his take on it? Something conventional?'

'Yeah, he's going down the route of revenge – either for sex or money. The victim was a financial advisor so he travelled and stayed away from home a lot.'

'And possibly played away?' Rob asked.

'Well, the possibility is there. But there's no evidence. No condoms, wife appears genuinely distraught, but had no suspicions. It's the same with chasing down any money problems. There are no complaints against him so Slater's looking at money laundering. But, we would need to find a second laptop or phone first.'

'And a second phone would also put more life into the theory that he was having an affair.' He paused for a moment. 'And I take it there's no sign of either?'

'There's next to no evidence of anything. The problem is that to all intents and purposes our victim was a perfectly normal independent financial advisor.'

'Who was killed in a less than normal way.' Haines took a deep sigh and they fell back to watching the film for a bit. Roger Moore was now in a nightclub with a beautiful seventies Bond girl. Even the decor looked dated now. Emma could sense that the film was heading to places where no film made today would head.

'How can you watch this, sir? Rob?' she didn't quite know what to call him.

'What do you mean,' he asked innocently.

'Well, it's very sexist, isn't it? All that stuff where the men clap their hands and the girls leave the room so they can talk business. It's awful.'

'Okay. Firstly, this bit is set in Cairo and it was filmed in the mid-seventies. That's pretty much the way the world was back then. And secondly, you see that pretty woman in the glittery black dress, that you probably think is a Bond girl? Well, she's a Russian agent and one who's more than a match for Bond.'

'I suppose that offsets things a little,' Emma said, slightly mollified. 'But that's still no excuse for every other woman to have a bikini. Or for any of James Bond's witty comments about women.'

Haines shrugged. 'It's what I grew up with. I know it's not politically correct or anything like that but I still like it. It's comforting.' A happy pause fell between them as Jaws, the seven foot killer came onto the screen. 'Anyway, how about some quid pro quo? There are rumours around that there's something really weird about this murder that happened at the motel. No one wants to talk about it, but if I'm going to give you the dirt on your new team...' He looked hopefully at Emma.

For her part, she weighed up the options. Even off on leave and under a cloud of suspicion, Rob Haines was still very well connected. He'd find out sooner or later. And she doubted that he wanted lurid gossip. The tension that she'd detected between Rob and Jem was probably from him being bored. Should she tell him? He was an off-duty police officer. More importantly, she was certain that he wouldn't do anything to compromise the investigation and he might even help.

'You're not going to believe this,' Emma said. She briefly outlined what they knew so far about the probable cause of death and how the body had been handled post-mortem.

'So, the chambermaid walked in and the body turned its head towards her and opened its eyes?' Emma nodded. 'All done with trip-wires and careful balancing? It's horrific.' He shook his head. 'I mean you expect some sort of dignity in death don't you? I mean, I know we're police officers so we see bodies in all sorts of places, shallow graves, dumped in the rubbish, just left where they are.' He stopped for a moment, lost in thought. 'Could it be a disgruntled undertaker?'

'Disgruntled or psychotic? I could ask Dani whether or not the body was professionally handled,' Emma said.

'Where there any indications from the scene of what kind of person this is? Was he angry, rushed, anything like that?'

'If anything, quite the opposite. From what Dani said he was very meticulous. He custom made some hooks and the bracket to hold the head. Dani was impressed by his skills – he sounds like someone you'd want to do your DIY for you.'

'I'm not too sure about that,' Rob said with a chuckle. 'I tend not to want murderers in my house.' There was a companionable pause between them, broken by Rob. 'Thank you for that. I know that you probably shouldn't have told me about this but I'm going stir crazy in here.' He nodded. 'I'll have a think. See if I can remember someone who fits the profile. I suspect they'd have worked their way up to a crime like this.' They watched the film for a few moments. 'Oh, now here we go. This is the car chase with the Lotus Esprit! This is the famous bit.'

'What, that white car that looks like a wedge of cheese?' Emma asked innocently.

'No taste at all,' Rob said, all mock offence. 'When I was a kid, that car was the one that everyone wanted. You could get a toy of it with all the bits, missiles that fired and all sorts.' He looked closely at Emma. 'You have no idea what I'm talking about, do you?'

'Not my era,' she said. 'And in case you've forgotten, I was a little girl, so not so much into the toy cars and James Bond.'

'Yeah, but you must have had friends, all of that?'

Emma shrugged. When the silence stretched a bit, she said, 'Shall we carry on going through the new CID line-up?'

'You always do that,' Rob observed, still watching the film. The car leapt spectacularly off a pier and went under water. 'Whenever there's anything about childhood or growing up, you suddenly clam up. Give a little shrug and change the subject.'

'What can I say? I wasn't that happy as a child.' She paused. 'Well, no that's not true. My parents moved around a lot, were quite chaotic, so I was always in and out of school and changed a few times. Made it hard to make friends.' She took a deep breath. 'But I had a lot of freedom over the summer holidays. Ups and downs.'

'Sounds like an interesting way to grow up,' Rob observed.

'That's one word for it. Anyway, I'm sure I've mentioned that I had a huge row with my parents after my GCSEs and moved out.'

'And you've never spoken to them since?'

'No, not really. I mean it's not like I've cut them off all together. They know where I am and I could probably find them if I wanted to. I've got an aunt, Belle, who's more settled down. I lived there over sixth form and she's always been my next-of-kin contact.'

'You don't even have your parents down as next-of-kin?' Rob shook his head, amazed at the depth of the rift. Something about her demeanour told Rob that the subject was closed. But he burned with curiosity to know the details about the family feud.

'Anyway, that's the whole story,' Emma said briskly, confirming Rob's suspicion that he'd gone as far as he could. 'Is it all right if I pick your brains about the rest of my team now?'

'Of course. Sorry to pry. Who else do you want the official Rob Haines' opinion for?'

'There's a guy called Brian Chisholm, he's in as a detective sergeant. I should know his name but I can't place him.'

Rob gave a low chuckle. 'Old Chisholm. I can't believe he kept his job.' Emma still looked confused. 'If I said Inspector Chisholm? Of the Domestic Violence Unit?'

'Oh, yes. Wasn't he... well, I thought he quit? Under a cloud?'

'He should've done. He took his work home, if you see what I mean. His wife filed for divorce and all the dirty laundry came out. He's just hanging on until retirement really.'

Emma's flesh crawled. She'd been in the same office as a wife beater? She'd taken orders from him, talked to him like a friend? She was now re-evaluating her relationship with the man. He'd come across as a bit of a dinosaur but nothing worse.

Rob saw her reaction. 'Of course, he's a bit of a test case. He had to go on all sorts of awareness courses and everything. I think all the higher-ups are watching him to see if he can be rehabilitated. How do you feel that he's coming on?'

Emma nodded. All her experience told her that once a man was a predator, that was how he'd stay. But, there again, those in charge obviously thought that Chisholm deserved a second chance. What she did know was that she was likely to keep a far closer eye on him in the future. 'I don't know. I haven't had to work directly with him. Now I know though, I'll keep an eye out.'

Her thoughts were drawn, as they often were to Gregory Watts. If her bosses believed in rehabilitation for a policeman, where did that leave him? Emma knew that his current pattern of chasing schoolgirls was already well established. She resolved that the best place for him was behind bars.

'It sounds fairly predictable so far,' Haines said, breaking into her thoughts. 'People who are waiting to retire but no one else wants on their team. But between them, they will bring in plenty of experience. I may not always have seen eye to eye with Chisholm, but he is a solid copper. Who else has been assigned to the sinking ship?'

'It's not that bad!' Emma protested. 'Anyway we've got one new sergeant, some woman Susan, call me Suse, Berman. And, when you give me your opinion, you'd better avoid the word "dyke" or any references to female golfers.'

'I'm not that bad.' Rob held his hands up. 'And it doesn't matter whose bed she chooses to spend the night in. She's proper canny that one. Ain't never going to be a raving beauty but she looks the part to get some credit for diversity. And she's dead ambitious to boot.'

'So, how should I deal with her?'

'Well, try to get on her good side. If she likes you, she'll take you up with her. She's always been right there, knowing what the latest buzz word is, what the management want to hear. Give her ten years and she'll probably outrank me. Don't let me take anything away from her, though. She's a good copper.'

'As long as you stay on her good side and don't get in her way?'

'Now you're getting it.' Rob smiled.

'Shame I don't like her then,' Emma admitted.

Rob nodded. 'She's not one for doing the right thing and sod the consequences, like you are. Much more in favour of working out the odds and seeing what's best for her.'

Emma went cold. Had he remembered more details about the raid? Even worse, had he figured out who it was who'd shopped him to Professional Standards? Stonor already knew so it'd only be a matter of time.

'Is it true what I heard about Andy Stonor?' Rob asked. 'Down to detective constable.'

'Yep.'

'Figures. I could never turn him, you know. God knows I tried, but with his family history.' He took a deep breath. 'I'll be honest, always gave me a bit of a worry that did. Andy, right there on the inside, knowing everything but not involved.' He rubbed his hand over his hair that was still short and stubbly. 'Oh, I know he would never rat out on a mate, on his team, but you know. It kept me awake some nights.'

Emma sat there, struck dumb. She really didn't know how to negotiate this one.

'What's up? Have I been a bit direct again?' Rob asked. 'I get these thoughts in my head and they come out of my mouth before I've had a chance to think. I did tell you about the fiddle, didn't I? Taking money and information from Billy King in return for an easier ride and some product for him?'

'Yes, yes, you did tell me. Even tried to recruit me, the night before the raid. You probably don't remember, you know, with the head and all.' There was an awkward silence. 'And it did take me a bit by surprise. You just talking about this like we're passing the time of day.'

'Yeah, I know, sorry.' There was another pause. 'What did you say?'

'When?'

'When I tried to recruit you. I literally have no memory of it whatsoever.'

'Oh, I...' Emma was stuck. 'I was going to think it over. You left it up to me. After the raid I was to join the evidence collecting team if I wanted to help divide up the spoils, and if not, I'd have escorted the prisoners back to the station.' She paused, knowing that she'd have to get the next lie spot on. 'I hadn't really made my mind up when it all went tits up anyway.'

And awkward pause fell between them. The raid hadn't gone off okay. The question still wasn't answered and it hung between them. The lie weighed heavily on Emma. She had made up her mind. And her decision had been to betray the man she was now watching a film with.

Eventually the silence became too awkward. 'We've also got a new recruit,' Emma said.

'Huh, what was that?'

'Detective Constable Nicholas Dent. I must be getting old, because he looks like he's about twelve.'

Rob Haines laughed. 'It'll only get worse from here on in. What did you say his name was?'

'Nick Dent. Surely you don't know him?'

'No, not directly. But he must've come up through the uniformed ranks. I can ask around.' He sounded conciliatory, backing away from the previous conflict.

'Thank you. It'd be nice to know who I'm working with.'

Eventually the Atlantis base was being destroyed and James Bond was escaping with his Russian lover.

'I'd better get off,' Emma said, keen to escape before any more awkward questions were asked. On the doorstep, however, she thought she might have one more attempt to mend fences. 'With the advantage of hindsight though, it's a pretty good job that Professional Standards were involved. On the night of the raid, I mean.'

'How do you figure that, then?' All of Rob's good mood had gone. He clearly still saw the past as us versus them.

'Well...' Emma faltered a bit in the face of his antagonism. 'If Professional Standards hadn't been on the ground during the raid, where would we be now? Glen Hargreaves would've walked Pietr Garoza straight through the cordon and out of trouble. You'd have woken up in hospital to him leading CID, completely in the pocket of Garoza. Between them they would, by now, be on their way to turning Bradwick into a major importing hub for drugs from Bristol down to Cornwall. With all the sex trafficking and violence that come with it.'

Rob Haines took a deep breath. He looked uncomfortable. 'Like I say, I have no memories for over twenty-four hours, either side of the raid.'

'What do your contacts say?'

'Well, the doctors and Jem want to keep me insulated from bad memories. Apparently it's better if they come back naturally, not forced. That's why I'm grateful to you for filling me in.' He stopped to think. 'I suppose you could be right. Obviously I never wanted Professional Standards to shut things down. I was working on a strategy to carefully extricate myself from the scheme. Move on up through the ranks. But I suppose you're right,' he finally conceded. 'I had my doubts about Glen, I remember that much. I underestimated how bad he was.'

Emma nodded, and slowly backed away. Something else had occurred to her. Without the involvement of Professional Standards, there was a chance she wouldn't have been with Rob Haines on the night in question. And if that hadn't happened, then the day after the raid, both King and Haines would've been dead and Glen Hargreaves would've had unchallenged control over CID, the drugs trade and Bradwick.

She shook her head as she walked back to her car. However badly her decisions had played out, at least she had avoided that particular outcome.

Chapter Ten

When Emma arrived on Monday morning, the preliminary results of the deep search on Fairthorpe's background were in. Despite his spectacular and unconventional death, he appeared to have led an exceptionally ordinary life. He had travelled up and down the south west, visiting people and arranging their finances – he did loans, investments, mortgages – the usual range of services. The problem was that there were very few complaints against him. Forensic accountants had started digging into his accounts but he didn't appear to be living outside his means. He drove a three-year-old Vauxhall Insignia and lived in a nice village in Gloucestershire, in a modest house.

Emma sat back and rubbed her eyes. It didn't make sense at all. Murder was a big deal. Despite what film and TV taught people, people very rarely just went out and killed someone. Usually, to become a murder victim, someone had to have seriously upset someone else. There were a few oddities, like people who'd kill over road rage or a spilled pint. But this wasn't a random event, like a pub fight gone wrong. No, the killer had gone to the motel with clear intent. He'd taken along a taser, a knife, a saw and a whole bag of DIY kit. All planned out in advance. That meant that the killer knew Fairthorpe, had a relationship with him and wanted him dead.

But why? That was the key question. An affair was looking increasingly unlikely. They'd found no condoms or second mobile in his personal effects. The technical teams were still working on his phone and laptop but Emma knew instinctively they'd find no trace of a lover. The wife had no suspicions and it looked like she was right.

Right now her best guess was organised crime. He worked with money and bank accounts, so he could have hidden ill-gotten gains in any number of places. If he'd been involved in money laundering and then moved on to skimming off the profits, then his murder would serve as a gruesome, public warning to what happens to people who cheat.

She wasn't the only one thinking this way. There were literally hundreds of actions on the system to check every one of his clients to see if they had any criminal links at all. She felt like crying. That was weeks of work and she could guess who'd be doing most of it.

She listlessly typed in the first name – a retired man from a suburb of Exeter. No links, nothing even vaguely dodgy. She was saved from further drudgery by the phone. It was Dani Price, the pathologist.

'I've got a weird one for you,' she said.

'What's up?'

'Well, this guy phoned through to the police. He was walking his dog along by the beach, when it turned up with a lump of flesh in his mouth.'

'Human flesh?'

'Well, that's the thing. It was burnt and had a bit of bone sticking out of it. Could've been a forearm.'

'I'm guessing, as this is the first that I've heard of it, it was a false alarm?'

'Yes. Good for a barbecue though. Someone got hold of a whole pig and blew it up.'

'Blew it up? What do you mean?'

'Well, we found a shallow crater and some scorched earth. It seems they tried to clear it up but there were still bits and pieces of bone and flesh around.'

'What are we looking at? Animal cruelty?' Emma was sick to her stomach at the thought of exploding animals.

'No, no, nothing like that. It was properly prepared and cleaned by a butcher. I'd be more concerned with someone handling explosives and setting off explosions.'

'Right then.' Emma got all the details of the location and time. It was in a quiet area of Bradwick, backing on to some waste ground.

Emma rubbed her eyes and thought over what she'd just learnt. It was actually useless information. She could pass it up to counter terrorism but without a time, date or person involved it would go nowhere. The area was a piece of scrubland outside the Seaview Estate, overlooking the sea. Any one of thousands of people could've accessed it. It could be anything from someone planning the next atrocity to kids mucking around with fireworks. She decided to create a report, circulate it to counter terrorism and put it out of her mind.

Chapter Eleven

She called up the next two of Fairthorpe's clients and ran them through the system but found no links. She was sure that she was barking up the wrong tree. More for a break than anything else, she went back to the initial report on the crime scene and skim-read it, paying more attention to the photos. Something wasn't right about the scene but she had no idea what, so she just let her mind drift as the pages scrolled past.

She realised what had been tugging at her consciousness. There had been a poster found at the scene. She called up the forensic report on it and frowned.

It was unused – no traces that it had ever been stuck to a surface, no holes from pins. One set of fingerprints, not on file anywhere. No folds or creases. But, crucially, the report did state that all the evidence pointed to it being fifteen years old. Most likely it was one of thousands that had been printed at the time.

An immediate question sprang to Emma's mind. Who on earth keeps a poster for a missing child for all that time? Not faded or creased, but kept flat somewhere, preserved. She could guess that at the time a local print firm would've printed them out and handed them to anyone who wanted one – shops, businesses or volunteers to stick them up. Getting hold of one or more would've been easy. It was the keeping of it that worried her.

She knew she was right about it being important and her boss was wrong. The whole crime scene had been staged. She didn't buy the idea that it was just a distraction. Even if the perpetrator had thought they'd done it randomly as a misdirection then Emma knew that it was a clue. Something might be buried in there, left subconsciously.

So, she pulled the keyboard towards her and started searching for the files on Callum Frost. On Saturday July 3, 2004 the Seaview Estate had been basking in sunshine. Children had come and gone from each other's homes, barbecues had been lit and a good time was being had by all. But, as the evening drew in and people drifted home it became clear that Callum Frost, aged twelve, was missing. The crisis spread slowly from a few phone calls to parents, to fathers and uncles walking round the estate in an improvised posse. Finally, when it was fully dark, the police were called in.

Thankfully, the officers on the ground had been quite forward thinking. A case like this, in a tight-knit community, it was always worth looking at the members of the public who got involved in the case. There were countless instances of people abducting children and then joining the search party, either to throw the scent off or to glory in the pain they'd caused. She called up a file and found a long list of people who'd formed the search parties, even down to the wives who'd manned the community centre, making tea and sandwiches. She hoped that one of them would leap out at her – maybe the passage of time would mean that someone who had been overlooked in the past was now of interest to police. She had just about given up hope when she got to the end of the list. She stopped and stared at the screen, almost unbelieving.

Albert and Margaret Watts.

Could it be? She pushed back from her desk and was about to go and ask DCI Haines to use his contacts to find out how they were related to Gregory Watts. Instead she slumped back down in her chair. She couldn't ask Haines. He wasn't dead, but in a professional capacity, he was as good as.

She checked the clock – it was a reasonable time for lunch. Without second-guessing herself, she left for lunch and went straight to the registry office. This kind of job needed to be done in person. Not only did her boss not want the Callum Frost trail followed, but going after Gregory Watts was even further from what she was supposed to be doing. There was no point in leaving a trail of either paper or email. She'd make sure that she was right before involving anyone else.

Soon she was in the registry office of Bradwick, a lovely old brick-built building, part of the town's Victorian heritage. She had navigated the various forms and the obscure filing system. Her lunch break had stretched so far that she'd have to work late to make up for it, but she was happy. She sat at the dusty desk, holding a piece of paper. The birth certificate of one Gregory Charles Watts. Mother and father listed as Margaret and Albert Watts respectively.

She needed to think. He would've been sixteen when Callum Frost disappeared. Was that old enough to become a predator? She shook her head. It wasn't about the age that Gregory had been, it was about his preferred victim. He was all about the schoolgirls, barely legal. She just couldn't see him being a predator after a twelve-year-old boy, then almost immediately switching to sixteen-year-old girls. In Emma's experience, if a predator had a type, then they tended to stick to it. And Gregory definitely had a type.

She wasn't going to get anywhere being away from the station staring at a piece of paper for too long, though. Now she had the information she needed, she pushed herself away from the desk and got ready to return to the station.

Back at her usual desk, Emma skimmed the rest of the file on Callum Frost. Mostly it was about what had happened in the weeks and months following the disappearance. There were pages of negatives and open case reviews. But no matter what was done, there was no progress. His bicycle had been found the day after the disappearance in a hedge beside a path that led to the beach. Even though the search then swung towards the sea, there were still no results.

So why, fifteen years after his disappearance, was someone bringing their attention back to the case? The most obvious outcome for the case was that Callum had either been abducted or had an accident and ended up being swept into the sea. She flicked back through the case notes and found the initial, rudimentary timeline and nearly groaned out loud. The last reliable sighting had been at one in the afternoon while the alarm hadn't been raised until after eight that evening. Seven hours later. If it was every parent's worst nightmare – a random abduction – then he could've been anywhere in the country before anyone even knew he was missing. Or dead, she thought bleakly. In the file it did show that the case had been referred to the National Crime Agency for profiling. Unfortunately, there were no other crimes that matched the pattern for several years either side.

Which left accident, she thought. Within a mile or so of the estate was a river that emptied into the sea and was connected to abandoned waterways from the Victorian industrial history of the area. Plenty of opportunity for a child to have an accident and be swept out to sea. Or worse, she reflected, letting the darker thoughts take over, plenty of places to hide a body.

* * *

At the end of the day was the meeting Emma had been dreading. The first-week review on the Fairthorpe case. With what she'd learnt from Rob, she looked at her colleagues with new eyes. DS Brian Chisholm – he had a long way to go before she'd ever trust him. She vowed to be professional around him, but no more.

Then there was Suse as well, quietly reading through some paperwork. Now Emma understood her far better. She was always on the ball, taking any opportunity to learn more, look for another angle. Anything to get ahead.

DI Kev Slater came in and called the meeting to order, breaking Emma's train of thought. As expected, progress was thin on the ground. It was left to DS Chisholm, as one who didn't really care about his career, to ask the awkward questions.

'Boss, I passed some queries up to you. Other forces, national agencies and even departments within our force are pushing back on the expense of tracking down hundreds of his clients.'

Kev looked slightly uncomfortable. 'Yes, I've dealt with some of them. And we've had some high-level discussions about the overall cost of the operation.'

'And?' Brian Chisholm asked pointedly, 'Was there any outcome from those discussions?'

'I was about to come on to that. I think we're going to have to screen the list first, informally.' When the people around the table looked confused, he pressed on. 'I've got copies of the entire client list here, enough for everyone. I want you to go through it and see if anyone pops out as being worthy of further investigation. We'll do the same with the national agencies and other forces.'

Brian Chisholm's face spread into a slow grin. 'You mean old-fashioned police work? Have a look and see who we think is moody, before going through the computers? Play our hunches?'

DI Kev Slater flushed. 'Well, I wouldn't put it exactly like that. But yes, that is the essence of the approach that we're looking for. Minimise the number of hits on the computer, minimise the cost.'

'Could I just point something out?' DC Nicholas Dent still seemed overawed at being in CID.

'That is how a case review works, Nick,' Kev said sharply.

'Well, if I was a dodgy financial advisor,' he said unsteadily, 'and I was getting involved in money laundering or something illegal, well I'd run it in parallel. I'd have one set of clean records – a group of clients that I dropped in on, had a cup of tea, and advised them properly, all above board. But at the same time, I'd run a second business, insulated from the first. Different phone, different laptop, different accounts.' He paused now he had the attention of the room. 'I mean, there might be a crossover. He could use the clean side of the business to the benefit of the dirty side, if you see what I mean.'

Brian closed his eyes and rubbed them. 'You know, young Nick, I'm not one hundred per cent sure I do see what you mean. How does this help us?'

'Okay, let's get specifics. He goes to see a little old lady, let's call her Mrs Smith. In order to invest her money, he gets her name, address, date of birth, etc. If he's good, he'll probably have copies of her documents, driving license, passport, proof of address, that sort of thing. He either trains her to give him all the statements when they arrive through the post or gets it sent to him direct. He can then open investment accounts using her name and details and then pass money through them. So we don't need to be looking for someone who's related to a gangster or organised criminal. We're looking for someone who has unusual activity in their name.'

'Like identity theft,' Kev said. 'Which puts us back to square one. We can't really check every account opened in each one of over a hundred names. And some of them might not remember if it was straight or not. Or, if he's as good as you say, they might not be aware of an extra account or two in their names. As long as their own money is invested and growing, they wouldn't have any reason to look deeper.' The mood around the table dropped. 'What else have we got?'

'Well,' DC Stonor said, 'we've tracked down as much CCTV as possible. There's none inside the motel itself, but the forecourt is pretty well covered. The trouble is that it's a petrol station on a busy main road and we've got quite a large window of time.' He looked at some notes. 'Body discovered around ten fifteen in the morning. So, according to our pathologist, it wouldn't work because of rigor mortis if he died any time before eight fifteen. But we don't know when he was attacked, and how much DIY our killer did before finishing him off. So we're checking from about seven up until ten.' He looked glum. 'That pretty much covers rush hour as you can imagine. At the moment it's really a case of recording as many names and addresses as we can identify. Once we get a strong suspect we can see if we've got a match. But it's nearly impossible to go back the other way and find the suspect from the list.'

'Anything else?' Kev asked.

Emma was getting fed up, so she asked, 'What about that poster of Callum Frost?'

'I still think that's a distractor,' Kev said. 'Put there just to confuse us.'

Emma wasn't going to be put off now. She knew that her boss was risk averse, but she couldn't afford to let him shutdown a valid line of enquiry. 'But we've got the results back from document forensics, and it appears that it was printed in the early noughties but it's never been used. No sign of adhesive of any type and no pinholes.' When there were blank looks around the table, she pushed on. 'Doesn't that strike anyone else as odd? I checked and a local printing firm ran off about a thousand of them for free. They were handed out everywhere, shops, restaurants, anyone who wanted to could pick up a stack and put them up in their local area. They turned up in pubs, shops, petrol stations, schools, libraries, everywhere really.'

Stonor and Chisholm both nodded. 'Aye. I remember, you couldn't turn round for seeing them.'

'So, who the hell gets one, and stores it away?' Emma tapped a buff folder on the table in front of her. 'There were no fade marks, no water damage, creases, nothing. Whoever had this poster took care of it, kept it flat and dark, and most likely they then brought it to the hotel where they killed Fairthorpe. Especially as that was a killing which was carried out with care and precision. This can't be an accident or a coincidence.'

'What do you want us to do though, Emma?' Kev asked. 'You said yourself they were printed for free and handed out to everyone. We can't trace one poster from a thousand.'

'No, but we could look into the disappearance again. It obviously means something to our killer. It was on the Seaview Estate, and I know some families stay there for decades. Maybe now someone will remember something? Or maybe say something that they were too afraid to say at the time? We might find a suspect who sticks out?'

'You'll have to be careful though,' Andy Stonor said, looking at Brian for confirmation. 'They have long memories on the Seaview.'

'That they do.' Brian took up the thread. 'And they see the Callum Frost case as a failure. The community failed to keep a child safe and the police failed to protect them, then it failed to find him or catch his abductor. There's a lot of resentment up there, even now.'

Kev nodded slowly, his lips pursed. 'Okay. So, Emma, this was your idea, so you run with it. But these two are right, you'll have to tread very carefully. Some quarters believed that the case was internal to the Seaview, and that message leaked out, so there's a lot of bad feeling up there. But, do what you can, go carefully and see what you can dig up.'

Emma felt like putting her head down on the desk and crying. But she couldn't, she wasn't allowed to in this environment. 'Will do, boss,' she said curtly. Damn, why did she have to speak up? She could have just done this quietly under the radar. But, on the other hand, she did have some information. She would have to tread carefully as the case was obviously still an open wound on the estate. That was the local knowledge that Haines would have supplied in the past.

An idea formed in her head and she decided right then to carry it out. She got up and found Kev Slater in his office. She knew that she was on thin ice but she also knew that she was right in what she wanted to say to her boss.

'Sir, can we talk about Rob Haines?'

'Rob, yes, of course.' He pushed his keyboard away and swung to focus on her. 'I was meaning to have a word anyway. You can't be seen to be too attached to him. He won't do any good for your career, and could easily drag you down with him.' She started to speak but he held up a hand. 'Before you say anything, there are things that you're not aware of. Haines was a divisive figure in the force, especially among the more senior ranks. Obviously, no one wanted him to be injured, we never want any officer to be assaulted. But his being off on leave has been a bonus for everyone. I'm sure you know that there is always a reluctance to move towards official sanctions on senior staff. We don't want dirty laundry being washed in public. If he does make a full recovery, instead of returning to work, he'll go straight into a corruption enquiry, suspended on full pay. Whatever the outcome, I wouldn't rely on him ever returning to work. So he's not someone that you want to be associated with whichever way it goes.'

'I'm sorry that you feel that way, sir.' She had to pause to tamp down her anger at the way her previous boss was being discussed. And she needed get her courage up. 'I was going to suggest that you brought him in to consult on this case. He has–'

'Did you not hear a word I said?' Kev snapped. 'This personal attachment to your previous senior officer will not be looked on favourably.'

'Okay, sir. Let's put my friendship with Rob Haines to one side for a minute. Let's look at this purely logically. We have no idea why this killer is targeting his victim. Without knowing this, we can't determine where he will strike next or who's in danger. Rob Haines, for all his faults, has impressive and deep local knowledge. He's been in the area for decades, and working for the police for a lot of that. His contacts are invaluable.'

'And I'll have you know that I have more time served than Rob Haines. He is a loose cannon with questionable judgement. As far as anyone can tell he ran the worst corruption ring that this county has ever seen.'

'That was all in the past.' Emma seethed. She knew that most of Kev Slater's time had been served behind a desk working a spreadsheet while Rob had been out in the community. 'And you know that he's a good copper, with the safety of Bradwick in his heart.'

'Right.' Kev's mouth set in a hard line. 'I've made my position clear. I can tell that you'll go your own way and ultimately it's not in my power to stop you pursuing any friendships that you might wish. But I hope I've made my opinion clear.' He paused to make sure that his words had hit home. 'And you might want to check with HR to see what would happen if you pass on confidential information about a case to someone not on the team.'

Emma went back to her desk without a word. She'd been humiliated – told off like a schoolchild. She'd tried to do the right thing and it had blown up in her face. She could've just informally talked the case over with Rob and kept her boss in the dark.

In the future, that definitely seemed to be the best approach to take.

CHAPTER TWELVE

Emma knocked at the familiar door. Every time she stood on the step she was transported back to the first time she'd called at his house. The night that she had destroyed his world. She couldn't help but wonder when or if he might recover his memories. But she was here now purely to be bloody-minded and to prove to herself that she wouldn't abandon her friends.

When Jem let her in, she recognised the feeling in the house. Haines was still in his uniform of tracksuit trousers and T-shirt.

'Emma, lovely to see you again.' As usual he was pleased to see her. 'Can you put up with another film?'

'No, not today,' she replied. 'I had another idea. When did you last leave the house?'

'What do you mean? I went up the hospital last week. Standard neurological follow-up appointment.'

'I drove him,' Jem said. 'What are you getting at?'

'Apart from hospital appointments, then. When did you last go out?'

Haines looked a little lost as if there was something he didn't want to admit.

'Come on! Let's at least go out down the café and get a coffee. You won't get any better if you're just sitting around here all day.'

Rob and Jem glanced at each other. Emma had no idea what unspoken message passed between them but there was clearly some secret that she wasn't being let in on.

'You can't tell me what to do. I'm your–'

'What are you, Rob?' Emma asked. He looked momentarily confused. 'I know you outrank me and you're still on the payroll.'

'What then, DC Angel?'

'Well, you have been replaced at work and I'm off work this evening. So I'm just here as a friend,' she said. She then looked at Jem and added, 'A friend of the family.'

Rob considered her argument. 'Like you said, I'm still a DCI, still on the payroll. But even as a friend you can't bully me out of my own home.'

There was a tense stand-off, broken by Jem. 'Oh, for God's sake, Rob. You are so stubborn. Go and have a shower, get some proper clothes on. We're going out.'

'But what about–'

'We'll handle that. You'll have me and Emma with you. We won't leave your side. It'll be okay.' She laid a hand on his arm and looked into his eyes. 'Trust me, Rob. It's taken Emma to make me see. We need to get back to some sort of normal.'

'Normal? You don't know if there'll ever be any sort of normal. The doctors are always hedging their bets with brain injuries.' He turned to confide in Emma. 'They say that the brain heals itself over time but can never give any specifics of what will repair or how long it will take.' He paused and took a breath. The two women were resolute, unmoved by his outburst. 'Stubborn I may be, but I know when I'm beaten.'

He stomped off upstairs to get ready to go out.

'What's the big secret?' Emma asked. 'Why doesn't he want to go out?'

'It's not really my place to say,' Jem replied. Then, seeing this wasn't enough of an answer, she continued. 'I will tell you, in broad terms, this injury has knocked his confidence. You know his moods and his memory aren't what they were. You promise me that you won't leave him alone?'

'We're only going out for coffee! It's not like a drug raid or anything.'

'I know. But promise me, okay. He needs support. I won't have this going wrong and setting him back.'

Jem drove the three of them to a pub in a village just to the south of Bradwick on the coast. It was somewhere they'd never been to before. Emma wondered why this fact was important enough for her to mention.

Finally they were sat at a table, making the most awkward small talk. Both Rob and Jem looked around all the time, watching every time a new customer walked in.

When Jem went to the loo, Emma seized her chance. 'Come on then, boss. What's the problem? You're here, with cake and coffee. But you and Jem are so jumpy. I've interviewed first time drug dealers who were calmer than you two.'

'I don't know what you mean,' Rob said to the tabletop.

'Is it some kind of PTSD thing? I know that I've been offered leaflets and counselling because I fought someone who was trying to kill me and witnessed a murder.' All she got back was sullen silence. 'Are you worried because you trusted Billy King and Glen Hargreaves and the whole thing blew up in your face? Now you don't know who to trust?'

'No, it's nothing like that.'

Emma tapped the table edge in frustration. 'I want to be a good friend to you,' she said. 'You trusted me before. And I've trusted you – told you what happened when no one else would. But I can't help you if you don't talk to me. Jem dropped hints but she said it's down to you. Your decision.' With an instinct born of hours spent in interview suites, she then went quiet.

Eventually, Rob Haines gave a rueful smile. He knew the tactic and it was working. 'I can't recognise faces,' he said simply.

'What do you mean? Since the accident?'

'Yes. I woke up in hospital and Jem was there holding my hand, sat by the bed. She had long dark curly hair, and the same clothes I remember, but her face.' He stopped and stared off into space, frustrated.

'You couldn't see her face?' Emma frowned as she tried to understand.

'No, it's not like that. I can see her eyes, nose, mouth but it's like they're all separate. I can't make them all fit together and then recognise that face as belonging to Jem.'

'But you were all right when I came round, weren't you?'

'You're forgetting that I may be on sick leave, but I'm still a detective.' He looked up as he remembered the day. 'My memory is a bit slow, but it's all there. When Jem opened the door, she said your name and that you were from my work. I can remember you, who you are, what your hairstyle is, how you talk – everything about you apart from your face.'

'So, if another short woman with blonde hair had walked in after Jem opened the door?'

'I'd have assumed it was you until she spoke,' Rob said, shaking his head.

A silence hung over the table and lasted until Jem returned.

'You told her then? Good. Maybe she can talk some sense into you about this.'

Emma picked up the hint. 'Have you told the doctor yet?'

'Told him what? I had a bang on the head and it knocked the ability to recognise people clean out. They already think I'm crazy because I had a concussion.'

Emma sighed, used to his intransigence. She got out her phone, typed in "can't recognise faces head injury" then slid the results across to Rob. 'Look. Over fifty million hits in Google. From the charity Headway and the NHS. It's a thing, and it can be dealt with.'

He took the phone and tapped a few times, like a sulky child. 'Doesn't look curable.' He looked from Emma to Jem and recognised when he was beaten. 'I'll make an appointment with the GP and he can refer me to a shrink.' He sounded thoroughly miserable. 'Actually, first I'll talk to my police fed rep.' Both of the women looked confused, so he continued. 'Photographs of people don't look like them any more. When I got home there were all these photos on the mantelpiece. Our wedding, Jem holding each of the girls in hospital, that kind of thing. Except to me, they could've been cut out of a magazine.' He shook his head, unaware of how upset Jem was looking. 'Thing is, I'm a policeman. You could show me a mugshot of Bradwick's most wanted and five minutes later I'd sit next to them in the pub, without a clue. If this goes on my medical record, I can't be a policeman. It's that simple.'

Emma and Jem looked shocked.

'Oh, come on! My career is over anyway. Between being too close to Billy King, and having Glen Hargreaves under my command, I'd be a fool to go back to work. Professional Standards would eat me for breakfast. Even if I did survive that, I would never get another promotion. Why do you think none of the rest of the team have been round to see me? They've all been done for the drugs and money that went missing. No, all I've got to do is figure out a proper exit strategy. And actually a medical reason might be just the thing I need.' He looked thoughtful.

'Yeah, but really, Rob, can you get out from under this?' Jem asked. 'I mean, I know you had your reasons, and we've had our arguments over that. But will they really let you go, keep your pension, all of it?'

'There shouldn't be but there is a definite ranking system of corrupt officers.' Rob leant in closer to make sure he wasn't overheard. 'But I was fairly low level.' Both women were shocked. 'No one I arrested didn't deserve it. It's not like those cases where they bang some bugger up for a murder they didn't do or even shoot someone on suspicion of being a terrorist.' He paused to think. 'I will admit that maybe some people who should've been arrested were given an easier time. But anyway. there isn't anyone left who can testify.'

Emma was shocked at how easily he admitted his guilt while she was struggling to live with her own. She had given the order that had led to the whole operation going wrong. But until Rob's memories returned there was nothing she could do.

'What? Is it the bang on the head thing again?' Rob asked, looking between Jem and Emma. Emma frowned at him, asking a question without words. 'You know about the frontal lobe injury, right?

My inhibitions are still a bit lower. It will gradually heal over time. But until then, you'll have to put up with me being a bit blunt.'

There was a slight pause as they all thought over what to say next. Finally, Emma broke the silence. 'Sir, I do have one question.'

'What's that, then?'

'Well, you always spoke your mind and told things the way they were. So if this does fix itself, well, how would anyone ever know?'

There was a stunned silence before Rob roared with laughter and actually pounded the table with his hand. When he saw the other two looking at each other nervously, he reined it in a bit. People on other tables had started looking over.

'Sorry!' Rob pointed at his head and shrugged. After a moment of silence, he picked up the thread again. 'Emma, how are you getting on with the new department? How's Slater shaping up?'

'He's still not being imaginative enough to crack this case.'

'That figures. I've been thinking about why he was chosen to replace me. For a start, he's squeaky clean, never put a foot wrong. Dead straight. And, of course, he'll be in the right place to follow the paper trail and see if he can find where we hid the money. See if we left any clues in the office.'

'This isn't a game, you know!' Emma was outraged at the cavalier way he was treating things.

'Oh, I know it isn't. It's also hard to take it at all seriously sat on the sidelines. My turn is over, really, and it sticks in my gullet. I did what I could to make this town safer, and now I get to watch it all fall apart as they'll be more concerned with chasing coppers and following the letter of the rules!'

Another awkward silence followed this pronouncement.

'Listen, both of you. This has been good to get out of the house.' He gazed around the crowded pub. For the first time, Emma saw an edge of fear in his eyes. She knew then that he was wondering if there was anyone there who he knew but didn't recognise. 'But the truth is that I need to get home.'

Emma looked at Jem with a question. 'Rob gets more tired now. He's meant to do stuff like this, push himself, but the truth of it is that his brain is rewiring itself and recovering from injury. We had better get home.'

Chapter Thirteen

Emma got back to work on Tuesday, feeling distinctly put out. She was still working through what Rob had told her the previous night. He couldn't recognise faces. She'd heard of super-recognisers who spend their time watching CCTV and matching them up with photos of wanted people. There was no reason why the scale of recognition shouldn't stretch out in the other direction. She had known that it was unlikely that Rob would ever return to work, but having it confirmed was a bit of blow. She also still needed to ask him about Callum Frost, but last night hadn't been the time.

Emma needed something to cheer her up and take her mind off the case. She had been tasked with investigating the Frost disappearance on the estate. The most obvious approach would be to pick a few random names off the list of those involved and re-interview them. And if one of those names happened to be Margaret Watts, well that was coincidence. And, further, if she happened to learn some details to add to her private file on Gregory Watts, then all the better.

However, before she went down that road, she had to mend some bridges with her boss, Kev Slater. She resolved to go through the list of Fairthorpe's clients and see who sprang to mind. She didn't have the depth of experience of some of the officers but if she could get one or two hits, it would help to improve her standing in the office.

Before she could really get started, she received a phone call. There had been a fire at a holiday park and now the fire investigator was requesting assistance from the police. It looked like it was drug related and Emma leapt at the chance to be out of the office.

She parked outside the gates and took a deep breath when she got out of the car. She was by the sea and the air was fresh and bracing. Much better than being in the office, glancing nervously at her boss's door, wondering how much harm she'd done to her career.

She turned to focus on the gates of the Sun View Holiday Park. Although this stretch of the coast had all the big names in the world of holiday parks, they were interspersed with smaller, privately owned concerns like this one. She frowned. They might not have the budget of a Butlins or Pontins but they certainly weren't making the best of what they had.

The gates were chained shut and even though the park had only closed the day before, it already looked abandoned. The sign had moss on it and the road looked uncared for.

As instructed, she opened a side gate and walked up to the main reception – a portable home permanently mounted on cinder blocks off to the right of the entrance road. Before she could go in, she was met by a technician in regulation white suit together with a harassed looking man who was in his fifties with balding hair and a pot belly.

'DC Angel?' the investigator asked.

'Yep, what have we got here?' she asked as they started walking across the grass towards a field with a wooden sign marked "caravans" at the entrance.

'Well, initially we thought it was a standard job for one of these parks – dodgy heater or gas cylinder, poor maintenance.' The short, balding man, presumably the owner, shot him a look of dislike. He shrugged, not bothered. 'But when we got in there we found broken up bits of glass and pretty quickly we realised they were the remains of test tubes, flasks, that kind of stuff. We figure it was a low budget remake of Breaking Bad.' He chuckled at his own joke.

They went through a gate into the field that had about a dozen static caravans along one edge. Towards the end of the row was the blackened shell of one caravan and the two adjacent ones were significantly fire damaged as well. 'Here's your crime scene,' the investigator said.

'Did you find any bodies?'

'No, they must've all legged it from the scene. Or it went up when it was unattended.'

'We'll put a call out for any suspicious chemical burns turning up at a local hospital,' Emma said. She spent five minutes looking around the place but there wasn't much to see apart from a twisted wreck of burnt metal. There was a very particular smell of burning mixed with the mustiness of damped down ashes. To get a break from the bleakness of the wrecked caravan she strolled further away and turned back to look at the row of other mobile homes.

'What are you thinking?' the investigator asked.

'I'm not one hundred per cent sure,' Emma replied. She approached the owner and asked, 'What about the people who rented it?'

'I only saw one lad, he paid cash for a couple of weeks. I saw other blokes turn up in cars at night and unload stuff but,' he shrugged, 'you know. They'd paid in advance. Probably just here for a party or stag do or whatever.'

'You allow that do you? Hens and stags?' Emma was already thinking that a stag do would be a weekend, not a two week stay.

'Yeah.' He looked around. 'I'm not exactly one of the big family parks that can afford to turn away large single sex groups. Anyway, he paid.'

'No complaints from the neighbours?' She looked pointedly at the other dwellings. They all faced away from her and were separated from each other by white plastic fences and low hedges. From what she could see, they were all sealed up. 'Were they evacuated by the fire brigade?'

He frowned as if seeing the caravans for the first time. 'No,' he said slowly. 'It's the end of the season, place is winding down a bit. Quite lucky really.' He paused and considered them. 'They're placed like that so the balconies face out over the sea. You can wake up and have your coffee listening to the surf.' A hint of pride crept into his voice.

'And who rented the caravan? What can you remember about him?'

'What do you mean?'

'Well, age, height, general description? What car did he drive? Did he speak with a pronounced accent? Would you recognise him again?' Emma couldn't believe that she had to spell it out for him.

'Erm, I only saw him once for about ten minutes. Average height,' he said, looking uncomfortable, 'well, taller than me anyway. Maybe a London or South East accent. Brown hair, clean shaven. Like I say, really unremarkable and I only saw him the once.' He paused as he recalled the questions. 'I think he had a modern estate car. Dark, maybe, like black or dark red. Not sure.' He shrugged again.

'Right.' Emma made notes in her book, even though the description was too vague to be useful. 'Don't go anywhere, we might want to speak to you again. Although I expect you'll be waiting here for the insurance to come through.'

He shook his head and looked back towards the entrance as if he wanted them to leave. 'I didn't pay this month as we're winding down for the end of the season.'

'Right, well, okay.' She waited for him to leave and then turned back to the investigator with a frown. 'Can you keep taking photos and samples for a bit?' she said quietly. 'I've got a funny feeling and I don't want the owner left here alone.'

The technician looked confused but agreed. On her way back out Emma looked at the reception area. Behind it, and screened off, was a much nicer mobile home, obviously where the owner lived. Parked next to it was a smart, modern four by four. Her suspicions growing, she turned right around and took in a clubhouse and a play area. The building was as dilapidated as the rest of the park and a swing in the play area was hanging by one chain.

When she got back to the car, she sat down and rested her head on the steering wheel. She knew what she had to do. She knew why she had to do it. It would be a major step to getting things back on track with Kev Slater. But it still didn't mean that she was looking forward to it.

With a heavy heart, she called her boss. 'I'm at the caravan park where there was the explosion. Can we get a warrant to have a full search of the site?'

'What's your reasoning?' He was abrupt and to the point, obviously still upset after their run-in yesterday.

'The owner is here and he's very edgy. His description of the person who rented the van in question was vague to the point of being useless. He says he rented it for cash and took no details. You should see this place, boss. It looks really rundown, the club house and playground haven't been used in months, I can't imagine he's had many paying guests over the summer season.'

'Okay, so he's a bad businessman.' Slater was determined to push her on this.

'It's more than that. The other caravans on the field are well sealed up. I mean, totally dark – I can't see anything. I'd guess that the curtains have been taped down. They, as opposed to the rest of the park, look like they've been cared for. No broken windows, nothing. And some decent-sized power cables going in. And, he's driving a nice new 4x4 and has a nice looking home on the site. There's money coming in from somewhere and it isn't paying holidaymakers.'

'And the evidence that we've got from the burnt caravan? Does that definitely point to a drug lab?'

'I've seen bits of flasks and test tubes myself. Packets of chemicals. I'm no expert but it looks like the type of equipment that was in my chemistry lessons at school. The guy from the fire brigade is still here taking samples.' She paused to make her main point. 'The thing is, if I'm right, the moment I leave and the investigator leaves, he'll start dismantling and hiding the evidence. Or, if that's too much work, he'll just do a flit himself and leave it all behind.'

There was a long, ominous pause as Slater weighed up the information. 'I'll start the paperwork and assign a couple of uniforms to park their car outside the gate. Let the owner know that he's not alone. And once we have a warrant, I'll get some of the drug squad boys to help us kick in some doors. See what else is in there.' There was another pause. 'You'd better be right about this, Angel.' You're running out of chances was the unspoken message.

'I am sure,' she said. Then, swallowing her pride, she continued, 'and I wanted to thank you for our chat yesterday. I didn't realise the full story behind Rob Haines or how deeply he was in trouble.' Had he believed her lies?

'And I'm sorry if I came across a bit heavy handed. I realised afterwards that one of Haines' strengths was to engender loyalty in his troops. It's no surprise that you still want to fight his corner, no matter how misplaced that instinct might be.'

'Well, I just wanted to let you know, sir, that I appreciate you looking out for me and telling me the whole picture. I'll be a lot more careful in future.'

'Well, least said, soonest mended,' Slater said. 'About this caravan park. You've got a good feeling?'

'Yes, sir. I can't see how someone would operate a lab like that under his nose without him being aware. When you factor in that the park is deserted but he has money, well the simplest story is that he's running the drug lab himself.'

'Right. I want you to sit tight till the uniforms arrive.' He paused, obviously making a snap decision. 'I'll let you know when everything's in place. You'll want to be there when the doors get kicked in.'

'Thank you, sir,' Emma said. Was he being nice to her and letting her see the result of her intuition? Or was he making sure she'd be there if it didn't pan out? Blame or glory? She didn't know what was waiting for her.

But she did know that she was determined to keep up her friendship with Rob Haines. She'd hate to see him dropped like a hot potato at a time when he would be feeling at his most alone and damaged.

Chapter Fourteen

Emma Angel had a few hours to kill but needed to stay close to Bradwick to be in on the raid at the holiday park. She drove over to the Seaview Estate, intent on talking to Margaret Watts. She was on much firmer ground than she had been a few months ago. With Rob Haines' sidelined, there was no one, apart from Andy Stonor, who knew about Gregory Watts. He was her nemesis – the one that she couldn't arrest for anything. Now, she had a clear field to pursue him on her own, until she had enough evidence to build a solid case against him.

Even so, she was far more nervous than she should've been. She stood outside a perfectly ordinary bungalow on the Seaview Estate. It had been built in the fifties and still had an original garden gate with green paint and a radiant sun design.

This was the house of Margaret Watts, the mother of Gregory Watts. Had he ever mentioned her name to his mother? If he had, no doubt he had painted her in the worst possible terms as someone harassing him. Was he here, even? She looked around but could see no big, flashy cars so maybe she was safe.

Now she was here, partly on the instructions of her boss. She knew that she was stretching the truth a little, but she was also eager to find out anything she could about Gregory. And she wanted to investigate the disappearance of Callum Frost. She kept telling herself that. It would be the only focus of her questions. Anything that she learnt about Gregory would be incidental. But possibly vital, if it didn't end her career first.

She made the approach up the path and knocked on the door, which also looked original. A short woman with dark hair in a neat bob answered. Emma couldn't stop herself checking for any features that might have found their way into her son, but she didn't see any.

'Hello, can I help you?'

Emma held out her warrant card. 'I'm Detective Constable Emma Angel from the police. Don't worry, it's nothing bad, I just wanted a chat.'

The woman's eyes narrowed slightly, the natural suspicion that people had on the estate for the police. 'What do you want?'

'Just a chat about some ancient history on the estate.'

'Hmmm. And you thought you'd come to me, did you?'

'It's about Callum Frost. We had a list of people who helped at the time, and we're just seeing who still lives in the area.'

She smiled, a tight smile that spoke of the pain that name still caused. 'Ah well, that was a long time ago although folk round here do have long memories. But this isn't the sort of thing to be talked about on the doorstep. I just picked up a Battenberg from the shop so you can come in and have some tea. Wouldn't want the neighbours to know what we're talking about.'

She was led into a smart home and when they were sat on sofas with cups of tea and squares of multicoloured cake, Margaret spoke, 'So what do you want to know about Callum Frost?'

'Well, do you remember the "missing" posters that went up when Callum disappeared?'

'Yes, terrible business. I know that they were probably helping, but can you imagine his poor mother? Every lamppost and shop? I know it'd be a comfort but in some ways it'd be a torment as well.'

'Yes,' Emma hadn't thought about the relatives. It was unimaginable what they'd gone through. 'One of the posters has turned up again, as evidence in a completely unrelated case.'

'Well, if you want a list of names who ever had one, then you'll be out of luck. They were everywhere those posters. We had a big stack in the community centre and folk were in and out all the time taking however many they needed.'

'I know. We've spoken to the printers so that's not what we were looking at. It's just that,' Emma leant forward, 'and this is confidential. There's been a nasty murder at the motel and that's where the poster has turned up. We have a list of names from the original investigation, everyone who helped out, but it's too long to be useful. What we need to know is if there's anyone we should be interested in?'

'And you want me to tell you who to investigate? Who among my friends and neighbours could've killed that poor boy?'

'No, not exactly. We just need a feel for what it was like.'

'It's all right, I'm messing with you,' Margaret said with a smile. 'I'm getting old and I'm stuck in this house all the time. You've got to let me have a bit of fun.' She smiled which reassured Emma slightly. 'Callum Frost, oh God, that takes me back. My youngest, Gregory, had just finished his exams, so he was home from school. His brother, Donald had left a couple of years earlier. But Greg, he never really relaxed. Even though he had just finished with education, he was still out every day. I was so proud of him, always grafting, always earning money.' She stopped for a minute, lost in happy memories of her sons. Emma's heart rate increased a bit. Margaret had brought up the subject – she hadn't even had to pry.

'So, were your boys around on that day?' Emma prompted.

'Don was about all day, bottle of beer in hand and a barbecue lit. Greg was out all morning and came back around lunchtime.' She stopped for a moment. 'That's the trouble about a day like that. You get interviewed by the police at the time, and then everyone talks about it. The press come sniffing around. By the time you've told the same story over and over, you can't really remember what happened, just what you said.'

'Was there anyone who stuck out as different or weird? Anything that you look back on now and think that it was a bit odd.'

Margaret shook her head. 'No, there's nothing. I mean, no one was behaving normally, not on the day or for weeks afterwards. I know it was the school holidays, but it felt so weird. It was like everyone was thinking about it but no one was saying anything.'

Emma felt her frustration build. But she had what she needed – she had a link between Gregory Watts and the Callum Frost case. She wanted to bring Margaret back to talking about the posters, to see who would've kept one. But she could already see some echoes of Gregory's behaviour. She was mischievous but also a bit manipulative.

'Did you know anyone who was a bit obsessive? Someone who was good with their hands, maybe good at DIY? But also a bit apart, kept to themselves?' She stopped and sighed. 'We're struggling a bit here to see who we're looking for.'

'Yes, well, that's a fairly vague description. Most of us on the estate, the old ones who know each other, well we respect each other. If someone needs space, we give them the space. So "kept to themselves", while it's a bit of cliché for a killer, doesn't really help. Likewise, you throw a stone round here and you'd hit half a dozen men who are handy. When you drive back to your station, look at the driveways you go past. This is where the self-employed live. It's not DIY, but there are builders, painters, plumbers, you name it. Although most of them are complaining about the Poles and Romanians taking their jobs.'

Emma tried to digest the stream of information. Basically, the killer could be on the estate, pretty much anywhere. They'd be going to work, owning a van, having plenty of tools and the ability to make any number of weird things for displaying bodies.

More to pass the time than anything, she asked, 'Is there a Mr Watts?'

Margaret went to fetch a photograph then sat down with it in her lap. 'My Albert. Lost him three years ago, the daft bugger. Still love him though.' Before Emma could find a tactful way to ask how, she continued. 'He never listened. Smoked all the time, drank and never watched what he ate. Worked up at the docks in Bristol and was within six months of retiring when he had a heart attack. I was hoping to retire with him, but, well, you know. We plan and God laughs.'

'I'm sorry to bring it up again.'

'Oh, don't mind. Everyone tiptoes around the subject. I loved the man and knew him for the best part of forty years. Still love the bugger even if he's not here.' She stopped for a moment to gather herself, then put the photo back on the mantelpiece. 'You asked about the whole Callum Frost thing? Well back then it was a close-knit community, people looked out for each other. After the disappearance, it all changed. I'm glad my boys were old enough not to worry. You see, they'd be able to go round to a mate's house or just play out without a care in the world. But afterwards, it was all different. You'd see kids being walked from one house to the next, parents meeting each other halfway. The whole estate got quieter after dark. I suppose that was the real tragedy. I don't think we ever got that back. I mean, they were all right when Al died – people came over, the funeral was huge, people looked in on me for weeks after, brought food for me.' She stopped for a second and judged Emma's mood. 'Oh, you don't want to hear me wittering on all day, do you?'

'No, it's okay. I like to listen. And I do need to learn more about what life was like on the estate fifteen years ago. And in this job, the chance to sit down for a few minutes with a snack is rare.' Privately she wasn't happy drinking weak tea and eating sickly sweet cake. But she knew that this was where the coal face was – this could be where the break in the case came, even though it seemed like wasted time in the moment.

She listened for a bit longer before the conversation naturally wound up. At the door, she asked the one question that mattered to her. 'Do you ever see much of your sons now?'

'Oh, well, you know. They pop round most weekends, have a meal and a chat.' She paused. 'I know I was a bit sharp when you knocked on the door but I have enjoyed our chat. Even with the community and my sons, I do get bored. You will come back, won't you? Have some more tea and cake?'

'Only if you really mean it, I wouldn't want to impose.'

'Of course I do. You can tell me what's going on in the town now, and I can fill you in about the past.'

'I'd like that,' Emma said. She was aware that she was adding extra obligations to her busy life. First she had Lukas to keep an eye on, then she needed to keep an eye on Rob Haines and now Mrs Gregory was on the list.

Chapter Fifteen

Emma retreated to a corner seat in the pub and closed her eyes for a moment as she sat down. It had been an incredibly long day, full of ups and downs, and she needed to take a moment. She was holding a cold bottle of beer and took a long draught.

She had a momentary respite from the celebrating around her. She could still remember the feeling on the holiday park when a whole group of officers from various teams had stood around on the grass. They had a Method of Entry Team, but it was hardly necessary. Their target was the row of caravans and they could almost have opened each one up with a tin-opener round the lock. Instead it was the formal battering ram, followed by a rush of uniforms and a shouted, 'Clear!'

Her heart had sunk when she peered into caravan number one. It was obviously in the middle of a refit. There was none of the usual furniture – no sofas, kitchen area or even bedrooms. Instead the space was open plan with a couple of workbenches set up on trestles.

Emma felt a squeeze on her shoulder and turned round to see an inspector from the drug squad. 'Don't look so downhearted,' he said. 'Look around this place. Who tapes the curtains shut when they renovate? And puts in some quality ventilation but all pointing out towards the sea?' He took an elaborate sniff. 'And I can smell something faintly, something familiar and illegal.'

'Thank you,' Emma said. 'I've got a lot riding on this. It was my hunch.'

'Well, let's see what's behind door number two, shall we?' he said in his best game show voice.

Door number two, as it turned out, had a fully set up cannabis farm, with lots of plants, all lined up in rows with high power lights and watering systems. They were fully grown, almost to the ceiling. The smell was overwhelming. Emma nearly collapsed with relief. There was a lot here, and it was only the second caravan. This alone was enough to justify all the officers involved.

However, when all the mobile homes had been opened, a range of farms had been found. Each one was at a different stage of cultivation, obviously being cycled through. The owner didn't even try to resist questioning – he admitted that with the turmoil in the drugs market he'd been dismantling the farms after harvest and converting them to laboratories.

The whole afternoon's work then led naturally to the joint teams all heading to the pub together to celebrate. For a moment she was happy to people-watch. She could see that Brian Chisholm was shaking hands and generally chatting with old friends from other departments. She did notice however that he had a soft drink in his hand where all his friends had pints. She nodded to herself – abuse and alcoholism often went hand in hand. Nick Dent was looking out of his depth and Suse was working the room, smiling and laughing, mostly with the more senior officers.

Feeling rebellious, she got her phone out to text Rob Haines. Nothing in particular that she wanted, just to check in with him and see how he was doing after last night's big revelations. And she needed to reassure herself that she wouldn't let the likes of her boss dictate who she could and couldn't be friends with.

'Why are you hiding over here in a corner, DC Angel?' Kev Slater had come over to her. She guiltily slid her mobile back into her pocket. 'If it wasn't for your hunch we wouldn't have had this good result.'

'Thank you, sir,' she said. 'I got lucky, and you did back me up with the warrant and the support.' She took a deep breath, to say the difficult thing. 'It was a team effort really.'

'Well, I'll drink to that.' He turned and drew her further into the pub. He started making the rounds, introducing her to people and buying drinks where they were needed. She started to see a new side of him, playing the politician as well as Suse.

Eventually Emma managed to pry herself away and went to perch at the bar. Ostensibly she was trying to buy a beer, but was quite happy to be ignored with the dregs of her last bottle. She needed a few minutes break from the clasp on the shoulder, hearty handshake and "well done" she'd been getting from some of the senior officers.

'That bad, is it?' a voice next to her asked.

'Just needed a break, really,' Emma replied, turning to see that it was the computer technician who'd decoded the computers. She'd remember his name in a minute.

'Pete,' he said, reading her face, 'from the IT department.'

'Oh yes, right. Now I remember. You had the computer and phone from the motel.' She paused for a second. 'What are you doing in here?'

'In a police pub, you mean? I do work for you. And sometimes I just get fed up of the banter and the jokes when someone has a spliff. I might be civilian staff but it's a better place to drink some nights.' He stopped to size her up. 'What's got you looking so down, anyway? Would it be fixed if I bought you a drink?' He indicated the empty bottle she was holding.

'I did a really good job today. Acted on a hunch and found a whole drug factory and cannabis farm set up as a holiday park. Owner arrested, drugs seized, job done.'

'And that made you miserable?'

'No,' she said in a lower voice. 'But then you end up in a pub with senior officers trying to buy you drinks and being all matey with you because one day goes well.' She sighed. 'Oh, I'm just being a bit down at the end of a long day. And yes, another drink would help. Thank you.'

She sat on her stool and had inconsequential chat with Pete. She was always a bit wary of people from work after her disastrous fling with a traffic officer. Once he'd understood that she wasn't going to drop everything to be with him, he'd turned nasty and nearly ruined her career. She still didn't like remembering that Rob Haines had intervened and smoothed it all out.

Emma tried as hard as she could, but couldn't help but like Pete. He was attentive and actually let her finish sentences. If he was putting on an act to impress her, it was convincing.

Still, the ghost of David from Traffic was looming over her, so she divided her attention between Pete and the rest of the team and made sure she left early and alone.

Chapter Sixteen

Amelia Spark felt good. She'd woken up early as she did every morning, put her jogging gear on and slipped out of the house. It was a good morning as her boy, who'd be three in a couple of months, hadn't woken. She had a long-standing agreement with her partner, Martin, that he'd take the early morning shift while she went for a run and then she'd be back in time to take over the morning routine and let him get ready for work.

She left the road she was jogging along and turned up a footpath. Soon, she entered a patch of woodland. The next ten minutes would be with leaf mould under her feet and trees overhead. She was relaxed – this was the same route that she'd run for years. However, when she rounded a corner, she stopped short. Something was wrong with her run.

Sat in the middle of the path was a man, who looked a bit like a tramp. She took a cautious step forward. Definitely homeless, she thought. God, why didn't they just get a job or something? Anything that would take them away from her route, her precious half hour of solitude before the day started.

The man just sat there, leaning back on his arms, legs out in front of him. She wasn't about to double back and ruin her morning. He was in the middle of a small clearing. If she was careful, she could skirt round the edge and stay out of arm's reach. Once she was past him, she'd put on some speed and get away from him and make up her time. She was irritated that he'd disturbed her and wanted to get back on track.

She took another step; she was nearly into the clearing now. Something was very wrong, he wasn't reacting at all to her presence. He was wearing a dirty raincoat with a ridiculous scarf wrapped around his neck. Despite his pose, sitting up, his eyes were closed and he hadn't moved. Was it possible for someone to sleep like that? Or be so drunk they'd passed out, she wondered. That was more likely, with a person like that with the pale skin and greasy hair. Maybe there was some new drug that they were using that made them do this.

She berated herself for being stupid and hesitating. She had already added precious seconds onto her time and would have to work hard to get home on schedule. She strode into the clearing, already angling herself to the left to skirt around him.

She was momentarily blinded by a flash.

A loud boom made her ears ring and her chest vibrate.

She took a step back, unsure of what was happening. Something fell around her, on her face, hitting the bare skin of her arms, it was in her hair.

Her sense of smell was assaulted. Blood, burnt skin, gunpowder. She immediately recalled childhood bonfire nights and that one time she'd burnt the roast. Wood smoke too.

Was she injured?

Her ears rang, but nothing else hurt.

Afraid of what she'd see, she looked down before opening her eyes. She blinked several times to clear the spots. Time to look up and see what had happened.

She stepped cautiously forward. The man was gone. He'd left his shoes behind but he'd gone, disappeared, literally in a flash.

Another step forward.

Her legs buckled. He had left his shoes, but his feet were still in them. And his legs. She got closer, unable to believe what she was seeing.

The lower half of his body was there as well – his hips and a short stump of spine stuck straight up. And there was a big red bowl of churned up meat. The inside of someone. His insides. Behind him were two hands, thrown aside. In between was a big charred area, a circle of blackened earth where all the twigs and leaves had been blown clear. The whole place was scattered with bits of flesh.

Bits of body that were now all over her skin, in her hair, on her clothes. She batted at her legs and flailed her arms. Her fingers got caught in the sticky mess that was her hair.

She screamed and ran back down the path, away from the horror. She continued rubbing at her arms and pulling at her hair as she ran.

When she'd failed to flag down the fifth car in a row, concerned residents had called the police about the woman covered in blood and shouting at the cars. Soon the whole circus descended and she was sedated by paramedics and helped to an ambulance.

Chapter Seventeen

Emma parked as close as she could on the residential street. She hadn't even made it into the office that morning. She'd been trying to get her head straight after the evening down the pub. She'd stayed longer than intended and she knew that it was because she'd enjoyed talking to Pete. She hadn't really decided what to do with that information yet. She didn't know how she felt about him, about the idea of a new involvement, especially with someone who worked in the same place. She had been trying to work it all out and also battling a hangover when her mobile had rung. She'd been summoned directly to this crime scene.

As she walked down the road trying to interpret the vague directions that she'd been given, she took stock of the scale of the investigation. One ambulance was trying to leave the scene, and two marked police cars were there, along with an incident van. People were starting to come out of houses and she knew it wouldn't be long before the press showed up as well. She stopped dead on the pavement. There, right in the middle of the street was a dark green Land Rover. Unmistakable were the black and white plates and regimental markings. What the hell was going on? Why had the army been called to the crime scene?

She quickened her pace and found a uniformed officer who directed her to a footpath between two houses. Soon she came out to an area of trees. It was right on the edge of the housing estate and the first section of the path was littered with plastic bags and larger items of rubbish.

There was her boss, Inspector Kev Slater, in his usual dull suit and tie, talking to a man in combat fatigues. DC Angel studied their body language and figured out that while there might not be a strict equivalence between police and army ranks, the two men treated each other as roughly equal.

The army man was younger with short dark hair and a stocky body. More than that, he had a way of carrying himself, an inner confidence that was missing in Slater. Emma had no choice but to hang back and wait for them to clear the path. There was no point anyway in barging in somewhere when the army were involved.

Soon enough the impromptu conference ended with shaking hands. As he passed, the army officer looked at her and said, 'The scene's all yours now.'

She approached her boss. 'What the hell's going on?'

'Well,' Kev Slater puffed himself up a little, 'we had a report of an explosion. Protocol clearly suggests that the proper thing to do is call in Bomb Disposal to make sure the scene is safe before putting any of my officers in danger.' Angel was thinking that it was overkill. Slater interpreted her expression and continued. 'It has been a common terrorist tactic, starting with the IRA, to detonate a small device and use that to lure the emergency services into the area and catch them with a secondary device.'

'So, what's the score now then?'

'The score, as you put it, is that your timing is spot on. The scene has been declared safe, although they did confirm that there is evidence that an IED has been detonated in the area recently, which combined with the witness reports means that we did have an explosion here.'

DC Angel nodded. She still couldn't believe that there had been a bombing here in Bradwick, her sleepy seaside town. She fell in behind Slater and kept walking up the path.

Soon they were past the range where it was easy to dump a fridge or television and the wood became cleaner and nicer. But for Emma the atmosphere was no better – she knew she was approaching a murder scene, the place where someone had died.

Soon they were at the police tape. They showed their warrant cards and were recorded on a clipboard before being allowed to proceed.

'I've got to warn you that this is pretty bad,' Dani Price, the pathologist, said as Emma approached.

'Hello to you too,' DC Angel said. 'Is it as bad as the motel? Or worse?' Emma still hadn't forgotten that she'd been the first one of the team to see what had become of Oliver Fairthorpe. She stopped on the path when she saw Dani's expression. 'How can it be worse than that?'

'Well, I'm not sure if it's worse or not, but the body is less intact.' She paused and indicated a second line of tape. 'This is the inner cordon, time to get suited up.'

'Less intact?' Emma asked as she shrugged her way into white overalls. 'That poor sod was beheaded.'

'Yeah, similar situation here, I'm afraid.'

Sensing that words would be useless, Dani waited for Emma to finish with the overshoes and hairnet. When she was done, Dani lead Emma into the clearing. 'Watch where you walk, we're still tracking evidence.' In the centre, like some macabre modern sculpture were a pair of jeans with trainers still attached. As she got closer, DC Angel could see it was actually the lower half of a body.

'Oh.' Emma moved a hand to her mouth, before remembering she was wearing gloves. 'Oh. My. God. Is that?'

'Yes, that's the lower half of our body.'

'Where's the rest...?' DC Angel couldn't finish the sentence as she saw the stumps of two arms lying behind the legs, as they'd been thrown aside. The more she looked, the more she could pick out odd body parts strewn around the clearing. A technician straightened from a crouch - he'd been photographing and documenting the head where it was lying, several feet from the body. 'What...? I mean, Dani, what's been going on here?'

She looked at a loss, and nodded at DI Slater, who was pale. 'Well, you saw the army were here, didn't you? The initial report was of a hysterical woman covered in blood running up and down the street. According to her, he just exploded.' He indicated the clearing and the body with a sweep of his arm. 'At first everyone dismissed it as some sort of hysteria, but when the other calls came in about a loud bang, well we had to take it seriously. That's when I took charge and called the army in. Ms Price, what are your initial thoughts?'

'Initial thoughts are that I've never seen anything like this. I mean, I talked to the army boys. Some of them have been out in Afghanistan, so they know what they're talking about. I've also read reports from combat medics, and articles about causes of death during war.' Emma couldn't help wondering at her morbid choice of reading material. 'Most injuries from IEDs are the loss of limbs, as they are usually triggered by either touch or step. In more elaborate devices, you get a tripwire. But in that case, the injuries are usually focused either on one side or the front or back, depending where the device was placed relative to the victim. But to have most of the torso destroyed, and the extremities left intact but thrown around...' She shook her head.

Something tugged at DC Angel's consciousness. She broke away from the group and backtracked to the obvious entrance to the clearing. On hands and knees, she searched the edges of the path where there were branches and tree stumps.

'Here! I need a technician!'

'What have you got?' Dani crouched next to her, looking but not touching.

'There, that glint of gold on the side of that tree stump? It's another brass eye, screwed into the wood. I think there's a bit of fishing line running through it.'

Dani turned to stare at DC Angel closely. 'You mean, just like the motel room? The first murder?'

'Yeah, you said tripwire and it set me thinking.'

'Good catch.' Dani squinted and tilted her head. 'That piece of fishing line leads up towards the body.'

Before they could explore any further, there was a crashing and a commotion on the opposite side of the clearing. Something about the raised voices made Emma turn and move towards the noise.

'You can't just come crashing in here, it's a crime scene!' One of the uniforms was trying to stop a large figure from getting into the crime scene. Emma's heart sank when she recognised Rob Haines.

'I know it's a crime scene. It's my crime scene. You obviously don't know who you're dealing with.' Rob had stopped grappling and stood back a bit. He was shouting at the young uniform. 'I could have your card on my desk this time tomorrow.'

'Rob, there'll be no need for that.' Kev Slater had arrived on the scene as well. 'I don't know what you're doing here, but I've got everything under control.'

'Ah, didn't see you were there.' Some of Rob's swagger disappeared, replaced by confusion. He peered closely at Kev, taking in his plain clothes and air of authority. 'I suppose you're in charge.'

'Yes. Do you remember that you're meant to be on sick leave while I run CID?' Emma hated hearing the tone in Kev's voice, as if he was talking to a slow child. This was her boss who was probably going mad being stuck at home with nothing to do. 'Honestly, you can't come in here, contaminating the scene-'

'What have you got there, Rob?' Emma earned a sharp look for talking over her boss, but she didn't care. 'Do you want to show it to our inspector, Kev Slater?' She knew that she sounded false but it was the best she could do. She'd read the confusion on Rob's face and knew that he had no idea who he was talking to.

'Oh, this.' Some of his animation returned. He locked eyes with Emma and gave the briefest nods of thanks. She could see some of the tension disappear from his shoulders. 'I found it pinned to a tree over there. I remember you were asking about the case. It was...' he paused to search his unreliable memory. 'Well it was a long time ago. And this poster is fresh, so it's a clue.' He brandished it proudly.

'A clue which you've contaminated already, making it useless,' DI Slater said bitterly.

Emma handed Rob an evidence bag and watched as he properly bagged up the poster. 'Right, come with me,' she said. 'There's plenty of cars around, we'll find a uniform who can take your prints for elimination. Won't be a problem.' She glared at Slater as she left.

'I'm sorry, Emma, I've messed this up, haven't I?' He shook his head. 'I still have friends in some parts of the police. I heard from the dispatcher about this crime scene as I was just sat at home staring at the four walls. Thought it wouldn't do any harm if I came over to lend a hand.'

'Well, if nothing else you put the wind up Slater and that can't be a bad thing. He's been so full of himself since he had to call in the army and everything.'

Emma quickly filled him in on what they'd learnt so far and how the poster confirmed the connection between the two crime scenes.

After a brief period of silence, Rob spoke again. 'I didn't really believe them at the time, but the hospital said there may be some temporary problems with inhibition. I thought it had passed, but it seems I've become worse recently. I hate being sat at home, feeling like I'm on the sidelines of everything.'

'Don't worry about it, sir. That bang on the head might have given you a few symptoms, but it hasn't changed who you are. You still want to help. You can't keep away from a good crime scene if you think you can be of use somewhere.'

'Nah, you're just being nice. This is just more evidence that my career is over.'

Rob stayed quiet for the rest of the way back. He silently submitted to having his prints taken on a new machine. When he was all done, he turned to Emma.

'Would you say that the victim was sleeping rough?' he asked.

Emma cast her mind back. She tried to filter out the horror – the lumps of flesh and bone that were dotted around the clearing. 'Well, his trainers were so worn there were holes, and his jeans had seen better days. I mean, the state of the body means it'll be hard to make a definite call now. Once we get the pathology report we'll have a better idea and be able to identify the victim. Why?'

'On my way to blundering through the crime scene I passed a makeshift camp. Old beer cans, fire, cheap tent, that kind of stuff. Might be nothing, but might tell us who the victim was.'

'Thank you, sir. Even if our victim wasn't sleeping there, then we might have a witness.' She was grateful – she knew that this was good information. Haines could've used it himself to repair some of the damage he'd done. Instead he'd given it to her.

Chapter Eighteen

'All right then, team, what do we know?' DI Kev Slater stood at a board with a pen in hand, poised to record the information. 'Dani Price is due in ten minutes, so we can cover the other physical evidence before getting the medical details on the body.'

'Do we reckon that they're the same perp?' DS Brian Chisholm asked.

'What do you guys think?' Slater asked.

'We'll wait for Dani, but we know that it looks like the bodies were handled differently and possibly not killed the same way. The locations are different as well,' Suse said. Seeing the looks around the table she held her hands up. 'For what it's worth, I think it's the same guy. But it's always worth seeing the other side of the coin.'

'We have a lot of points in common,' Emma said. 'The tripwires are, according to scene of crimes, identical in both cases. And there is some kind of theatrical setting of the scene as well. Attention to detail.'

Kev nodded. 'Nick, have we got anywhere on an identity for our victim?'

'Yes, thanks to Emma, we found a campsite near the crime scene. We found a biscuit tin there which had the documents for one John Garner. I had to do a bit of digging around, he was a hard person to find. He signed on for Universal Credit, had at least one ex-wife and a girlfriend. He was officially of no fixed abode, but when the weather was bad he tended to sofa surf. Anyway, I've managed to dig up photos and prints – he had a habit of getting drunk and scaring the tourists on the seafront, so we know he's our man.'

Kev Slater looked thoughtful and rubbed the side of his nose. 'Is there any way we can connect this Garner character to Fairthorpe? It might provide another link to suggest that these two crimes have the same perpetrator.'

'It's hard to see how a twenty-seven-year-old drifter has anything to do with a financial advisor in his forties,' Emma said. She knew she was on shaky ground challenging her boss. But she needed to break his fixed thinking and get him to broaden out the enquiry.

'Well, Emma, they were both murdered and their bodies were displayed in bizarre and graphic ways. And we have the same hook and wire arrangement at both scenes. So there has to be some connection between them. What else links the two crimes?'

Too late, she saw the trap that had been laid. She had started walking into it and now couldn't avoid it. Before anyone else could take the flack, she said, 'The same poster was found at both crime scenes. Callum Frost.'

'Actually, we have to take DCI Haines' word for it that he found the poster at the second scene,' Kev Slater said.

'Sir, whatever you may think of Rob Haines, he's still a serving officer. If he says he found the poster on a tree near the scene, then that's what happened.'

'He's also suffered a head injury and his behaviour is, uh, erratic.'

'I don't think that this is the right forum to discuss another officer's medical condition.' Emma was resolute. To cover her embarrassment, she shuffled through the forensic reports. 'Ah, here it is. The poster was torn from a nearby tree. The techs found that tree, matched the missing piece of paper perfectly. Even better, there was a fragment of thumb print on the head of the pin and that matched prints which were found at the first scene.'

'Well, I think that's the final piece of evidence,' Kev said, moving past the fact that he'd been proved wrong without a comment. 'Fingerprints, posters and the tripwire arrangement, we can treat these two as the same case.' There was an awkward pause. Emma wondered if she was about to get carpeted for arguing with the boss. 'Ah, here comes Miss Price now. Let's see what else we can find out.'

'Hello, everyone,' Dani said. 'I did hope I wouldn't have to come back here and do this again, but it looks like we have another one. I had to liaise with both scene of crimes and especially the army on this one. They have a lot more experience with improvised explosives and especially with looking at the after-effects and determining what happened.' She was rambling so she pulled herself up and took a deep breath. 'Anyway, this isn't very straightforward or easy to do. As far as we can tell, the body was split down the back and the explosive placed alongside the spine, or more likely, tucked in front of the spine.'

'Eww,' Suse said. 'How would you even do that?'

'Well, the explosive was probably in a flexible plastic pipe to make it easier to shape it to the body.'

'This isn't the kind of thing you could normally do first time and get right is it?' Brian asked.

In reply, Dani looked at Emma. 'I think you can take this.'

For a second, Emma was confused. Then she remembered the last phone call she'd had with Dani. 'The exploding pig!' she exclaimed. Then, seeing the confused faces around the table, she continued. 'A dog walker found the remains of a pig that had been blown apart by some means. I filed a report but we really had nothing to pin it to, until now.'

Brian nodded. 'Practice runs. Makes sense.'

'As much as any of this makes sense,' Suse said.

'Anyway,' Emma said, 'I'll find the report on the pig and assign it over to this case.' She looked at Dani. 'Maybe you could take a second look and highlight any similarities?'

'Of course.'

'I've already checked around the local butchers,' Emma said. 'There are plenty of hog roasts and that kind of thing going on. Unfortunately it's not that difficult to pick up a whole pig. For all we know, he went through an intermediary like a catering company. So that's a dead end. But we can check to see if it is the same guy.'

Emma sat back from the table. It was all going very well – they were identifying who had been murdered and where, when and how the act had been carried out. They were still, however, completely in the dark about the why, and of course the identity of the killer. She stayed on the sidelines as the meeting carried on, learning that John Garner had probably been tasered and then stabbed before being arranged in the clearing.

She did pay more attention when Nick Dent asked a question though. 'Where did the explosives come from? I mean, what kind of explosives were they?'

'What do you mean exactly?' Dani asked.

'Well, are we dealing with a home grown terrorist who's cooking up explosives in his garage? Or a rogue soldier who's been light-fingered in the armoury? Or do we need to start checking through the reports of thefts from quarries and the like?'

'That's a good question,' Dani said. 'I've got a report here from the army.' She leafed through some paperwork. 'It looks like a weird mix – the explosives were commercially available but the whole switch activation method was home-made.' There were frowns and mutters around the room. Dani continued, 'It kind of makes sense. Whatever firing mechanism he used, had to be abandoned at the scene and most of those have serial numbers and manufacturers that we could trace. But they're not that complicated to make, and of course that eliminates another route for tracing him. Once again, he has shown good workmanship – it might not be a professional job, but it's still very well put together. He's displaying a lot of skill in making things.'

'Is there anything on it we can trace?' Brian asked.

Dani shook her head while scanning the document. 'Battery was a standard one, from any branch of Halfords. Other bits were pretty much home-made or just plain untraceable. It's not like a remote control bomb where you could recover parts of a phone or a timer. It's just a mechanical switch to send electricity to the detonator.'

Nick nodded and Kev said, 'Nick, we need a national search of missing explosives from quarries or similar locations.'

'I'll add it to the actions,' Nick said, making notes.

Emma mentally detached herself from the discussion around her which was mainly concerned with the minutiae of running an investigation. She had the same overwhelming feeling of disgust about this individual. Whatever his reasoning, here was another victim who wasn't allowed to rest in peace but who continued after his death to form part of some twisted plan.

Maybe Slater was right. Maybe there was a link between Garner and Fairthorpe. Obviously, in some way both of them had upset the killer. And upset him seriously enough that he would spend a lot of time and effort to desecrate the bodies after death.

When the meeting was over, she caught Dani's eye and led her over to her desk. She had a hunch to follow-up on from Rob so she didn't want to do it in public.

When they weren't being overheard Emma asked quietly, 'How was the body handled? When it was all set up to, you know...?'

'Explode? I'm not sure what you mean.'

'Well, someone suggested to me that maybe an undertaker or other professional might be involved.' She checked to make sure she wouldn't cause offence. 'Maybe even someone who works in a similar job to you? Maybe a porter or something?'

Dani stopped and thought. She wasn't one to take offence, she was used to considering all the angles. 'I'd say it was a fairly clumsy job. They didn't really make much effort to close the wound once they put the explosives in, no neat stitches or anything. And I suppose the redressing of the body could be described as slapdash.' She thought for a moment, reconstructing the scene in her head. 'No, I can't see it myself. More of a gut reaction than anything, but I don't feel that it was a professional.'

'Right. Okay. I'll close that avenue. Thanks, anyway.'

CHAPTER NINETEEN

It had been a very long day trying to get to grips with the new murder that had happened the day before. When she finally got home, all she wanted was some time curled up on the sofa with Florence the cat and a bottle of beer. A bit of down time to process everything.

However, when she got in, her housemate, Lucy, was waiting for her in the kitchen. Emma had forgotten that she'd promised to go with her to a monthly meet-up of car enthusiasts. It was a get-together of young adults who could easily get into trouble with the police. With a combination of education and bribery, the police arranged these meetings to try to keep them on the straight and narrow and earlier in the year, Emma had worked with them to identify Dark Car Man – a dangerous predator who'd been killing young women in Bradwick.

Now she remembered that she'd promised to go back with Lucy. As the case had been closed by CPS, due to the only suspect being dead, there had been no real publicity. But the teenagers, especially the young women, had been asking for news from the police. So Emma had promised to go along to the next meeting and tell them what she could. Only, with the recent murder, she'd completely forgotten that it was that night.

It was a favour she owed, and given that the meetings were only monthly, it couldn't be put off. 'Okay, yes, I just remembered,' Emma said. 'Give me time to shower and change and I'll be right with you.'

Soon enough, Emma found herself with Lucy in a car park on the outskirts of Bradwick. As before it was occupied by modified cars and their young owners. Emma was uncomfortable addressing them as a group – she wasn't sure of the protocol as this was a crowd standing around in a car park, not a formal meeting with a stage and lectern. There was nothing to do but to start talking and hope they quietened down enough to listen.

'Some of you may remember me from before, when I came here asking for help with some photos. We had a car we were trying to trace. Dark Car Man's vehicle in fact.' There were nods and murmurs around the group. Most of the conversations had stopped, and more people were joining the crowd, drifting closer. 'Well the good news is that, thanks in part to your help, we caught the man responsible. And it turns out he was guilty of the attacks on young women in the area. We found enough evidence to be sure of that.'

'How come we ain't heard nothing about it? What's going on? Usually you get something in the news about how an arrest has been made, then they go quiet before the trial.'

'Ah, yes.' Emma hadn't had time to work out how to break the news. 'Unfortunately the man in question took his own life before we could arrest, question or charge him. But we are confident that we had the right man and as a result the town is now safer.'

'Well, who was it? We have a right to know who's been killing women in our town!'

'We're not releasing his name at the moment.' Emma was resolute. 'He still has relatives living in the area and, bearing in mind the strength of feeling these attacks have raised, it wouldn't be fair to expose them by naming him.'

The crowd of teenagers erupted into expressions of distaste and discontented murmuring. Judging by how this simple statement had turned the mood ugly, she was glad that she hadn't told them the name. She could see a mob forming already.

'Okay, so does this mean that we're safe to walk home at night now then?' This was from a teenage girl with coffee coloured skin and a haze of frizzy hair.

'Erm, well, obviously we'd always advise, in the police, that you exercise reasonable caution.' Emma cursed herself – why hadn't she seen this coming? The feminist, radical part of herself wanted to say that women should go where they wanted to, when they wanted to, wearing whatever they fancied. But the sensible, police part of her needed to keep people safe and keep her conscience clear should there be another attack. She also knew that although she had the skills to defend herself and the training to spot a dangerous situation, not everyone was so lucky.

'So that's it? The same useless advice? That doesn't tell us anything!' The frizzy haired girl turned and stalked to the back of the crowd.

'Wait!' Emma took a breath. 'I'm a young woman too, you know. And I want to go out to a club without worrying about what's in my drink. I want to be able to say no to the losers who try to chat me up without being worried that they'll be waiting outside with their mates at closing time. I'd love to wear a miniskirt and walk home at two in the morning and feel safe doing so.' The teenager had stopped and was now listening intently. 'But what do you want me to say? I could say that you should retake the street and walk where you want, when you want, wearing what you want. But then, how do I feel when I'm taking your statement in the sexual assault suite the next day? Regardless of the politics, of what's right and what's wrong, at the end of the day we have to do two things. We must campaign for change but at the same time we have a responsibility to keep ourselves safe.' A stunned silence settled on the crowd. Emma seized her moment to wrap things up. 'Right, that's all I wanted to tell you. Any questions?'

'So, he's really gone then? DCM?'

'Yes. We know who he was and that person is dead. We've seized the car. Have there been any more sightings?'

There were shaking heads and murmurs but it did appear that she could at least close off the case of the DCM.

She wandered away from the crowd to commiserate with Lucy. 'Well, I made a right mess of that.'

'No, don't say that. These kids, they're bright. They know bullshit when they hear it. You did the right thing by being honest with them. And they needed to know. It's been a big part of their lives.'

Emma walked with Lucy and watched her working, stopping to chat and talk to the youths. Emma had been sceptical when Lucy had first explained the scheme but now she could see the value of it. Children could easily grow into adults viewing the police as the enemy, some force to be railed against. But projects like this were collaborative, they worked with the young people who could easily go into a life of petty crime. Hopefully projects like this would divert some of them.

CHAPTER TWENTY

Emma had had another very long day. The Garner murder meant that she had spent over twelve hours at her desk, primarily updating the computer system. Now they had two murders, work was being done quickly by all the associated agencies. The post-mortem was completed on the remains – at least as far as it could be. Likewise, a profile of John Garner's life was rapidly being assembled. All across Bradwick, and further into Wootenshire, uniformed officers were taking statements from the many people John had known.

He had lived a complicated, messy life. Sometimes he lived in his camp in the woods, drinking cheap alcohol and taking legal highs. Often in this phase, he'd been arrested for public order offences. This had made formal identification very easy from his fingerprints. But at other times, he had lived with one of several girlfriends, or his ex-wife had put him up. Factor in a few other friends who let him occasionally kip on their sofa and it was hard to build up a coherent picture of his life.

Even more difficult to see was any connection between him and Oliver Fairthorpe, who had lived a neat, organised life by comparison. Although the official protocol was to enter all the information onto the computer and let it find the links, no one could resist trying to find that one nugget of information. It meant that by the end of the day, everyone was tired and frustrated.

On top of all the computer work, the technicians had completed an accurate map of the crime scene, marked with the positions of all the major body parts. The route was popular with joggers, so it had been a simple matter to set a tripwire across the path and wait for someone to come past. They had found most of the tripwire leading to the detonator and car battery hidden behind the body of Garner.

Still, she tried hard to push all those thoughts out of her head. After the debacle at the crime scene, she definitely wanted to go round to see Rob today. She couldn't imagine how he'd be feeling now.

'Oh, Emma, lovely to see you.' Jem had answered the door again. 'Rob, it's Emma,' she called through to the living room.

'Hi, Rob,' she said as she walked in and sat in the armchair. He barely raised his eyes to her, still watching the TV. 'What's up with you?'

'Well, I'm not used to being rescued, especially by you,' he said, still not really looking at her. 'And I made a right idiot of myself in front of the new boss.'

'It's not that bad. You found some good clues. And I know that you did it for all the right reasons. The same reasons that you always do things – to do right by Bradwick.'

'That's nice of you to say, but I probably did more harm than good.' There was a further silence, awkward this time. 'I had some memories come back,' Rob said finally.

Emma's stomach turned over slowly. How much had he remembered? Had he worked out that someone had betrayed the raid on the industrial estate? He was unconscious for most of the important events, but if he remembered enough to piece it together, then where would that leave her?

She needed to say something, and soon. 'So, what have you remembered? Does it come back chronologically, so you remember the most distant stuff first?'

Rob studied her carefully. He could tell that something was worrying her. 'I remember that last day a lot more clearly. You being absolutely resolved to find Dark Car Man. And you finally identified him as Reg Patterson. My mentor, the one who brought me up through the force, taught me all I know.' He paused meaningfully. 'And set up the whole operation with Billy King and passed it on to me.' There was another pause. Emma didn't want to prompt him, she wanted to see what came back. From the corner of her eye, she could see Jem waiting in the doorway, waiting to see what would happen. 'That evening, we argued over whether it could be him or not. Then we went round to talk to him about it and we found the garage. With all his tools and everything. The diary. And then we ...' he paused and faltered, and this time, Emma stepped in.

'We went into the house and found his body,' Emma said gently. 'Do you remember that?'

'Yes, I remember. It's weird, because I really can't understand how I ever forgot it. Do you know what I mean? I've seen plenty of dead bodies, it's part of the job. But Reg? My mentor and friend? Now I've remembered, I can't believe I ever forgot. And then we had our chat in the garden. I know you told me when I asked, but I remember it for myself now. The ultimatum I gave you.' He paused and sighed. 'And then I came home.' He looked at Jem who nodded.

'I remember, you were late back,' his wife said. 'Nothing out of the ordinary there. You were upset, obviously. But you also had the big raid the next day.'

Rob thumped the arm of the chair. 'And that's it. Then I woke up in hospital. I've pieced it all together, but there's still a big gap, forty-eight hours.'

Emma released the breath that she'd been holding. But she could see that the memories were returning. Sooner or later, they would have to face up to the elephant in the room.

She couldn't imagine what Rob was going through. Was he sitting there talking to a stranger who he knew to be Emma and another stranger who he assumed was his wife? Or had he just assumed that they were who they said without being able to recognise them. She was beginning to understand why he was so tired all the time and reluctant to go out.

'Would you mind going through the raid again,' Rob asked. 'I feel like it's right there. Like a song I can't quite place, a word that I can't quite recall.'

Emma glanced at Jem. She was leaning on the door frame and hugging herself tightly. She nodded. 'Well, obviously you kept me with you. We were going to the raid, having a final check around the perimeter. Billy King was there, and that made you angry. I mean, I know it was his tip-off, but if he'd been sensible, he'd have been miles away. So, you went to talk to him. I don't know what you said, I waited in the car.

'But I could tell that something was wrong. He had these two bodyguards and they were behaving oddly. Not just standing back and checking out their surroundings, but they were looking at each other, and moving around too close to you and Billy.' She paused, trying to judge Rob's mood. He was attentive, but she could tell he remembered nothing. 'Then, well, you know.' She paused, not wanting to go back over the fight again. 'They tried to kill both of you and I immobilised both of them.' She rubbed a thumb over her knuckles, tugged on her ear.

'I know all that,' Rob said. 'I mean, I don't remember, but I remember you telling me, reading the reports. What happened next? How did it all go wrong?'

'I had to call in an ambulance because you were unconscious. And then, because the emergency services arriving would tip off the dealers in the warehouse, I started off the raid as well.' She paused a moment, putting herself back in the alleyway, watching the chaos unfold. 'The first thing that happened was that Greg Hargreaves left with Pietr Garoza.'

Rob nodded. 'And he was promptly arrested by Professional Standards. The idiot. I honestly thought I'd trained him better than that but he got greedy and impatient. I mean, leaving an active scene with a pocket full of cash and escorting our principal target out as well. It's just stupid. If I'd been there, I'd have run it straight, waited until the raid was over, then sorted out the cash, arranged for someone to take the product when everything was quieter.' He shook his head, more than anything disappointed in his former colleague. 'Did you see how he got arrested? Were they waiting for him?'

'No, I didn't see that part. He left and then ran back in pursued by other officers. It all went wrong after that – police fighting police, complete chaos. Just as I had to trigger our raid really, Professional Standards had to do the same thing.'

Rob ran a hand over his hair. 'So they were just waiting in the wings to run alongside our operation. They must have had some really good information.'

'Yes,' Emma said, going deliberately quiet. There was nothing she could say even though there was so much she wanted to. She had to let Rob get there on his own, if he ever did.

'I don't know. It's a lot to take in, isn't it? Not only was Hargreaves bent, well I mean, I know that he was, he worked for me. But he was trying to clear me and Billy out of the way. And while that was going on, someone else was working to bring him down.' He shook his head again. 'I thought I knew what was going in my team, but everyone was running their own agendas. I still can't believe that Glen arranged to have me killed. I worked with him for years. I thought I knew him.'

'Yes,' Emma said again.

'You've gone quiet,' Rob observed.

'Well, I...' Emma faltered. 'I mean, like you say. It was all going on behind the scenes. I don't think any one person had the whole picture.'

'Hmmm.' Rob was obviously not convinced but also couldn't find the words, the memories, to probe any further. When the silence had stretched to an uncomfortable length and Jem had gone to put the kettle on, Rob said, 'So, how bad was it back at the station?'

'What do you mean?'

'Well, with the whole crime scene thing.'

'Oh that. No one's really said anything about it.'

'Oooh.' Rob winced. 'It's that bad?'

'Bad? What would you prefer? To be the butt of the jokes around the canteen?'

'Actually, yes. The humour in the station is the most important thing for morale. If people joke about it, then they're okay about it. Not talking is the worst outcome. I really have to apologise for the situation I put you in.'

'Not at all.' Emma shook her head.

'I was just bored and fed up with the drips of information that I was getting. It all just built up in my head and, I don't know, I just wanted to do something rather than nothing. I wish I could get my hands on the files. I just know that if I could see everything, I might be able to find a connection.'

'Well, it would be brilliant if you could. At the moment we've got two bodies, same MO, probably same killer and no links between them. We've got a settled, family man in a travelling job and a drifter who never left Bradwick.'

'I take it everything's gone into the computer?'

'Yep. All of Garner's drug dealers, friends, sofa-surfing mates, all of them, together with all of Fairthorpe's clients.'

'It's hard to see how they'd move in the same circles. Might be something random like they were in the same queue for coffee.'

Emma shook her head. 'I can't see Garner as a Starbucks kind of a guy though. Unless Fairthorpe got his coffee somewhere like McDonald's.' She blew out a big breath. 'This is just pointless. Could be literally anything.'

'Yeah, that's true. There's one thing that me and Slater agree on, you can't ever get inside the mind of a killer, not really. In his mind, all this makes sense, but we can't know his reasons.'

'It's the most frustrating case that I've seen. One of the links is the two posters of Callum Frost that have come up. Were you there, sir?'

Rob closed his eyes and rubbed a hand over his face. He took a deep breath, then slowly got up from the sofa to go and stare out of the window. 'You wait. You just wait, till you get older. Then you'll have the one that got away. The case that should've been cut and dried and somehow never quite closed. I tell you even now, what fifteen years later, I could tell you all the details of that case. When he was last seen. Even back then we had an idea of how these things worked – we had details on all the members of the search parties. You have no idea, it changed everything up on the Seaview Estate. The advantage of that place was that it's an old-fashioned estate, you know, kids playing on the street, everyone in and out of each other's houses, that kind of thing.' He paused to gather his thoughts. 'I suppose you want to know what happened. Well, I'll take it you've read the official report. It was an ordinary evening, early in July, good weather. The kids had a couple of weeks to go before breaking up for the summer, spirits were high, exams were over. Well, it comes around to nine o'clock and Callum's not shown up, has he? He'd been out earlier, with his friends.

'Long story short, he'd wandered off somewhere. No one's sure of the last time they saw him but by the time the police were involved it was full dark and he hadn't been seen for hours. That first night was chaos – the men on the estate had all been down the pub. No one coordinated them, they just split up into groups with torches and spread out around the area. Some into the scrub to the north, others down to the beach and the cliffs, others around the estate. No idea who'd looked where or if any area had been missed. For all we know some areas were covered three times while others were left.' He stopped and sighed. 'By the morning, everything was far more serious. We had a base set up in the community hall, maps divided into search areas, the whole lot. But by then too many people had been traipsing all over for the dogs to have much luck. It was mostly residential so not much in the way of CCTV.'

'And no one ever found him? No leads at all?'

'No, he vanished off the face of the planet. You don't really know what to do with a case like that. Do you leave it a week, or two, or a month before you throw in the towel?'

'Officially, sir–'

'I know, I know. It's an open case even now. But realistically there comes a point where you can't just throw more men at the problem. You have to admit that a child has been lost and won't be found.'

There was an awkward pause between them. Finally Emma asked, 'Why now though? Why is someone bringing it all up again?'

'These posters? Do we know where they came from?'

'Local printing company knocked up thousands back in 2004, days after it happened. Did it as a favour to the community. And, before you ask, no they didn't keep records. Most of the local shops and pubs had a stack. Volunteers came in, took a handful and went about sticking them to walls, lamp posts, anywhere they could really. The one interesting fact is that it appears that these posters at the crime scenes are new.'

'New as in reprinted?' Haines asked.

'No, new as in never been put up before. No holes, tape marks, creases, sun fading or water damage – nothing. Someone, somewhere has at least two of these that they've kept for the last fifteen years. Until now.'

'And we have to assume that person is also our killer.'

'They're certainly someone that we'd like very much to talk to.'

Chapter Twenty-One

Emma sat at her desk while her stomach contracted and somersaulted. She had made her preparations, marshalled her arguments. Now all she needed to do was the difficult thing. She went across the office and knocked gently on Detective Inspector Kevin Slater's door.

'Sir, I've got an idea, but I don't think you'll like it,' she said as she entered his office.

'And why don't you think I'll like it?' Kev asked, looking up from his desk.

'First, I think it might be a way out of the fix we're in with the two murders.'

'You think we're in a fix?' Kev asked innocently.

'Oh, come on, sir. You know what's going on out there. We've two bodies with no connection between them apart from one killer seems to be responsible for both. I know we're all working really hard, collecting evidence, entering it into the computer and hoping for that connection to turn up. But we have to face the fact that it might not.'

'Well, this is a turn up for the books. You were all for us taking this case, bringing justice to the families. Wiser heads were warning that this might happen. That we might be mired in a case that turns into the next cold case, that drags on for ever.' There was an awkward pause between the two of them. Finally Kev broke it, saying, 'Well, what is this terrible plan that I'll hate? I presume you think it'll be the saving of us.'

Emma swallowed hard. This was the point she'd been putting off, even while she was making preparations for the meeting. 'Rob Haines,' she said simply.

'What about him?' Kev was tense now.

'We need his help. We need him to look at the case files. He knows this town, this county better than anyone. He might have a unique insight.'

'From him?' Kev sneered. 'From what I've heard he doesn't even leave the house.' A momentary pause. 'Unless, that is, there's a crime scene for him to mess up somewhere.'

'He wouldn't have to actually be operational,' Emma said. She had to bite her tongue. She would've loved to lay into Slater about how unfair he was being. But she needed him to be onside for her plan. She needed it, Rob Haines needed it, and the case needed something to give it a shot in the arm. 'We could see if he could be set up and work from home. He might never need to come into the office.'

'I still think he'd be a liability,' Slater said.

'You know, I think a big part of the problem at the crime scene was that DCI Haines was on the outside of everything. He got frustrated sitting at home.'

'That might his problem, Emma, but it isn't mine. We're not here to make people feel better, we're here to solve crimes.'

'And I still feel, sir, that Haines might be our best hope of doing so. Even if he doesn't solve the whole thing, he might have in his head the one fact that leads to the killer.'

'That's just your opinion though, Emma,' Slater said, standing up to bring the meeting to a close.

It was time for her final gambit. Something that she had worked out late last night, sat on the sofa with a bottle of beer and a purring cat on her lap. She thought that it was risky, but would probably work. She got up and went to the door. At the last minute, she turned back and said, 'You know sir, if you did go through with this, then something odd would happen. You'd still be the head of the MIT and even though Haines is a DCI you'd be his boss. He'd work for you and anything you turned up would be to your credit. Chances are he's out of the force soon anyway so you'd take all the kudos.'

Without waiting for a reply, she went back to her desk. She started poking around in the case, taking the door-to-door enquiry reports and skim-reading them before putting them on the computer. She wasn't really paying attention – she was more concerned about how Kev Slater would react. He could easily be offended that she'd suggested that he'd be motivated by getting one up on a senior officer. Or he might not even care. But, she thought, that wasn't true. She could tell that he was ill at ease around officers with more experience. She remembered how puffed up he'd been that he'd needed to call in the bomb squad.

The man himself, DI Slater, broke into her thoughts. He was stood by her desk, waiting for her to finish what she was doing. She looked up.

'Ah yes, Emma.' He was hesitant. 'I've been thinking about what you we're saying, and well, there might be some value in it. But you'd have to check with technical first, to see if it can be done from home. Don't want the old boss roaming around here like a dinosaur. And we have no idea how the CPS will react to this. Any information that comes through this channel will have to be double-checked by regular officers. We'll just use him to sort the wheat from the chaff.'

'I'll see what can be done, sir,' Emma said with a straight face. She'd already checked with Pete and it was possible. He'd gone into a long discussion of secure VPN's and virtual desktops, none of which she'd understood. But she did know that it was possible for Rob to see the files without ever setting foot in the station.

'Right. Yes. Well, if it can be done, and if Rob agrees, then we might as well see if he can make any sense of this mess. And if he can't, well, nothing ventured and all that.'

Without another word, he retreated back to his office. Emma knew she'd won the battle but wondered what the cost would be later on. She wondered if this was how people like Suse saw the world – as a series of battles and strategies. She'd agonised over the best way to get around Kev Slater but, from what she'd seen, other people did it completely naturally.

However she felt about it, she had won for the moment. Now, all she needed to do was to put the wheels in motion and get Rob set up with a new laptop. But, as she reached out for the phone, it rang. Feeling slightly spooked, she picked it up.

'It's Sergeant Kelly here.' Emma knew he was the desk sergeant who knew everything that was going on in Bradwick. 'I thought I ought to give you a heads-up. I've taken the decision not to send anyone onto the Seaview Estate single-crewed. You know that lad who was taken into hospital yesterday for an overdose?'

'Yes,' Emma said with a sense of dread.

'Well, he died overnight. Tensions were already high over there, but now they're approaching boiling point.'

'Thanks for that,' Emma said, already working out how it would impact their work.

'No problem. You take it easy if you're going over there.'

She hung up and sat back a bit. She'd seen the news reports last night – a fourteen-year-old boy had been found collapsed on one of the pieces of rough ground that dotted the Seaview Estate. The story was still new and details were sketchy as to what exactly he had taken. But with everyone getting their news online, word spread like wildfire. He was found with a syringe as well as a number of so-called legal highs. The fact that he was just a child and had died overnight was serious.

She knew that with the dealers vying for position by means of revenge beatings and intimidation the estate was already a powder keg waiting for the match. Now it appeared that the dealers were also targeting new customers and maybe even bringing in drugs with different formulations and strengths.

A sudden wave of depression swept over her. Police briefings were all about strategies and initiatives. Targets had to be met, arrests made, drugs taken off the street. She imagined that on the other side of the fence, dealers were worried about territory, who was trying to take their place and about their bosses. But all of that ignored one thing. That in the middle were fourteen-year-old children who were the casualties of this war. Families that had lost a son, a cousin and brother. Schoolfriends who'd lost a mate to kick around with. Somehow all of that got lost in all the talk of targets and task forces.

She shook her head to try to dislodge her thoughts. She knew what she needed to do. Walking across the room, she stopped by Brian Chisholm's desk. 'Sir, I've just heard that the fourteen-year-old overdose victim died overnight. I've a contact on the Seaview, so I wanted to drop in and get a feel for the current mood. Maybe see if I can smooth things over a bit?'

Kev nodded. 'Do you need any backup? One of the DSs or maybe a uniform?'

'I think it'd be more dangerous to appear as police, if you know what I mean, sir. I'll just go on my own, have a drink with my contact and see how the land lies. In normal circumstances the police aren't welcome on the estate, so I'd like to keep it under the radar for the moment.'

'OK.' Brian nodded decisively. 'Keep in touch though. And be careful. Don't go anywhere without your radio. I mean it.'

'I won't sarge. I'll just be popping round for a chat with a friend.'

CHAPTER TWENTY-TWO

Emma took her own car and drove to Margaret Watts' house. On the way through the estate there had been groups of people standing around the green. They just appeared to be talking to one another, some smoking cigarettes, but Emma was uneasy. With a trained eye she could see that the groups were mostly men, and also mostly younger. It was worse than she'd anticipated. She knew that when the sun went down the mood could change, become uglier.

'Oh, Emma, it's you.' For once Mrs Watts looked uneasy. She hung onto the edge of her front door. 'Are you sure this is a good time to come round?'

'Are you going to invite me in?' Emma was suddenly nervous about what she was doing there. She was exposed standing on the doorstep.

'Of course I am. It's just a strange time to have police on the estate.'

Soon they were settled down in the front room with rich fruit cake and cups of tea. Before she could ask why the police were persona non grata, Margaret told her.

'It's silly really. The people stirring up trouble around here are usually the first to avoid the police if they can manage it. They like to solve their problems on their own, if you know what I mean. But now they're saying that you should've been here to crack down on the dealers. They think that if you were, Jordy would still be alive.'

'How bad is it out there?'

'Have you seen Twitter? Hashtag Justice for Jordy is trending in this area.'

'Trending?' Emma asked, amazed.

'Less of that!' Margaret said with a smile. 'The community centre did computer courses and set up a website. I'm not too old to learn new tricks. And I love Twitter – we've set up groups to organise local events. Anyway, there is a lot of ill feeling starting from the fact that beat police haven't been seen around here for many years.'

'It's just hard to know what to do next,' Emma said. 'If I'm being honest we want to come here more often. But it's a hostile environment and we're so often single-crewed that we don't. We also have our own resourcing issues.'

'Well, you'd better find something and find it quick. The mood round here is ugly.'

'If we could have maybe a couple of days to sort things out, we could make moves towards arresting the dealers, try to get some of the worst stuff off the streets.' She paused for a moment. 'But we won't be able to do that if we're policing a small riot and processing a station full of people for breach of the peace.'

Margaret Watts looked shifty. Finally she said, 'I do know one of Jordy's relatives – an aunt. I mean, we're both on the same community committee but I don't really talk to her.'

'But you could?' Emma asked hopefully.

'Maybe. I mean, the whole family will be in turmoil.'

'But do they really want young people causing trouble on the estate?' Emma pressed.

Margaret sighed. 'No one wants to see that. Can you wait here for a bit? I'll see if I can get hold of the aunt and maybe a couple of others. If you talk to them, promise that you'll find this dealer, maybe we can calm things down.'

'Yeah, I can wait here.' Emma sat in the front room unable to relax. The chairs were overstuffed and all the surfaces and walls were cluttered with plates. She sipped her rapidly cooling tea and ate another slice of cake.

'It's no use,' Margaret said as she came back into the room. 'The whole family has so much to do with undertakers, hospitals, the police, you name it. A sudden death like that shakes everything up. They won't, or can't, come to meet with you. But the nephew, Jordy's cousin, has said he'll get onto Twitter and all the rest and try to calm things down. Straight from the family, it might help.' She stopped and looked awkward. 'Listen Emma, there's not much good you can do here. You know me, I'm a very polite person and known for my hospitality. But right now...'

'No, no, you're all right. I understand. It would be bad all round if someone called round and found me here.' She got up and prepared to leave. 'Anyway, I ought to be out there, chasing up some of my informants. See if they know who's supplying this stuff. The sooner we make some arrests, the better.'

With more awkwardness than usual, Emma got up and left. She looked both ways on the way to her car, feeling like she was being watched. But the street was quiet – most of the residents were the other side of the estate. She hoped that Jordy's cousin would be able to calm things down.

She knew where she had to go and drove straight there. Away from the residential estates of Seaview and Coopers End was a more picturesque part of town. Here, up a cobbled side street, was the holiday cottage with a view of the sea where she'd last seen her friend, Lukas.

As soon as she knocked on the door though, she knew that it was empty. Her career of banging on doors and looking for people had given her an instinct. She looked through the window and confirmed exactly what she'd thought, the house was empty. She peered more closely inside. It wasn't only empty, but professionally cleaned. There were no personal possessions, not one used coffee cup, to be seen. There was a key safe on the wall by the door, the holiday rental had ended and the house had been turned around for the next occupant.

She walked back to her car and prepared for the next stage of locating Lukas. She called him, left a voicemail, then backed it up with a text message. Then she drove to the right part of town and started banging on doors where he'd lived in the past.

Unsurprisingly, the only real answer she got was that he was 'shacked up with a posh bird' and hadn't been seen for ages. It was getting late in the day so she had to decide what to do next. She sat in her car and weighed up her options. She should really head back into the station, call Pete, and get things underway with the laptop for Rob. But, she had a nagging worry about Lukas. With only ten minutes left before the technical department clocked off, she called Pete from her mobile, told him to go ahead, and to leave the paperwork on her desk if anything needed signing.

Now the time was about right to go and try some of the dodgier pubs. The trouble was that she was on her own and the mood was already quite ugly. On the other hand, her concern about her friend was mounting. Usually, if she put a couple of hours work into it, she could find him. Either he didn't want to be found or something was wrong. She decided to try a couple of the less dangerous pubs. While she was there, she'd also try to find out who was filling the gaps in the drug market.

Two hours later, she had to admit defeat. No one had heard or seen of Lukas recently, wherever she asked. She'd also tried to push her contacts on who was currently dealing, especially around the estates. But word had already spread of the unrest. No one was admitting to anything. If they had supplied those drugs they'd have to choose between an angry mob or a lengthy prison sentence.

Emma sat in her car outside the last dodgy pub on her mental list – The Greyhound, which was a flat-roofed, prefab building in a part of town that was definitely not on the tourist route. She couldn't remember a time when it had taken her this long to hunt down Lukas. She had a bad feeling that she'd learned not to ignore.

She could go home and try again tomorrow, but she knew she would never settle so instead she drove back to work, grabbing some fast food on the way to the station. It felt different now that it was early Friday evening. There were fewer civilian staff and the uniformed officers were gearing up for work.

As a police officer, Emma knew how to handle a missing persons case. She also knew that she could use her name and rank without making it official just yet.

She started calling the various departments within the police who might have seen Lukas Mills, or picked him up somewhere. She was working on auto-pilot when she dialled through to the Bradwick Hospital.

'Yes, Lukas Mills is here. On Ward four west, admitted two days ago. Suspected overdose, but still being held for observation.'

Emma thanked the administrator who'd answered the phone and automatically hung up. She knew she ought to go and see him, but she was still in shock. Lukas had always seemed so indestructible, stumbling his way through life in a charmed fashion. What had gone wrong?

Her thoughts were interrupted when Brian Chisholm banged his way into the office. 'Right. Who's coming down the pub? Got a proper result this afternoon!'

'What are we celebrating?' Nick Dent raised his head from his computer monitor.

'I've been out all afternoon, real police work. Drinking pints with all sorts of undesirables who've been my snouts either now or in the past. And under one rock that I turned over I found the lowlife who sold poor old Jordy Peters some very dodgy drugs.' He smiled smugly. 'I managed to persuade him that his best chance lay with us. We may have to move him out of area when we want to lock him up.'

'You promised to get him locked up out of area?' Nick said, sounding impressed.

'Well, to be honest, people on the estate would be likely to have a cousin or brother somewhere in a local prison. He'd be safest a long way away from here. Of course, I'll have to go to court for the remand hearing and ask the judge. But it'd be worth it. I've had a quick nose round his house before calling in the specialist search teams. The dealer wasn't the sharpest knife the drawer, drugs and weapons all over the shop.' He stopped to look around the room.

'But the details can wait till tomorrow, tonight I'm off to the pub and I'm buying, who's with me?'

'I can't, I've got to visit a friend in hospital,' Emma said, making the decision immediately. She found herself irritated that she'd failed to defuse the situation on the estate and that none of her contacts had turned up the dealer. Her annoyance also spilled over to Brian Chisholm. She thought that she owned the problem on the estate, but obviously he had taken it on himself and done what he could. She'd only really informed him as a courtesy, a matter of procedure. She certainly hadn't expected him to steal her case and make a success of it.

Chapter Twenty-Three

Emma quickly found her way straight to the correct ward at the hospital. She hated that she was so familiar with the place – it was almost like a second workplace for her.

She went onto the ward and read the board to see where he was and soon found Lukas in the middle of a bay of six beds, all occupied. Before he saw her, she had a chance to observe him. He looked strangely vulnerable, pale, with bruises under his eyes. He was wearing a hospital smock and none of his usual jewellery and bangles.

'Angel! You're here! Finally!' She went over and gave him a hug. Despite his appearance there was a bit more meat on his bones.

'Lukas, how are you feeling?'

'Like crap, if I'm honest,' he said, his voice still slightly hoarse. 'Well, I landed up in here, didn't I?'

'What happened?'

'What do you mean? Do you mean that as a friend or as your job?' he asked playfully. Emma punched him lightly on the shoulder. Although he was lovely she was coming to realise that he was more like a little brother to her. Someone needed to look out for him. He continued. 'It was all going well, then Kelly just decided that it was time to go home. I think something happened and she had to go back to London. And that's when I realised...' He paused and Emma decided to wait him out. 'It was just a holiday fling. Well, for her anyway.' He looked dejected.

'Did you fall for her?' Emma asked gently.

'No. Yes. I don't know.' He took a breath to gather his thoughts. 'I think I fell for the whole thing. I'm not explaining really. She had a car. I know that sounds silly but she had this little Peugeot and it started every time. Most of the time, I know someone who I can blag a lift off, or I walk somewhere. And the cars are always a bit old or lashed together. And then you'd wake up from a party and the usual hassle would start again, you know. Who's got space, can you get a lift home. Sometimes you'd hitch to get back home.

'But with Kelly, we'd wake up one morning and she'd have a bunch of friends who were having a party down in Cornwall or Devon. We'd pack a load of stuff, chuck it in the car and drive down there. Have a beach party, sleep around the fire and just drive back with no drama.' He stopped and shrugged. 'I dunno, it probably seems really trivial to you, but it was a glimpse of another life. Sleeping in a bed, knowing where you're going to be next.' He shook his head.

'And then she went home?'

'Yeah. She rented a holiday cottage with a hot tub, sea view and bit of rough boyfriend. When she needed to go back, she just packed up and left it all behind.'

'And you ended up in here?' Emma knew that she had to choose her words carefully. 'Were you trying to...? I mean, was it...?'

'No, no, nothing like that, babe. You know me, life is out there for the taking. I'll bounce back, not check out. No, I just went back to my old life, my old haunts. But, well, I saw a paper while I was in here. That guy Jordy. It's a different world out there now. Half my dealers had disappeared, there were new people, new drugs. I just wanted to get out of it for a bit. Get out of my own head.'

'Except you woke up in here?'

'Yeah. Out of practice and a few weeks of clean living. Well, not clean maybe, Kelly like a bit of coke now and again. But she had London dealers, proper stuff.' He shook his head again. 'But it's a different world down here. Legal highs and drugs cut with God knows what.'

'What are you going to do now?'

'I don't know. I'm basically okay now; they've flushed out my system and taken blood for testing. I think they'd like to kick me out but they need to be sure that I'm going to somewhere safe with a low chance of ending up back here again.' He shrugged expressively. 'Of course, there's bugger all funding for social care so I could grow old in here!'

'You can't come and live with me,' Emma said hastily. Her new resolve to treat him as a brother wasn't up to being tested by sharing a house with him. 'I've got two good lodgers and we're all settled.'

'No, you don't need to worry about that, babe. I can see that having a homeless ex-druggie sleeping on your sofa isn't a good look for a police officer.'

Emma laughed. She liked his sense of humour and was glad that he wasn't going to impose. She'd picked up on something though. 'You said ex-druggie. Does that mean?'

'Yeah,' he sounded resigned. 'I mean I can't carry on like this. I think that's what my time with Kelly showed me. I'm nearly twenty-eight, I'm gonna be thirty pretty soon. It's a bit sad to be kipping on people's sofas and not knowing where I'm waking up.' He swept his hand around to show the ward. 'Trouble is, I don't know how to go from here, to having a stable kind of life. I haven't really got a CV, most of my experience is in petty crime. There are large gaps.'

'You could go home?' Emma said. 'I know you have family up there. You could even move back home.'

'Yeah, but my family are as bad as yours. For a start it'd be tough being nearly thirty and living at home. And then I'd hook up with my old friends.' He shrugged. 'I'd be bored and fed up and then, well, I know myself, I wouldn't be clean for long. No,' he said firmly. 'I don't know what the answer is, but it's not going backwards, not going home. I've got to stay around here and find a new way.'

'But you do have skills, don't you?'

'Well, if you count being good at organising road protests.'

'Hey, that shows initiative and that you're good with your hands.' When he looked sceptical, she continued, 'You're talking to the queen of reinvention here. I'm sure we can figure it out.'

'First thing we have to do is to get me out of here.' He leaned forward and lowered his voice. 'They're even talking about a psych evaluation. I need to avoid that kind of stuff. Anyway, now it's the weekend, it's not very likely that they'll discharge me before Monday.'

'I can have a poke around at work,' Emma said. 'Maybe talk to some colleagues who are more community minded.' She thought of Lucy who worked with teenage drivers and tried to stop them from getting into trouble. 'Don't pull that face at me,' she admonished. 'They're good people and they know all the schemes, grants, all of that. If you want to get straight and make a change, you'll have to sit down with some of these people and make some plans.'

'Yeah, maybe.' He brightened a bit. 'It's got to be something though. I'm actually getting bored of the same people who have the same parties in the same pubs.'

They chatted for a bit, just small talk about people they'd known while growing up. A nurse came in and gave Emma a look that said it was time. She knew she'd been given leeway on the visiting hours, but it was getting late.

'I'll keep dropping in and see if I can get something sorted,' she said.

'Please do. I'm kind of going mad in here. I've even started reading books.' He indicated a novel on his bedside table – something lurid with guns and action by the look of the cover.

Chapter Twenty-Four

Emma was back in Rob Haines' front room. As usual Jem had provided tea and biscuits and withdrawn. Rob was kneeling beside the TV cursing at the large, unorganised piles of DVDs. 'I was looking for Moonraker – would you believe it, there's a box here but no sign of the disk.'

'Listen, boss, there's something I need to tell you before we settle down to watch a film.'

Rob straightened up and went back to his armchair where he settled in with a sigh. 'Well this sounds serious. I'm not your boss any more, but I can still tell when you think you've fucked up. What's on your mind?'

'I went to Kev Slater with an idea. I half expected him to either shoot it down or give it time to think it over.'

'Okay,' Rob was nodding. 'What's it got to do with me?'

'I asked him if you could help us on the case.' A look of panic momentarily flickered across his face. 'It's okay. You wouldn't need to go back into the office. With the Internet now, you could get a laptop connected up to the police computer. You still have your access rights so you could keep an eye on the case. Maybe give us some insights?'

Rob laughed, a low, throaty chuckle. 'Christ! Poor old Kevin Slater. He must be proper stuck on this case if he's even considering bringing me in. I wonder how he'll square that away, what with me being under investigation and all?'

'Well, you wouldn't be operational. No going out there and meeting the public. You'd just sit here with your laptop and tell us where we're going wrong.'

'You're really that stuck?' Rob sounded concerned now.

'Well, we've got two murders. Absolutely no connections between the two victims, different locations, possibly different methods of death and yet we're certain that we're only looking for one killer.'

Rob sucked in through his teeth. 'And if he's already killed twice, then he might carry on.'

'I have a feeling someone like this will carry on until he's caught,' Emma admitted. 'And so far we have no idea how he's choosing his victims or how he's picking the places he leaves them, nothing.'

'Right. So, do I expect a phone call from Kevin at some point in the next few days?'

'Not exactly. It's all been agreed by him. Just needs a phone call to the IT department and you'll be all set and ready to go. Something should happen by the end of Monday?'

'And it needs my approval,' Rob said darkly. 'You did all this without even running it by me?'

'Well, I thought he wouldn't buy it. Or he'd talk to you.' Emma was flustered. 'I never imagined he'd roll over and just say yes. And then I could hardly back down and say I hadn't checked with you.'

'And now you'll be properly snookered if I turn around and say no, won't you?'

A silence fell between them. Finally, Emma said, 'What are you going to do?'

'I'm wondering if I could go back to work. If I'd make a difference? Would I still be any good? And how would it sit with the whole mess that is the medical case and the corruption case that are hanging over me? It's going to be hard to argue that I can't work while I'm still helping.

'On the other hand, it'd be good to get my feet back under the table, even if it's only for one case. Remind myself that I'm still useful. To be honest, I'm tempted to just accept, sign whatever I need to and sod the consequences. Then I could have my swan song.'

'It was just a feeling. Even killers who try to be random have a reason. There could be anything linking those two. A drinking den that you shut down years ago, or some old scandal in Bradwick's history. If we knew what you'd find, we wouldn't need to ask, would we?'

'Well, I suppose that is true.'

'And I've seen you work your magic before. You know just who to phone and what to ask.'

'If you're going to flatter me, then I suppose I've no choice. Make the phone call and get the ball rolling.' He stopped for a minute, unsure how much to reveal. In the end, as he always had, he just charged ahead and hoped for the best. 'I made a proper mess of that crime scene though, didn't I? I am sorry about that, causing trouble between you and your boss.' He tapped his head. 'It is getting better. I'm not as tired and the headaches are happening less often. But I probably had better keep my head down for a bit. I honestly can't believe I did that. I went to the crime scene without checking in with the SIO, no rubber gloves or overshoes. Just blundered straight in like a civilian.' He shook his head in bewilderment. 'So, this could be a good thing. Get me back in with the higher-ups at the station and hopefully stop me doing any more damage.'

'Well, let's just take it one step at a time. Get you set up and see what you can do when you have access to all the case files.'

After that, Emma relaxed and actually enjoyed spending time with Rob and his dodgy taste in films.

Chapter Twenty-Five

Emma was sat at her desk, scrolling through the latest list of information that had come back from the fruitless searches into Fairthorpe's clients. None of it looked at all useful.

Likewise, the file on Garner was looking thin. His lifestyle meant he had a lot of contacts but it was hard to pin down any actual enemies. She briefly considered asking Lukas what the deal was but she didn't want to bother him until she could find something that he could do with the rest of his life. Besides which, something didn't feel right. There was an ongoing battle for control of the drug trade in the town, but it wasn't as sophisticated and involved as these last two murders. There were brutal stabbings and beatings over turf – she'd noticed that King Kabs were being singled out for revenge attacks – but nothing this complex..

Besides which, Garner was a low-level user, there was no sign that he had ever dealt at all. This murder might be making a statement to establish rights over turf, but if that had been the case then the victim would have been a dealer, not some no-mark user who was homeless half the time.

Her musings were interrupted by the other person in the room, Brian Chisholm, muttering 'Yes!' under his breath. Emma turned around just in time to see him actually punch the air.

'What? Are you telling me that you have a lead in this case?'

'You bet I do. There is a link between our financial advisor Fairthorpe and our down-and-out Garner.' He paused for dramatic effect. 'John Garner has an aunt, one Joanna Shaw, who was also a client of the late Oliver Fairthorpe.' He looked smug, and deservedly so.

'How the hell did you tease that out?'

'List of all known contacts of Garner, cross referenced manually against the master list of clients. Not subtle, took ages, paid off.' He paused, sizing Emma up. 'Needs two people to interview the aunt. Fancy coming along?'

Emma considered for a moment. No doubt this was a golden opportunity. She could be right there at the beginning of the end of the case. On the other hand, she would be alone with Brian Chisholm. Even being in the same office gave her the creeps. And she was still irrationally annoyed that he'd taken the Jordy case out from under her. But, would he really attack a fellow officer while on duty? That was a whole different level to what he might do at home. He almost certainly wasn't dangerous.

He saw the indecision on her face and smiled ruefully. 'The rumour mill working overtime then? I see that you've heard about me and my past history.' He grinned, more wolfish than reassuring. 'I promise, I won't bite.'

She gathered her coat and handbag. She needed to get on with him. 'It's okay. I used to work with Rob Haines. I know how to handle a dinosaur.'

They left together, both laughing.

After an uneventful journey, for which Emma was grateful, they pulled up outside a nice bungalow in a village just south and inland from Bradwick. They made the usual introductions and reassurances before all getting seated around a coffee table, hot drinks to hand.

'I'm afraid we have some bad news, Mrs Shaw,' Brian said. 'We found a body a few days ago and all indications are that it's your nephew, John Garner. We're having trouble tracing people, so you might be next of kin.'

'John?' She didn't show a huge amount of surprise. 'Poor thing. Always felt sorry for him, but well, you know. We just kind of drifted apart. You know how some families are. Different paths.'

'So, just to clarify,' Brian said, 'when was the last time you saw John Garner?'

For the first time, Joanna Shaw looked a little uncomfortable. Both Emma and Brian caught it. She looked sideways at her superior.

'Mrs Shaw? Is there anything we should know?' He was all concern and caring.

She looked out of the window, as if she might bolt and leap through it. 'It's kind of awkward, you know. Family rows and all that.'

Emma said, 'It's okay, we hear all sorts. And we keep it to ourselves. Unless it has a direct bearing on the case, then we'll just forget all about it.'

Mrs Shaw took a deep breath. 'You have to understand, his father, my brother Gordon, was an accident really. I was already sixteen when Mummy got pregnant, so when I left for university there was a toddler running around. I didn't really get to know him and what I did know, I didn't get on with.' She shook her head. 'I'm sorry to say that Gordon was one of life's unfortunates. He never really took responsibility for his own failings, always blamed someone else. So, I grew up, married, got settled down and got on with my life. Of course, I bumped into Gordon at weddings and funerals, you know. But we weren't close. And then he died, what must be over ten years ago now.

'Of course, I knew he had a child, but as I said, he didn't really take any responsibility. He brought the mother and baby to a couple of family events and then she just disappeared. I did feel bad for the child, especially after Gordon passed, but the mother wasn't interested in Gordon's family. When he grew up I tried to help but he was worse than my brother. I haven't spoken to John in well over five years. Some people will just bring you down if you let them. I'm afraid that I rather cut him off the last time I saw him. He only ever came around when he was short of money. And if I wouldn't lend it to him, well, I have some strong suspicions that he stole things. Eventually, enough was enough and I told him exactly that.'

'And you haven't spoken to him since?' Brian asked.

'Not at all. We were never close, but he hasn't got his parents around, so I felt that I should try to look out for him.' Her jaw set firm. 'But, I did my best and it wasn't enough.'

Emma's heart sank. This was meant to be the big break. But the link between the two looked as if it only existed on paper. While Chisholm and Mrs Shaw carried on talking, Emma subtly looked around the room. It was outdated but well decorated, with flock wallpaper and a deep red carpet. She had been to the camp where John Garner had slept occasionally and could see the gulf between the two people. It was obvious that he'd lived there for some time, with a cheap tent augmented with bits of tarpaulin. There were muddy patches where he'd walked about – it was obviously a well-used place. It was equally obvious that he'd had nothing to do with his aunt for years.

Her reverie was broken by Brian moving the interview on. 'The other thing I wanted to ask was about your financial advisor, Oliver Fairthorpe?'

'Oh, yes,' Joanna said. 'I got the letter the other day. Such a terrible shock. What did you want to know?'

'Well, we've got his files, but we'd just like to know what your impression was of Mr Fairthorpe?'

'My impression? Didn't really form one. He was professional and responsible. My husband died about nine months ago, and well, I thought I'd better do a proper job of sorting out all the money. Pensions now are so complicated, not like they used to be. And there are all these warnings now about scammers and people waiting to steal your pension fund.' She stopped to dab at the corners of her eyes with a tissue. 'Sorry. It's still so recent. But I had lump sums and decisions to make so I called a professional. And that's what he was.

Absolutely fine, good advice. I've got a nice lump sum, money put aside for emergencies and a monthly income.'

Emma's heart sank even further, but she knew she had to be thorough. 'So, you ended your relationship with John Garner before you met Oliver Fairthorpe?'

'Oh God, yes. I'll be honest, I haven't thought about John from one month to the next. I suppose in hindsight, he might've turned up if he'd heard I had a lump sum. But if he had found out then he would've spent it all on drink and drugs. I'm sorry if I sound harsh, but that's about all there is.'

After that there was nothing to do but make small talk about how terrible it was to have two murders in one town. As soon as they were in the car, Emma and Brian looked at each other.

'Well, that was a bust,' Emma said despondently.

'Nah, it's all part of the game. You get leads and you check them out. One at a time. Not all of them play out, but you have to go through motions, tick them off. It's the job.' He shrugged.

'But it seemed so certain. A definite link.'

'It's just weird coincidences. You think about it, Fairthorpe had hundreds of contacts on his books. And our man John Garner, he must have known half of Bradwick. His kind always have someone they can bum money off, or a night on the sofa, or spot them some drugs. Think about those two big groups of people. It's statistics isn't it?' Emma turned to look at him, surprised at his comments. 'I'm not just an ugly face, you know. I know things, I can do the maths. And some days that's what this job is. Just maths. Chase up nine crappy leads before you can find the one golden one.'

There was nothing more to be said so they headed back to the office in silence.

CHAPTER TWENTY-SIX

Emma had found herself relying more and more on Margaret Watts' advice. Having the second body and crime scene to process had taken some of the focus off the drug problems. The Seaview Estate had gone from threatening to boil over back down to its usual simmering resentment. As often happened, the resentment following the death of Jordy had settled down. Members of the family had repeatedly appealed for calm and there had been a memorial service. On the police side of things, the arrest of a dealer had helped as well. He had not been a master criminal – a search of his house had turned up a range of different drugs, a selection of weapons and a list of contacts. This last item had been a goldmine for the drugs squad and had led to a major operation. It had done the police a lot of good as a whole to be seen to be arresting people on the estate.

Emma's last visit to Mrs Watts had been awkward. She had fled from the bad feeling on the estate and probably shouldn't have been there at all. She was glad she had the chance to make amends when she pulled up on a sunny afternoon.

'Emma,' Mrs Watts said as she opened the door. 'I am so glad you stopped by. I've been feeling awful about the last time you came round. I was rude to you and I hope you'll accept my apology.'

'Really, it was thoughtless of me to impose at such a time. I should've known that you would have contacts with Jordy's family. And I can come round here for a cuppa and go away again. But you have to live here, it's a different thing. You did the best that you could.'

'Well, least said, soonest mended. Come on in and I'll put the kettle on.'

Emma knew that was the beginning of a sequence that was far more complex than her own habit of putting a bag in a cup. She followed Margaret through to the kitchen and watched her warming the pot as the kettle boiled.

There was the obligatory small talk – Emma learned that nothing much had changed in her sons' lives. Greg had produced another grandchild, a beautiful boy in her opinion.

'What's going on with you then, Emma?' Margaret asked. 'You look like you've got the weight of the world on your shoulders.'

Emma sighed, she wasn't really sure where to start. 'You know when I came over here to talk to you after Jordy died?' Margaret nodded. 'I really thought I could come in here as a shining knight and fix everything. Calm down the tensions on the estate, arrest the dealers, sort everything out.'

'You know what I've learned over the years, love? Doesn't matter what you do, the dead are still dead. You could've done all that and while it would be a big comfort to the parents and would've stopped someone else going through the same, it wouldn't have brought Jordy back. Nothing would. I know when something like this happens all of us feel that there's something more we could've done, we all want to <u>do</u> something. It's natural isn't it.'

'Yeah, I know what you mean. I should be used to it, but a fourteen-year-old boy, it's so senseless. Such a waste.'

'I kind of hope you don't get used to it. I've never done any kind of emergency services job but I can't imagine anything worse than not being upset by the death of a child.' She paused and studied Emma. 'So, why the long face? The news is all over the estate. There have been a series of dawn raids. People have been arrested, drugs and weapons off the streets. Surely that's a good thing?'

'It's just me and the people I work with. I got the call and thought that it was my problem to solve. But when I tapped up all my contacts, tried to see what was going on, I found nothing. And to make it worse, one of my people, well, really a friend, I found him in hospital.'

'Oh no! What happened?'

'Same as Jordy by the sound of it. But Lukas got lucky this time. He dodged it and is now recovering.'

'And your nose is out of joint because someone else solved the case? I thought you lot all worked as a team?'

'Well, we should, but everything kind of fell apart a few months ago. Most of the team were suspended pending an enquiry and they cobbled together a new group of people. But we haven't really bonded as a team.'

'And how much have you done to help that?' Margaret asked.

'I know you're right. I've got reasons to dislike each of them. I don't trust them or their motives.' She paused, unsure of how much to reveal. In the end she decided to push on. 'All my annual performance reviews say that I'm not a team player. I'm happiest going off on my own and fixing things. I don't like relying on other people.'

'Emma, why did you join the police? I mean really?'

'Really? In truth I did it at first because I was having a row with my parents and it was the one thing that I knew would piss them off. And it worked, they don't talk to me at all.' She paused, lost in the memory. 'And then I found out that I was good at it, and I enjoyed it. I know it can be a crappy job but it's my job.'

'I see you and I can tell that you've set your path to be in the police. But you've got to work with people. Give the others you work with a chance to show what they can do. I mean, they caught this dealer so they're not all bad.'

'Change the habit of a lifetime you mean?' Emma said with a laugh.

'Yeah. I know that people, especially round here, have a low opinion of the police, but they do have training and selection procedures and everything. Those guys that you don't want to trust or work with are police officers. As I said, you'll have to take a step or two towards them first.'

'I suppose I know you're right. And, they did catch the dealers and calm down the estate.' She was downhearted and couldn't really explain why. Rob had changed and wasn't the same man she'd known three months ago. Lukas was in hospital and threatening to change. Her team at CID were all different. And they had a killer on the loose who was targeting people where and when he wanted.

CHAPTER TWENTY-SEVEN

Emma was torn. On the one hand she wanted to check up on Rob and see how he was getting on now he was all set up to work on the case. She was eager to find out if he'd made any progress. But, she knew that he wouldn't react well to pressure. And she also knew that if he did find anything, then she'd be the first to know. After a couple of days of leaving him to it, he called her.

He'd been rather cagey but had insisted on meeting her at the Grand Imperial Hotel on the seafront for afternoon tea. It didn't sound like his sort of thing and, when pressed, he revealed that there were other people she needed to meet. Although she was curious she couldn't get any further details out of him.

Just over an hour later, Emma walked into the lobby of the hotel rather cautiously and took in the surroundings. It had been a proper seaside, Victorian hotel in the middle of Bradwick for years. Now it was trading on past glories while also trying to be modern and up to date. The effect was confused – framed photographs of elder statesmen competed with modern signage for wall space. The bar was over to the left so she went through and looked around for the rest of the party. Rob Haines walked up beside her and said hello.

'Is that them over there?' Emma asked. 'Marnie King and Kev Slater?' She looked at Rob with confusion – had she said the wrong thing?

'Yep,' he said. 'And don't worry, I was expecting to see them so I can roughly guess what they look like now.'

Marnie King stood up and waved. When they were close enough she said, 'I've ordered afternoon tea for four. Come and sit down, we've got everything here.' As they slid around the table, they nodded to DI Slater who was already there.

'I must say that this is quite irregular,' Slater said when they were all settled. 'I'd much rather meet somewhere that we could take notes or record the interview. Rob isn't even on active duty.'

Rob bristled at this but it was Marnie who spoke first. 'This isn't a meeting. I simply invited a few friends over for afternoon tea.' She paused to see if Slater would argue, but he kept quiet. 'First of all, I'd like to thank you, Emma, for what you did on that evening.' Emma frowned at Marnie, so she continued. 'I spoke with the coroner and pathologist and they agreed that my Billy died instantly. There was nothing more that you could have done. If you hadn't been there that evening, then I would never have known what happened, who killed him. You arrested the man who killed my husband and I won't forget that.'

'I was just–'

'I know, doing your job.' Marnie looked around the table, taking in the difference between Rob and Slater. 'But we all know that there are many different ways that you can do the job of police officer. If it wasn't for you, then the likes of Hargreaves would be running the CID. And we can all imagine how that would work out.'

'It wasn't just me,' Emma said, keen even now to distance herself from the Professional Standards investigation.

'Anyway, I wanted to thank you. I know nothing will bring him back.' Marnie paused again and considered the table. 'And I wanted to let you know that I'll be taking over the business.'

'The business…' Rob couldn't find a tactful way to finish the sentence with Inspector Slater present.

'King Kabs,' she said with a knowing look in her eye. 'Since my Billy passed away there's been chaos, lots of chancers starting up rival outfits. Well, I've sat down with the accountant and thrashed it all out. I've bought Tom Quinn out of his share of the business, given him a fair price for his house, and arranged for him to move to Spain. He should have enough money to buy a villa and a bar.'

'This isn't the seventies, you know,' Rob said. 'We do have an extradition treaty with Spain now.'

'Oh, he's not afraid of being arrested by your lot,' Marnie said airily. 'No, he's seen his two best friends, who he's known since school, killed within weeks of each other. There's nothing left here for him and if he's going to wait for someone to stick a knife in, he'd rather do it somewhere sunny.'

'You do know that we've put Garoza behind bars, don't you?' Rob Haines leaned forward to make his point. 'His whole operation is too busy fighting with itself to worry about things going on here in Bradwick.'

'And you know he's not the only player on the field. There is a power vacuum here as much as there is in Birmingham. He's much better off with a new start somewhere the weather is better. It'll take him years to get over this.' The warning was clear to them – he was a victim in all this and off limits to the police.

There was an awkward pause. Eventually Rob broke the silence. 'You do realise, don't you, that any deals that were made in the past were strictly between Billy and me. Unfortunately with me on sick leave, Hargreaves suspended and Billy no longer with us, well...' Rob shrugged apologetically.

'I have been made aware of what went on the past,' Marnie said. DI Slater looked like he'd rather be anywhere but with the three of them.

'Just to be clear,' Rob said. 'I know in the past that things were a bit lax with the recording of money and drugs seized in raids–'

'DCI Haines, are you saying what I think you're saying?' Slater pushed himself back from the table as if to distance himself from the conversation.

Before Rob could answer, Emma spoke. 'I'm sure you're aware, sir, that Rob is recovering from a head injury. Maybe that has affected his memory. I do know he's more likely to speak without thinking and I don't think we can't attach too much weight to his words.'

Rob looked thunderously angry, his gaze flicking between Emma and Kev Slater. Marnie King was sat back, quietly observing the row among the police officers.

'This is why I wanted a formal interview where everything was recorded,' Slater said as he stood up. 'I can't be here and listen to things that might need to be actioned later. I am aware of your injury, Rob, so I'll let that previous comment slide.' He turned his attention to Emma. 'But, I don't think this is somewhere that serving officers should be. I wouldn't want you to be put in an awkward situation.'

Emma seethed. Her boss had no idea of the many difficult situations she'd been in, of the secrets that she kept, or of the decisions she'd made and what they cost her. 'Thank you for your concern, sir, but I'd like to finish tea with my friends.' She paused for a moment. 'I'm not taking notes and I'm not on duty.'

'Right.' Kev Slater nodded icily to the group. 'DC Angel, I'll see you in work in the morning.'

Emma bit the inside of her lip. She knew that Slater's parting comment was a reminder that they'd be in the same office – it was a warning that she'd be called into a meeting with her boss. She shrugged half-heartedly at Marnie, although she was also angry at her for calling this meeting and inviting Slater without warning Emma or Rob.

'Well, sorry about that,' Marnie said unconvincingly. 'Where were we?'

'I was just saying that if you've come here with your hand out,' Rob answered, 'then you're going to be disappointed. For years I've been aware that things couldn't carry on the way they were. The world has moved past the age of brown envelopes stuffed with cash and packages of drugs going missing.'

'Rob's right, you know,' Emma said. 'Phones and airwaves track where we are, pretty much twenty-four seven. They're now talking about trialling body cameras for all of us. It's going to get more and more tricky to break the rules.' Emma was very aware that she had admitted to considering doing what Rob had done, with the same justifications. But that could never be right, sitting down with self-confessed drug dealers for the good of the town.

'Can I put my cards on the table here?' Marnie asked. 'Now that Slater's not here, can I speak freely?'

Rob shrugged. 'I'm on extended sick leave at the moment. There's not a lot I could do even if I wanted to.'

Both of them turned to look at Emma. She slumped slightly in her seat. 'I'm going to get carpeted by Slater over this anyway. I might as well hear you out.' Marnie raised her eyebrows at her. 'I can't promise that I won't take action until I know what you've got to say. But I suspect that you're just going to confirm what we were thinking anyway, and we haven't moved against you yet.'

Marnie considered this and nodded slowly, setting her large earrings swinging. 'As I said, I'm taking over the business. I've got a lot of Billy's old operation back under my control, although there are a few who'd like to freelance.' She glanced nervously at Emma. 'I am truly sorry about that fourteen-year-old on the estate. Should never have happened. I leant on some people I know, to make sure that a message got back to the police. But that incident was the kind of thing we can expect if the market remains in chaos. I'm sorry, but you might see more injuries as I clamp down at first to make sure they know who's in charge.' She stopped to take breath. 'But, as soon as I can, I'll go back to the old-fashioned way of doing things. We won't involve children, won't sell around the schools, the arcades, those kinds of places. Try to keep the town as safe as we can. I'm a mother, I know what that poor woman must be going through losing her son like that.'

'This is all very admirable, but I don't see how it affects us,' Emma said. 'What do you want and what are you offering?'

'Straight to the point, I like that. Right, well, as Rob will know, we have the taxi market all sewn up. So we have bodies on the ground, we hear things, know who's coming in and who's leaving. We can see what you never will. And we could continue to feed that information back, both formally and informally, however you want to do it.' There was an ominous pause. 'In return, we'd like an understanding. That we do what we do and we'll try, as I said, to be sensitive. So, it would be counterproductive if you were to investigate us too heavily.' She spread her hands wide. 'If that were to happen, then we'd be back to the chaos that we've seen unfold over the last few weeks and months.'

Emma and Rob sat back and digested what had just been said. Emma said, 'so, you want us to look the other way while you pass us information to take out your rivals?' Was this the beginning of the slippery slope that first Patterson, then Haines had been dragged down? After the events of the last few months, she was very wary of doing anything that wasn't strictly on the straight and narrow.

Rob held up his hand. 'No, there'll be no need for that. I've spent a lifetime dealing with the Slaters of the world. You don't talk about doing a deal with criminals. You give them all the spiel about intelligence-led policing and prioritising resources to maximise results.'

Emma nodded, even though she wasn't sure that it was in line with her ethics. Marnie seemed happy though. Emma decided it was time to burst her bubble. 'I suppose I can try to run that past Slater see what we can get away with. But, I have to warn you, Marnie, there will be no free pass on this. If we catch one of your people obviously guilty, then they'll have to be arrested and run through the system. It'll be up to the CPS what happens to them. Likewise, if one of the other agencies catches someone, then we'll have no choice but to act. Are we clear on that?'

Marnie pursed her lips, but nodded.

'It's not all bad,' Emma continued. 'We can prioritise the attacks on taxi drivers and their vehicles. Especially if you give us information as to who might be behind them.'

'I have a fairly good idea of where you might start looking,' Marnie admitted.

'Right, then. But you're going to need to play this as a long game.' Emma tried to work out the right way through the maze, the best way to say what she needed to. 'No revenge attacks, no more beatings and houses being torched. If you want to get rid of someone, pass the information on to us. It'll take longer but it'll mean the town is safer. And you'll get the high ground. If you give me a list of drivers who might be cooperative, we can spread them around, get them signed up.'

Marnie narrowed her eyes as she considered this offer. 'You know I don't have to accept this, don't you? I could just seize control anyway.'

'You could.' Emma nodded. 'But then you'd be up against the police as well as everyone else.'

'What you're offering would give me an edge,' Marnie admitted. 'It'd take longer to get established, but I should be able to get back to where we were before.' There was a long pause. 'Okay then. No more attacks, and I'll get some information over to you about who might be attacking us. And details of which drivers might want to go on the books as informants.'

'And we'll be free to do our jobs?' Emma pressed. 'If we catch someone being naughty, then we'll arrest them.'

'As long as you don't target us, then we can live with that,' Marnie said. She let out a big sigh. 'Damn! You drive a hard bargain. Can we relax and have some cake? I meant what I said, I'll always be grateful to you.'

Chapter Twenty-Eight

Emma was looking forward to going round to see Rob after the meeting with Marnie the day before. She had dreaded going into work, but Kev Slater had been absent on some management training course. However, he'd still managed to make his displeasure felt as Emma was assigned only the dullest of desk-based work and no one in the office would meet her eye. She had no way of knowing what her boss had said, but it was obvious which side everyone in the office was on. Only Andy Stonor had the decency to look embarrassed about it.

Despite all the fallout, she was still glad she'd gone to the meeting and that she'd reached an agreement with Marnie. Whatever happened, Bradwick would probably become safer as a result. She was keen to get Rob's opinion and see a friendly face after a gruelling day at work. Even the thought of sitting through some misogynistic seventies film didn't dent her optimism.

However, all that flew from her mind when she opened the door.

'Oh! Emma. What can I do for you?' Rob said, obviously upset.

'Rob, what's the matter?' Emma asked.

'When were you going to tell me?' Rob asked. 'I've been doing some thinking about that raid, that night when everything changed. I've thought over what you said and some memories have come back. Now, I only have one question.

'How did Professional Standards get there so bloody quickly? I know that the word around the station is that Andy dobbed us all in.' He shook his head. 'But that doesn't make any sense. I've always got on well with him, all things considered. He was settled in the department, he'd made his decisions and I'd made mine. If he was going to do anything, then he'd have waited until I left. He didn't have much time for Hargreaves. And, he's not the type to hang around. If it was Andy, he'd have transferred out of area.' Rob paused and stared at Emma. 'Is there anything you want to say here?'

'Rob, boss, well.' Emma was flustered. She'd rehearsed this in her mind and it hadn't gone anything like this. She gathered her thoughts. 'Yes, I was approached by Professional Standards. Of course I was, the new one in the team, so it made sense to recruit me before I got embedded.'

'So you admit it then?' Rob couldn't keep the excitement from his voice.

'Yes, I admit it,' she snapped back at him. 'But, just stop for a minute and think it through, try to see the whole picture. By the time they came to me, they had most of the picture. They knew what was going on. All they needed was the proof.'

'Which you were happy to hand them on a plate!'

'I was never happy about any of it! But if they knew that much and I rebuffed them, then what would've happened next? Answer me that, Rob. They would've kept going, kept digging.' Emma was into her flow now and wouldn't be stopped. 'When they finally got there, they'd have taken all of us down. And they'd have landed particularly hard on me, because I turned them down in the first place. You know how most officers retire or resign or use some trick to get out from under? Well, most likely if I hadn't cooperated I could've been looking at prison time.'

Rob opened and closed his mouth. He worked through what she'd said and saw the logic in it, but he still stung from Emma accusing him of using tricks to escape justice. Finally he said, 'So you were selfish, then? Just looking out for number one?'

'In this case, yes. When the alternative was to look at jail time. Oh, I know it wouldn't have been long. Odds are that I'd have been out of prison by the time I was thirty. With a career as a bent cop and a stretch inside on my CV. Doesn't look particularly good, does it?' She took a deep breath. She wished she was having this argument anywhere but Rob's front doorstep.

'Okay,' Rob gave a little ground before going on the offensive again. 'But why that raid? Why couldn't you have let me have my moment in the sun? You could've brought Glen Hargreaves to justice after I'd been promoted.'

'Now who's being selfish?' Emma asked. 'What you're saying is that you wanted your nice office and rank of superintendent, safe from all of the shit you'd had to do to get there. And then, once you're cosy and safe, then I can do the right thing?'

She couldn't stay there, couldn't see how they would ever agree. She turned on her heel and stalked off. She left rather faster than she should have done. Before she had an accident, she came to a halt in the car park facing out to sea. Watching a storm brewing over the waves, she did something she rarely allowed herself to do. She cried; released all the tension and let the tears flow down her face. Soon she felt just a little better. Not perfect, as she had managed to alienate both her current and her previous boss within twenty-four hours.

She took a deep sigh and flicked down the vanity mirror to repair her make-up. She knew what she needed and it started with going out and getting drunk with a friend. After that, well, she'd see. She texted Pete and arranged to meet up.

'So, what brought this on?' Pete asked as they fetched their third drinks of the evening. It was obvious that all was not right with Emma.

'Ancient history coming back to bite me,' she replied. 'I just lost a friendship with someone I really respect. And I managed to piss off my current boss as well.'

'No chance you could repair the friendship?' Pete asked.

'I have no idea. He accused me of betraying him, and he was right.' She swigged down the rest of her beer. 'I have no idea what's going to happen next but I don't want to talk about it, if that's okay.'

'Fine by me,' Pete answered. 'But I'm here if you need me.'

'I need more to drink,' Emma said. 'At least it'll be better in the morning.'

Chapter Twenty-Nine

Emma woke up with a hangover, but not as bad as she was expecting. She remembered going out to get drunk after the row with Rob. But, with a combination of her job and her upbringing, she never wanted to get dangerously, black-out drunk. She rolled over and found a space where she expected Pete to be. In his place, on the bedside table was a glass of water and strip of paracetamol. Thanking him silently, she took a long drink and some painkillers.

For a few seconds she wrapped herself back in the duvet and luxuriated in the warmth of the bed. She reviewed the previous evening and hoped that Pete was one of the good guys. All the evidence seemed positive so far and she wasn't regretting her decision to pursue him. Then, as she was sleeping in a T-shirt, she slipped on some tracksuit bottoms and went off to find out if Pete had scared her housemates yet.

She found him in the kitchen and he'd already figured out where the coffee was. The cat wound itself around his legs, purring.

'I found a cat, and the food was there, so I fed her, him, it?' Pete said.

'This is Florence,' Emma said. 'Did you see the sign?'

'Sign?'

Emma picked up a piece of card that read "Florence was last fed in the morning". 'So, if you didn't turn it over,' Emma said, 'I'd guess you've just been outwitted by a cat!' She went on to explain that on the advice of the vet, Florence was on a diet. All the housemates worked shifts and the cat had caught on to this, getting fed around the clock. She was now on a strict two meals a day, unless she could mug someone like Pete.

'She was very convincing,' Pete said.

'Yeah, she is. That's the problem,' Emma said. 'Thanks for the painkillers and coffee.'

'Well, I figured you'd have to get up for work. I'm on flexitime but I didn't know if you'd be on shift or whatever.'

'It's Tuesday morning and we're in the middle of a complex case, so yes, I will be needed in the office.' Her heart sank at the thought. She was almost certainly going to be carpeted by Slater. Not only had she ignored his advice and accepted a meeting with Haines, she'd added a potential drug kingpin to the mix.

And she was now not talking to Rob Haines anyway. She supposed she could tell Kev Slater that she'd broken off her friendship with Haines – that might make him happy. But the truth of it was that more than anything she wanted to keep her private life well away from Slater.

'You look miles away,' Pete said.

'Oh, just considering going back into work, with the same load of problems and a hangover.'

Pete looked sad, in an over exaggerated way. 'So, nothing that happened last night helped, at all?'

'Oh, don't say that,' Emma said, reaching up to give him a peck on the cheek. 'I do feel a lot better, just to have a few hours away from thinking about it. A few hours where nothing mattered. A tonic for my soul.'

'Soul? That's a bit heavy, isn't it?'

'Sorry, I get a bit mystical when I'm tired.' Emma sipped at her coffee. 'I really don't mean to chuck you out, but I do need to have a shower and get myself into work.' In her mind she had memories of the row with Dave that had spelled the end of her relationship, such as it was, with him.

But Pete merely shrugged and said, 'No, even with flexitime I need to get back to my car and drag myself into work. I'll be working late tonight as it is.'

'So, boyfriend, I'll give you a call later, when I know what I'm doing.' Even though she was looking for it, she didn't even see the slightest flinch.

'Okay, girlfriend,' he replied and kissed her.

She wound an arm around his waist and leaned into him. 'And you're all right with that?'

'Of course. I'm a grown up. I don't want to be casual. it's nice to be part of something.'

Emma nodded. 'I've tried casual once. Didn't work.'

'Can I ask?' Pete said tentatively.

'Oh, he was an idiot. We had an on-again, off-again thing. But then he wanted me to drop everything when he felt like it. Always on his terms, not mine. And then he revealed his true colours when I stood up to him.'

'Hey, listen. I get it. I know I have a desk job and it's basically nine to five, but I still work for the police, I know what you do. You'll pull long shifts, cancel at short notice and have to work nights. I'm not stupid, I can see what you do is important to you. And I'll try not to be an arse about it. Okay?'

'Thank you.' She reached up to kiss him again. 'Anyway this is all very good but I'm up to my eyes in a murder case so I really had better get a shower and get ready for work.'

* * *

Soon, she was back in the office and at her desk. She didn't have to wait long before Slater called her in.

'I honestly thought you had better judgement than that, DC Angel.'

She suddenly realised that he'd been at the meeting too. But her poor choice wasn't in attending the meeting but in not leaving when it became clear what was going on. 'I know you think it's misplaced, sir, but I didn't want to leave Rob Haines alone with Marnie King.'

'You know that it shows poor judgement, yet you did it anyway.'

Way too late, she saw there was a better gambit. Why had she come into this with a hangover? She mentally kicked herself. 'Anyway, sir, if we'd both left, then there'd be no one on our side who could know what they were talking about, would there? The more information we have the better.'

Kev Slater looked more interested. 'Is there anything to definitely tie Rob Haines to any corruption?'

Emma forced herself to at least look like she was reviewing the conversation. It wouldn't do to be seen to be supporting Haines. 'No, sir. There was nothing that could be of use to the ongoing Professional Standards investigation.'

Kev Slater nodded with a sour expression on his face. He recognised that her over-formal words were hiding something. 'Well, was there anything of value from the meeting? Or was it just tea and cakes?'

'Yes, it was very valuable,' Emma argued. 'Marnie suggested that some of her drivers could be signed up as Confidential Human Intelligence Sources. The more regular, established ones.'

'Hmmm, I suppose that could be useful,' Slater admitted.

'Definitely useful,' Emma said. 'Think what they must hear in the back of their cabs? It might be good to have a few on our side.'

Kev didn't say anything, a sure sign that Emma was right.

'Anyway, Marnie will hand over a list in the next few days, then we can check things out and then set them up.' She paused for a second or two. 'But obviously, you'd have the final say, you know. If you don't feel it'd be appropriate.'

'No, no, we need some ears on the ground. We've been playing catch-up on the drug problems in this town. Getting ahead of some of them is just what we need. A good result, a shot in the arm for the crime statistics.' He paused this time and studied Emma closely. 'But, while this might be a step in the right direction, I won't forget that you went behind my back to go to the meeting and then defied a direct order to leave.'

Emma bit her tongue. She had been off duty and at a private function. He had no right to talk to her like that. But she knew the Slaters of the world wouldn't listen. He'd made his mind up and marked her card. She nodded to her boss, to give a semblance of politeness, and left the office.

When she was back in her seat, she wanted to put her head on the desk and cry. First, Rob was no longer her boss and now her new boss had isolated her at work. Worse than that – she couldn't now go running to Rob and ask him how to fix this problem. He would be the one who'd know how to either charm Slater or undermine his efforts to ostracise her at work.

With a grim resolve, she continued through the task of following up on Oliver Fairthorpe's clients, checking through the house-to-house statements following the explosion and cross-referencing crime reports from John Garner's associates. All of it was tedious and mind-numbing and there was no promise of light at the end of the tunnel. Whoever this killer was, he was still one, if not ten, steps ahead of them.

Eventually she made it to the end of the day without any great breakthrough being made. She went home and slumped on the sofa. Even Florence could detect her mood and came to sleep next to her on the sofa. She wasn't a cat that'd sleep on a lap but she would lean against someone now and again.

Lucy came in too and got straight to the point. 'Wow! You look really down. I thought dragging Pete back here last night would've put a bit of a smile on your face.'

'Oh, trust me, without that, I'd be suicidal by now.'

'What's up then, love?'

Emma outlined everything that had happened. Aware that Lucy also worked for the police, she was careful with what she said about the corruption within the former CID. But the overall message was clear – Emma had been in a difficult situation between doing the right thing and being loyal to her team.

When she moved on to the other troubles with Lukas, she said, 'You move around in those community based circles, Lucy. Can you think of anywhere that we could put Lukas, keep him out of trouble?'

Lucy thought for a moment, then said, 'You know that holiday park that you raided a while back?' Emma wanted to point out that it wasn't a solo raid, but also didn't want to break Lucy's flow. 'Well, the owner rolled over, pleaded guilty. Of course, with a site like that the Assets Recovery Agency swooped in and got an interim court order, freezing his assets. His lawyer went to court and argued that his residence wasn't part of the business. Anyway, long story short, the CPS, assets branch of SOCA, and a whole bunch of lawyers are arguing over the place.

'Now, I've got this contact called Trevor, who does lots of the community outreach projects. He's been looking out for a site to do some more in-depth, residential work with troubled teens. Maybe even something like a halfway house for when they get out of care and have nowhere to go.' She stopped to draw breath. Emma didn't prompt her as she could see where this was going. 'Now, all the legal arguments are going to take a while, so he's applied to act as administrator for the place. Basically his remit will be to preserve it so it doesn't lose value until it all shakes out. Do you want me to put him in touch with Lukas?'

'What and have Lukas live there?'

'Basically, yes. It needs a caretaker. Trevor's in his fifties, has a family and all that so all he'd be able to do is look in from time to time. If someone was living on site, then they'd be able to do the maintenance and keep an eye on things. You know what it's like, once a property is deserted then it goes downhill.'

Emma nodded. She knew that Lukas would have to be careful. Maybe she'd have a quiet word with this Trevor character. Keep her friend away from temptation. She knew what that world was like though – plenty of opportunities to volunteer and keep busy. 'Thank you, Lucy. If it all works out then it could be the best thing for him.' She handed over Lukas' mobile number and his details at the hospital, currently the best place to find him.

That done, there was nothing to do but to finish the beer and go to bed.

Chapter Thirty

From the outside Jenny Plover had it all. On this Monday morning she was driving down the road in her sports car, top down and hair flying, on her way to her high-powered job.

Inside the car however, she was suffering. Two co-codamol hadn't touched her headache and she planned to take two more when she got to work. Her throat was sore too – why did she only smoke when she drank? At least she'd had a shower this morning so hopefully work would be none the wiser.

The bloke from last night though, he might be more of a problem. What had he been? Builder, roofer, even someone who worked on the roads? Whoever he was, he'd definitely been a bit of rough. She was, unfortunately, used to this morning-after combination of hangover, sore throat and shame.

She decided to enjoy the weather and the feeling of wind in her hair, even if she'd have to brush it again when she got to work.

As she passed under a bridge, there was a falling blur and a loud thump which disturbed her reverie. She instinctively jammed on the brakes. The car, travelling at nearly seventy, bucked and started to slide under heavy braking. Something wet landed on her head so she shut her eyes, steered for the hard shoulder, and hoped for the best, bracing her arms. All around her she heard strange thuds and other wet noises as more things landed on the car.

There was a bang and the car left the hard shoulder and bounced over some gravel. The wheel was wrenched from her hands as she tried to steer back to the right. Finally she came to a stop.

Silence. Not quite silence; she could hear the traffic to her right, slowing down with a few blasts of horns. She was wet and cold, with something dripping from her hair. Something sticky. There was a horrible smell, a mixture of metal and something else she couldn't identify. Her shoulders, arms and hands ached from wrestling with the steering.

Cautiously, she opened her eyes, wiping something from her face to see clearly. Blood. Was she injured? Nothing was actually hurting but there was red sticky liquid everywhere.

There was an arm resting on top of the windscreen. As she watched, its balance shifted and it fell, bounced off the steering wheel, and came to rest on the dash, between the wheel and the screen. Its hand was up, fingers slightly curled, as if it was asking for something.

What a stupid, dangerous joke, she thought. Fake blood and a rubber arm. She could've been killed. Kids today were so irresponsible! As she calmed down, she saw a scar on the forearm, nestled among the ginger hair. And it had dirty, bitten nails. Just how realistic could a rubber arm be?

She identified one smell – the blood – coppery and acrid. Then another smell hit her – vomit. As if someone had been sick in her car. With a horrible sensation the truth dawned on her – the grey, red, slippery mess all over her car was someone's body and the intestines had split open.

Unbelieving, she looked around. There were unidentified bits of body all over the car, hanging off the bonnet, the mirrors. Blood coated everything. A leg was perched on the seat next to her.

With shaking hands, she released her seat belt and gingerly eased out of the car. She tried to avoid touching anything as every surface was slick with blood. But then, so was she, it was all over her.

She looked back the way she'd come and wished she hadn't. There was a long slick of blood and entrails leading to her car. There was a bridge that she'd just passed under, with a plastic barrel hanging off it. Drips of blood were still falling from the lip.

She stood there in the sunshine, buffeted by the traffic going past at speed. Finally, a lorry stopped on hazards and gave her a respite from the noise of the cars.

She was shaking uncontrollably. She turned away from the bridge but there was a head lying on the hard shoulder. It looked at her, the eyes staring blankly out from under a mop of curly red hair. He was battered and bruised and utterly dead. He looked like a young lad. The head of a young lad, she corrected herself. And the arms, legs and internal organs of a young lad.

Still shaking she stood there as her brain tried to block the memories – blackness came down and she didn't see any more.

Chapter Thirty-One

'Well, I see our killer has left us an abundance of evidence this time around,' Emma said as she approached the scene. She had parked further down the road and walked up the steep incline onto the bridge over the fast A road below.

The news of another grisly murder had blown all the politics and disapproval from the office. Instead of worrying about who she was friends with, what decisions she made, it was a case of all hands to the pump.

Kev Slater turned to face her, turning his back on the road and the scene of carnage below him. His face was pale and he was visibly shaken. Further down the road, technicians were just retrieving a large blue barrel that had been suspended upside down over the road. 'He must have parked here with a van and a body already dismembered and stuffed into the barrel. Somehow he got the barrel up onto the railing and balanced. Then, as soon as he saw a car approaching, he'd just have to nudge it and over it goes. There's a loop of climbing rope at the bottom to stop the whole thing hitting the road.'

Emma looked at the road below, which had the nearside lane coned off. She could still see the gruesome bloodstains on the tarmac, alongside the fresh rubber skid marks. A temporary tent had been erected over the car where it had come to rest on the verge.

Something didn't quite add up for Emma. She couldn't figure out what, but something about the timeline niggled at her. There were figures in white working on the car, so she climbed over the barrier and picked her way down the slope from the bridge to the main carriageway. The going was tough, with wiry grass and rocks interspersed with whatever rubbish could be thrown out of a car.

Finally she approached the tent, where she was stopped by a scene of crimes technician, in full white suit. 'Sorry, miss, but you can't go any further. Not without suiting up.'

'It's okay,' Emma said, holding up her warrant card, 'I just wanted to know, how did the body hit the car?'

'What do you mean how?'

'Well, did the car drive into the falling debris? Or did some of it hit the back of the car? What happened?'

The technician frowned. 'There's a sizeable dent in the bonnet that's most likely where the head struck. Some of the limbs are still in the car and there's a fairly even spread of blood and intestines right across the vehicle, front to back.'

Emma nodded. If this was another in the series of murders, then she was getting a feel for how precise their killer was. This hadn't been left to chance. 'So, it had to be timed then?'

'Timed?' Behind the face mask and hood, the technician frowned.

'Well, you're up on the bridge, with a dismembered body in a barrel. You're watching the traffic, waiting for a convertible with the top down. How lucky would you have to be to hit it squarely like this one did?'

The technician scooped the hood back from her head and pulled down the mask. She had a wide face with a scatter of freckles across it and auburn hair. 'It's not luck, it's physics.' She frowned at the bridge. 'What do you make that height? Ten, eleven metres? Maybe twelve?'

'If you're balancing the barrel on the railing, let's add a metre on and say twelve to thirteen,' Emma replied.

'Okay, and until this happened traffic was flowing well, let's say sixty-five miles per hour or so.' She already had her phone out and was tapping. She muttered as she worked, 'Metres per second, not miles per hour' and 'gravity is nine point eight'. Finally she looked up, triumphant. 'If I was planning to drop a body into a convertible car, I'd walk back somewhere between forty-five to fifty metres from the bridge and leave something as a marker. I've rounded up to allow a bit of time for our killer's reaction time, the barrel to move and the contents to start sliding out. Could be as simple as a bottle to catch the sun or a coloured piece of paper. When the car passes that, then over goes the body. Come on, I'll get an evidence kit and we'll go for a walk and see what we can find.'

A few minutes later, Emma had chills running down her spine. She was crouched beside a busy road with the technician, looking at a poster. It had been attached to a board and post and turned to face the bridge, away from the flow of traffic. It had the face of a child and the simple words "Missing" and "Callum Frost", top and bottom, white on red.

'Fuck,' Emma said quietly. 'I mean we thought, but fuck. It is him.'

The technician nodded. 'I'll get the camera and accurately measure the distance from the bridge. Although we already know that he got his maths just about spot on.'

Emma stood by the poster, occasionally buffeted when a large lorry went by. How callous was their killer? To stand on a bridge, dismembered body in a barrel, and just wait for a convertible to come past was cold. But to use the poster of a disappeared child, somehow made the whole affair more chilling. The eyes on the poster stared back at her. He was accusing the police of having failed him. She knew she was being sent a message by the killer, they all were, but they had no way to decode exactly what it meant.

Chapter Thirty-Two

Dani Price was back in CID to explain another murder. 'In terms of the whole set-up, everything was a lot simpler this time. It looks very much like our killer has a pattern – the body has marks from a taser. From what was left of the remains it looks like asphyxiation by compression. Most likely something held over the face. From there, the presence of ice crystals and the changes in the cells indicates the body was frozen, then cut up into pieces.'

'How long would it have taken to defrost?'

'At room temperature?' Dani frowned. 'At least twenty-four hours. The process wasn't completely finished, there was still some ice deep in the tissue.'

'So,' Emma said, 'he must've been watching the weather forecast. Waiting so that he could choose a day when it would be sunny enough that there would be someone driving past with the top down on their car. And then he'd have to get the body out the day before.'

'Makes sense,' Dani said. 'Well, just as much as anything in this case does. I've looked for the tool marks on the bone but there's nothing really indicative there. It could be a basic saw bought from B&Q or a bone saw like I've got in my lab. I don't think it's likely that it's proper medical or butchery equipment though.'

'Why not?' Emma asked.

'Well, whoever did this had no medical or butchery skills. He missed the joint on several occasions and, in other places it's clear he just cut his way through the tissue with no regard to the underlying physiology. To be crude, this body was just hacked apart.'

'Any further on an identity yet?'

'No, we're assembling a pack for missing persons. The head sustained damage but we've got a good artists impression. Aside from that, we have a young male, between eighteen and twenty-three years of age. Slightly thin, but otherwise in good health. All indications are that he was from the UK, but we can test for that if missing persons comes up as a blank.'

All around her, people were taking notes. Emma summarised, 'So, he somehow finds this guy, tasers him, suffocates him and chops him up. Then he puts him into the freezer in pieces and waits for a nice sunny day to tip the body onto a convertible car?'

'Pretty much. If I had to choose, I'd say that he froze the body first, then chopped it up. If he had somewhere private, he could've put the frozen pieces into the barrel and let them defrost in there. Would've saved a lot of mess.'

Brian was frowning. 'He must've used an engine crane or something similar to move the barrel around. Even a small person is one hell of a weight to be lugging around and balancing on railings.'

Dani nodded. 'There were fixings on the edge of the barrel that could easily have been attached to a crane or hoist.'

'The barrel,' Brian said. 'Could that be traced somehow?'

'Afraid not, it's a fairly standard industrial barrel. Any farm supply store or warehouse would sell you one for under fifty quid. It's a standard item; food safe or for drinking water.'

Emma's heart sank. They were battling someone who was always one step ahead. He appeared to have no remorse, and no inclination to stop killing. And he was so calculating that the chance of him making a mistake was vanishingly small.

'Any chance of tracing the crane or lifting equipment?' Brian asked. 'Did it leave any unique marks or anything on the edge of the barrel?' He sounded hopeful, but Emma could detect an undertone of desperation in his voice.

Dani shook her head. 'Not a chance. Given the poster that was used as a marker, and the fingerprint evidence, it's the same man as the motel and the woods. He's good at DIY, so we can assume he rigged up a simple pulley or lever system. The only ray of sunshine is that he almost certainly had to use a vehicle, a van of some sorts.'

Nick nodded and made notes. 'I'll get onto the CCTV and see what we can run down. Looking for a van, maybe a small one, or a pickup with a blue barrel on the back.'

Emma nodded with the rest of them. But she had a horrible feeling in her stomach that any leads would be dead ends. Maybe when they identified the body it would give them a connection – with three people it was more likely than two. But it wasn't hopeful.

Chapter Thirty-Three

As was usual the day after a murder, the office was buzzing. People stayed late and arrived early. Emma had just got some coffee when Nick stood up from his desk and went towards the whiteboard.

'I've got a victim for us,' he said. 'Timothy Philips. Twenty-year-old lad, brought up in Liverpool, came down here for a dodgy job delivering leaflets, signing people up to do fascias and double glazing. Mother hasn't heard from him for over a week. But look at this photo.' He put a picture on the board and it was obviously a match to the head. Ginger hair, young, thin face.

'That's good,' Brian said. 'We need to get onto his boss and find out which area he was leafleting. He would've had a fixed route. We can get uniforms out to ask who's got a leaflet and who hasn't.'

'Unless he was just grabbed off the street,' Emma said darkly.

'This is still a murder enquiry,' Kev said as he walked to the centre of the room. 'As I said at the beginning, we'll ignore all the window dressing and get down to the core of the case.' He tapped the whiteboard. 'We have a victim. Because of the freezing, we have to establish where and when he died. Brian is right, we can build up a timeline for him, based on the route he should've been working as he delivered leaflets. Maybe our killer made a mistake and grabbed him as he went about his job. If nothing else, it'll give us an area to look for. We need a formal interview with the mother, pin down when she last spoke to him. The same thing with the boss. Let's not sit around moping and get out there and do our jobs.'

Chastened, Emma turned back to her desk and brought up her list of actions. She knew that at some level Slater was right. They needed to do the hard work, go through the basics, try to find the mistake. With three victims, it was more likely that there would be a crack in the case.

But, she also knew that this killer was striking at random and carefully working out his next move. The odds on him either making a mistake or deciding to stop were slim.

The whole team worked hard all day and a basic timeline was emerging. Tom Philips had last spoken to his mother over a week ago on a Wednesday evening and reported for work on the following Thursday. His boss drove a minibus around, dropping off his charges and picking them up at the end of the day. Tom hadn't been there on the Thursday evening, but this wasn't noteworthy. 'I'm a businessman, not a babysitter,' the boss had growled. It was a low-end job, cash in hand, paid daily. An employee not turning up was just par for the course in the world of temporary zero-hours work. So, they knew that at some time on the previous Thursday, Tom Philips had met the killer. Presumably, given what the pathologist had said, he was killed and frozen that day.

Emma had a flicker of interest when she learned that the victim had been working the Seaview Estate on that day. Could he have met John Garner? It was more likely that there was a connection there than with Oliver Fairthorpe.

Now the day was over, she had an invitation. It was Friday evening and she returned to the Sun View Holiday Park. She headed straight for a group of people by the dilapidated play park.

'Angel, babe, you made it,' Lukas said, pulling her into a hug. 'This is Trevor, my boss.'

A large bear of a man, with a short grey beard, came forward and shook her hand. 'Lovely to meet you,' he said. 'And I must thank you for introducing me to Lukas. We've been looking for a site like this but having a live-in caretaker makes it a lot easier.'

'I'm glad I could help,' Emma said, looking around. The site definitely looked a lot more cared for. 'Are you well settled in now, Lukas?'

'Yeah. I've got the owner's old caravan, behind reception. Proceeds of Crime have seized his possessions into storage so it was just an empty shell when I moved in.'

'But we know the community furniture recyclers – they take in furniture that people want to throw out and restore and resell what they can. They've been really helpful. I mean, it's all pretty basic and second hand but it's not bad.'

Lukas laughed. 'I've lived on road protests and squats. What I've got here is luxury!'

'And how are you coping? Keeping busy?' Off the drugs, she really meant to say, but Lukas understood.

'Yes. I'm having a bit of trouble sleeping. And working outside is tiring. But it's just basic gardening really, trying to get this place under control before the winter.'

'That's really common, the trouble sleeping,' Trevor said. 'After an overdose or when someone's trying to clean up, the body has to re-establish a normal pattern without chemical inputs.' Trevor indicated the barbecue. 'Come and get a burger.'

Emma got some food and circulated. She had strange feeling that a lot of the young people there were the sort she was likely to arrest at some point in the future. But they were the ones that she didn't really want to arrest. She could see what Trevor, and the other adults here, were trying to achieve. Early intervention so that these people didn't have to take that first step onto the carousel of police cells, court rooms, probation service and maybe even prison.

'Do you think you'll cope with being here over the winter?' she asked Lukas.

'Yeah. I've got no illusions. A nice autumn evening now won't be anything like a grim February in a storm.'

'And you won't be inviting your friends back for wild parties? I've raided this place once, I don't want to do it again!'

'No, no.' He looked a bit sheepish. 'I feel bad but I've been ghosting all my old friends – not replying to their messages. No one knows where I am, but then the people I know drop in and out anyway.'

'It's the best way for someone trying to get their life back on track,' Trevor said, joining the conversation. 'A clean break at first. Then, with distance, you can see who's worth keeping and who's not.'

Emma nodded, thinking about the fact that she'd made her own clean break from the world of her parents. Well, clean except for Lukas, who she couldn't drop, even if she'd wanted to.

Chapter Thirty-Four

Rob Haines had expected that giving up his computer would result in some big operation. But instead, one boy who looked about twelve came and took his laptop, all packed up into its case with mouse and power lead. When he left, Rob felt deflated.

There was no need for him to give up the computer, he knew that. But every day that he looked at, or walked past the spare room, it was an admission that he couldn't do his job. Long gone were the days when he could work a case by putting in sixteen to eighteen hour days, fuelled by little more than coffee and enthusiasm.

Now, if he looked at that tiny screen for more than an hour, a headache would creep in behind his eyes. He'd tried, obviously, powering through with painkillers, but it had just got worse. Eventually it was so bad that he found he wasn't concentrating, the words on the screen were just flowing past without meaning.

In his wilder moments, he imagined a way that he could get back to work. Maybe there'd be some work around for the weird thing with the faces. He'd looked on the web and there were some universities developing training programs. There had to be a way he could be useful. But this, his inability to work solidly without breaks or painkillers, was the nail in the coffin of his career. He knew that.

But he wasn't beaten yet. The one thing that drove him was still there – the case needed to be solved. From what he'd seen and heard, Kev Slater wasn't making any progress. And he wasn't doing it to help out Emma Angel either. That bridge was burned now.

No, he was doing it for himself and for the town. It was the same reason he'd gone into work every morning. Now that the technician had left with his laptop, he went back upstairs to his makeshift office. It had been his daughter Abby's bedroom, but she was now settling down in Cornwall so he'd taken it over as his workspace. The bed was still there, pushed up to the wall. He'd bought a new desk, chair and other office essentials and squeezed them in. Although it looked clear, he sat down at the desk and opened a drawer.

He took out a stack of 5x3 postcards. Each one had been filled in with his handwriting. What he'd found was that if he worked in thirty to forty minute stretches, he could transcribe the detail from the computer onto the index cards. He had locations, witnesses, victims, suspects, forensics, every fact broken down, one on each card.

Now he set to work attaching them to the wall. He had three areas on the wall, one for each killing. He tried to arrange things logically – victim at the top, then witnesses, then locations. He found that, unlike the glow of the computer screen, ink on paper was kinder on his eyes. He worked away for two hours. Finally he needed a break so he stood up and had a look from a distance.

Several cork boards competed for space on the walls with a selection of Post-it notes and other postcards that had been stuck up with Blu-tack. He'd even included a map and attached photos of the victims with string pointing to where they were killed.

It reminded Rob of when he'd started working and how old-fashioned things were even in the nineties. But it made sense to him. It was also another reason for Rob not to return to work.

Looking at the wall again, he knew the answer was there, but just out of reach of his conscious mind. Like having a word on the tip of his tongue. He stretched and went to gaze out of the window at his back garden.

Then, when was ready, he turned back to the wall. And he saw it immediately. A link, very faint, but definite between the three cases. Something that no one else had mentioned.

He needed to be sure that he'd seen what he really thought he had seen. He tracked a finger across all three columns, all three murders.

He tapped on each of three cards. The pattern he thought he'd seen was definitely there. It was tenuous but it was there. He searched among the paperwork on his desk for his mobile. He needed to make some phone calls. It was time to do some work and see what it meant.

CHAPTER THIRTY-FIVE

The next week started well for Emma. She had a formal letter from legal stating that the judge had dismissed the case that Trevor Swain had tried to bring. In addition, she'd had a quiet meeting with the chief constable where she'd been awarded a commendation for her actions in saving DCI Haines. It was bittersweet now that they weren't talking. However, this turned out to be the high point of a week that slowly went downhill.

As it went on, the case progressed slowly. There was now a map of the Seaview Estate on the wall. Every confirmed leaflet drop was marked with a pin and some even had a time next to them, when Timothy had canvassed someone to sign up. These pins had been joined up to an approximate route. The problem was that the route petered out in the middle of a road that was primarily retired people and self-employed. The last house to definitely receive a leaflet belonged to a carpet layer. He'd spent the whole morning installing a new carpet in an office with a fitter's mate, CCTV, and a caretaker who'd let him in.

The theory that Timothy had been abducted in the middle of his round made no sense. If that was how it had happened, then someone must've done it by car. In an area without CCTV. Another dead end.

There were several overlaps between his route and acquaintances of John Garner, but none of them had panned out to anything.

A particular low point in the week was Thursday morning when Kev Slater stopped by Emma's desk with a nasty little grin on his face. 'Heard from your boyfriend recently?' he asked.

'You mean Rob Haines?' she asked icily.

'Yes, that's him. Word is from the technical department that he's handed his laptop back. Signed off from the whole project.' He looked smug. 'What was that, just over a week?'

'Any idea why, sir?' Emma wanted the conversation to be over but she also wanted to know what was going on. Rob still wasn't speaking to her.

'I thought you'd know,' Kev Slater said. 'No word came back. Must be his medical problems.' With his bombshell delivered, he stalked back to his office. His barb had hit the mark. Emma was plunged further into depression.

The only real output from the murder enquiry was a lot of paperwork. The numerous house-to-house enquires threw up many leads. There were some cars on the route to the bridge that were fitted with dash-cams. All they really showed was that the quality wasn't good and the van couldn't have been on the bridge over the main road for long. Ten minutes before the body was dropped, there were no vehicles or people waiting on the bridge.

Emma had the feeling that she was missing something but she couldn't put all the pieces together. The news about Rob had further darkened her mood and she was finding it hard to concentrate. She was so isolated from her team that she was considering putting in for a transfer.

The only thing that stopped her was that they had a murder enquiry to complete. She might hate her current boss, be having a row with her previous one, and not be talking to any of her team, but she still had a job to do. She hoped, with hope that decreased daily, that by slugging away at it she'd be able to crack the case open.

This was mirrored by the mood in the office. They were all working hard but it was with a kind of fatalistic desperation. They knew the case was approaching a dead end and could do nothing to avert it.

The only thing that kept her sane was Pete. She was coming to depend on him with a speed that alarmed her. He was easy-going enough to spend an evening sat on the sofa with the cat and rubbish on the TV. But equally he could be dragged out for a drink. It was as if he could sense that she was under a lot of stress and gave her the space to be herself.

After her disastrous relationship with David from traffic, part of her wanted to keep her distance. But, so far she'd had no problem with Pete – he was good to her and more importantly, got on well with the cat, Florence.

Later on Thursday morning her phone pinged with a text message. She assumed it was Jem still trying to walk a line between the two of them, but it wasn't.

Rob: Are we talking to each other?

She pushed back from the desk and turned the phone over in her hand. She put it back on the desk. She'd never known her old boss to apologise so her curiosity was piqued. She ran a thumb over her knuckles and stroked her ear. It must be something important.

Emma: Well you texted me.

Nice and neutral, she thought. Not giving any ground, but keen to find out what was going on.

Rob: Can we talk about the last time you came over?

Oh no, you don't, she thought. He wasn't going to weasel out of a proper apology. She texted quickly, before he could carry on.

Emma: We should meet. Not do this over text.

Rob: Where?

Emma: Susie's Café on the seafront.

This last message caused a longer pause. Emma wondered if she should suggest somewhere else. If Rob still wasn't leaving the house. She decided to dig her heels in as she knew that she couldn't defend what she'd done, but she wasn't going to give Rob a free pass either.

Rob: Thirty mins?

Emma: Yes.

It was done. All she had to do now was to get to the café and see if Rob would actually apologise or not.

Chapter Thirty-Six

Haines was rapidly approaching his fiftieth birthday and felt like a kid again but not in a good way. He had been driven to this café by his wife, not his mother, but that was about the only difference. Jem had agreed to give him space to sort things out with Emma, but she was still there for support. She was sat closer to the door so that she could intercept anyone that Rob might know. Of course, she didn't know everyone that Rob did, so it wasn't a perfect solution.

As he waited for Emma to arrive, he looked at his wife. She was staring out of the window, her face in profile to him, catching the autumn sunshine. His brain felt fractured in two. One part, the instinctive one, saw a woman who was tall and beautiful and about his age. She had worry lines and hair that was greying around the temples but still fell past her shoulders. Even though he could remember when it had been a rich chestnut brown and had more body, this part of his brain was staring at a stranger while he waited for Emma to arrive.

The logical half though, knew that his wife, Jem, had brought him here. She had worn that precise dark orange top, that she insisted was burnt umber, even though he had no idea what umber was or why anyone would burn it. He knew that she'd brought him here, got drinks and set herself up at that table.

He could feel the two halves of his brain rubbing up against each other, like the rough edge of a broken tooth. That woman was both a complete stranger and logically his wife – at the same time. It was no wonder he was always tired.

At least he felt better about meeting Emma. He knew she would be here and she would be punctual. All he had to do was hope that no other short blonde woman walked in at the same time.

As if summoned by his thoughts, someone did choose that moment to walk through the door. Not only was she short and blonde, but there was something about the way she carried herself – both with authority and slightly beaten down. And definitely annoyed, he added to himself. He glanced at Jem and she gave the slightest of nods, that wouldn't be seen by anyone else.

* * *

Ignoring him, Emma went to get a drink before sitting at his table. It was between lunch and evening rush so the three of them had the place to themselves.

'Emma, good of you to come.'

'Are you expecting me to apologise for what I did?' she asked. On the walk over, she'd been stewing over what had happened. She'd had no choice. 'I explained myself last time we met.'

He nodded slowly. 'No, not expecting you to apologise.' He took a deep breath. 'I worked out everything that you said. I took it one step at a time and worked out that I put you in an impossible position. Once Professional Standards get their hooks into you, they won't let go. If you hadn't handed us over, your career would've been finished. And every operation that you went to and joined in with the corruption, well you'd have been in a hard place when it all blew up.'

'Sir, you're rambling.'

'Sorry. Yes. Well. You were in an impossible situation and you pressed the nuclear button because sometimes that's the only way out.'

An awkward silence fell across the table. Finally Emma said, 'Rob, you texted me. You agreed to come here. Was it just to explain, or was there something else?' She had noticed that he hadn't actually apologised but knew that it was as close as she was going to get.

'Yes, you're right,' Rob admitted. 'I think I might have something. Did you ever play Top Trumps when you were a kid?'

'Top Trumps? I saw them around the playground, but I don't think I ever actually played with them.' She frowned. Was he losing the plot completely?

'No, I don't suppose you did. It was more of a boys' thing from the eighties. You got a deck of cards that'd all be about a theme, like tanks or sports stars or dinosaurs or even Star Wars.' Emma nodded. Definitely a boys' thing. 'You'd read out one category, like top speed, and everyone else playing said what they had. Whoever had the highest value won the trick.' Rob fished in his pocket and pulled out three postcards that were covered in his handwriting. 'I wasn't entirely honest,' he said. 'I gave that bloody laptop back because it gave me headaches. But before I did, I went through all three files and transferred all the information to these index cards.' He looked embarrassed. 'I find them easier to handle than computers at the moment. Anyway, I've got the three victims here. Take a look.' He passed them over. 'It's like they've come from three different decks, there's nothing in common at all.'

Emma took the cards and flicked through them. She knew the details, had lived with them for weeks. 'A financial advisor who covers the whole of the south west, some guy who's a homeless functional alcoholic and a kid from Liverpool in a crappy job. We've been working them for weeks. The closest we got to a link is that our killer doesn't like transporting the bodies.'

Rob nodded. 'So he either doesn't drive and did the last one from a hire van, or he wants to keep hold of his car or van and not contaminate it with DNA and other trace evidence.'

'And if it's the second option, then he could've moved the engine crane and the sealed barrel without too much risk of contaminating his car.' She paused and studied Rob. 'Is that why you brought me here? To go back over the victims and tell me what I know? That there are no links?'

'No. Like I said, they're from different decks of Top Trumps. It's like trying to play a tank against a dinosaur.'

Emma struggled to see his point. 'So, what, he was aiming at someone else and got these guys by mistake? The first one was in a hotel, did he just get the wrong room?'

'No.' Rob Haines took a deep breath to get his frustration under control. 'No, I think he meant to kill these people but they weren't the killer's primary focus. Take look at these cards.' He handed three new ones over.

Emma obediently flicked through the three new cards. 'This is much better, Rob. We've got three females.' She laid them out side by side. 'They're all about the same age. Two have children, one doesn't. All born and grew up in the same area. Off the bat I'd say it was likely they were all in same year at school, they might have even known each other.' Her heart sank when a theory occurred to her. 'Have you found three new crimes for me to investigate? I'm not sure we could investigate six murders at once, even if these three are more clearly linked.'

'No, Emma,' Rob said. He wasn't even trying to avoid being patronising. 'They're from this case, look at the names at the top of the cards.'

'Eileen Sanders, Amelia Spark and Jenny Plover. They look familiar, but... Oh fuck! How the fuck did we miss this?'

'Each of them found one of the bodies.'

Rob and Emma stared at each other. He now knew that he was right and she had that shiver down her spine that meant he'd found the one fact that would prise the case open.

'My God! Of course they did. You know what it's like, you take a statement from the person who finds the body. But pretty soon you've got scene of crimes, door to door, forensics, and pathology. That initial statement probably doesn't get a second look. Certainly you don't investigate the dog walker or whoever it was who made the first call.' She paused again, shaking her head slowly as she looked at the three cards. 'But this, it's immense. I mean huge. If there's a link between these three women, then were they the real targets?'

'Targets? I thought they might be involved. You know, in on the murders, sent there to make sure the bodies were discovered.'

'Okay, Rob,' Emma said kindly. 'I know you're a seasoned officer, but cast your mind back. The first time you went to an RTA and had to deal with a dismembered body spread all across the road. How did it affect you?'

Rob nodded, seeing her direction now. 'I won't bullshit you, Emma, it was a proper wake-up call. Bad dreams, off my food, all that stuff. I mean, obviously, I pushed through it and carried on. It's what we did.'

'And that was when you were prepared. You knew it was your job and you knew that you could do something to help. And you had support as well, even if it was just your colleagues. Just think for a minute what this case must be doing to those three women who found the bodies. This makes sense of the theatrics of where and how they were found. Bodies as puppets, exploding and dismembered bodies. What if the victims weren't the dead people but the people who found them?'

'That would explain the lack of a link. He just needed a body that was conveniently in the right place at the right time to be found by one of the women.'

'And if you look at all three, they made their discoveries when they were in the middle of predictable routines,' Emma said, getting excited now. 'Eileen was at work cleaning rooms in the hotel. All he'd have to do is to work out which floor she was working and when she was on shift. I bet she works the same pattern week in, week out. And the other two, well Amelia was out on her daily run and Jenny was commuting to work. For any of them, it'd only take a week or two of observation before our killer knew exactly where to leave the body.'

'And then he'd have to find the victim to fit the time and location,' Rob said. 'In the case of the hotel, if you don't care who you kill, then all you need is a person staying on their own on the right floor, at the right time. Saves all the effort and risk of killing someone elsewhere, freezing and storing the body and then having to transport it.'

Emma nodded. 'Likewise poor Mr Garner. He was obviously sleeping in the same wood that Mrs Spark ran through. Once the killer knew that, his job was even easier. Wait until Garner was sleeping out in the woods, kill him early in the night, then he could set everything up by torchlight and be ready for the morning.' She stopped as a thought occurred to her. 'Do you think he stayed around to watch the discovery?'

Rob pursed his lips and thought for a moment. 'The hotel room was almost impossible to observe. And in the woods we threw a cordon around it and the army were there too.' He shook his head. 'No, I don't think he was there. We don't know what is motivating him, but I don't think he's like an arsonist who likes to watch things burn. Something more complex is going on here. He's deliberately giving these women nightmares.'

'More than nightmares,' Emma said. 'This is a short cut to PTSD.' She paused. 'What do you think we should do next?'

'This is too big for you to go off solo on,' Rob said. He sounded better disposed towards her tendency to go it alone than he ever had when he was her boss. 'If you start interviewing one of the women, then they might immediately phone the other two and tip them off. If you're going to get anywhere, then it'll have to be simultaneous interviews. I've made some discreet enquiries, they were all at Bradwick High in the same school year. I'd lay good odds that they knew each other.'

'I suppose I'll have to take it to Slater,' Emma said uncertainly.

'How will you explain my involvement?' Rob asked. 'I really shouldn't have kept all the handwritten notes.'

'No, but I'm sure when they see the quality of the information, it'll be fine. I'm not going to leave your name out of it – you need to get back in with CID. And, it's not like you've discovered something that we didn't know. We had all the same information so it's not new. If it goes to CPS, then your name might get left out to make sure it's watertight in court.'

'If you're sure, I would appreciate it. They're going to make a decision on my case soon. I'll need all the favour I can get. But you be careful – you'll be making an enemy of Kev Slater.'

'I think I've already done that.'

They both laughed at that, and Emma considered her next move.

Chapter Thirty-Seven

Emma could hardly contain her excitement all the way back to the station. This was right, she knew it was the big breakthrough that the case needed. She would take this to Kev Slater and then they could make some progress.

She hoped she could gloss over the fact that Rob had been working unofficially on the case. The quality of the information would surely override any minor infringements that had taken place.

Finally, she got to her desk and saw that Kev was in his office. Without sitting down, she went straight across with her pocketbook in hand.

'Sir, have you got a minute?'

'Of course, constable, sit down.'

'I got a call from Rob Haines today,' Emma started, unsure how much to admit. 'About the case.'

'I thought we'd already closed off that avenue. I got word that his psych report looks like he's heading for retirement on medical grounds. We can't have someone like that with access to the police computers.'

'But,' Emma said, panic setting in, 'we've got a big breakthrough. He's found the first thing on this case that makes any kind of sense.'

Kev Slater held up his hand. 'No. I don't want to hear it.' Emma frowned at him. 'The minute I hear that, I become part of a chain of tainted evidence. Anything that comes from this, has to come from good, clean information. If we find the bad guy, then his defence team goes through all the evidence with a fine-tooth comb. And I don't want to be the investigating officer when they find out that an unauthorised officer found key evidence.'

'But this is good information. It could help us to catch the killer.'

'No, DC Angel, you are wrong. It could help us to identify the killer. But to catch him, we need solid verifiable evidence. That will stand up in court.'

Emma ground her teeth. She was a detective constable. She had been on the witness stand more times than she could remember. She knew that it would be easy to go back over the evidence and link together the three women who found the body. All it would take was a follow-up interview to find out why they had been targeted. It would be easy, although heartbreaking, to keep Rob Haines' name off the paperwork. But she could also see that Kev Slater's mind was made up.

'I hear you, sir, loud and clear,' she said, with only the slightest hint of sarcasm. 'I'll just go back to my desk. Check the outstanding actions.'

As she got up to leave, Kev Slater said, 'Just one more thing. I know that you have some kind of special relationship with Rob Haines. And you know that I've warned you about this in the past. But you have to bear something else in mind. He's off on medical leave right now and within weeks, if not days, he'll be a retired police officer.' Emma struggled to keep herself under control as he adopted what he obviously thought was a fatherly attitude. 'Listen to me. I'm at the end of my long career, and you're at the beginning. More than the arrests you make, there is one thing that will affect your career. You have to decide who to hitch your wagon to. Which senior officers will help your career and which will take you down. The world is full of retired officers with bitter opinions and no power. So, go back to your desk and think about that.'

How dare he? He hadn't earned the right to come across as a father figure to her.

Emma slumped down at her desk and let her head hang back, eyes closed. Anger, resentment and embarrassment swirled through her. And frustration. She knew how to solve the case but she was being patronised by her boss. She could feel everything slipping away from her.

'That bad, huh?'

Emma opened her eyes. Suse Berman. 'Yeah. It's okay though. Just another day at the office.' She mentally toughened up. There was no way she was showing weakness in front of the detective sergeant.

'Well, if you're sure,' Suse said, before walking back to her desk.

Emma looked around the office. Suse Berman, purely focused on statistics and furthering her career. Brian Chisholm, someone who'd be in court for domestic abuse if he had any other job. Even though he was supposed to be reformed, he still made her uneasy. She had the feeling that he was just spinning his wheels until retirement. And rounded off by the other two constables, Stonor who had looked the other way and Dent who was freshly minted.

She took a deep breath. It was not time for her to strike out alone. She was part of a team. She just needed to find a way in. She took a breath and felt tears prick at the corner of her eyes. She went back over Slater's words as she left his office. She knew it was true. Haines' was finished. Any sway he had had in the force was on the wane.

With great reluctance, she got up from her desk. There was a huge distance to cover between her desk and that of Suse Berman. She knew she didn't agree with her motivations, but they did have common ground. They wanted to solve crimes, and ultimately, like Haines, keep Bradwick safe. Keep it being the same town they knew now.

'Hey, er, Suse. Truth is, I'm not okay.' Suse frowned, waiting for elaboration. In reply Emma glanced at Kev Slater's open office door. 'I'm just going for lunch.'

'I need to grab a sandwich too,' Suse said smoothly. 'I'll walk down with you.'

Soon they were perched on high stools with coffees that were too hot and sandwiches that were disappointing. They watched the shoppers on Bradwick High Street. 'So, what's up then? You don't usually seek me out, do you?'

'Well, that's… it's just that…' Emma wasn't really used to straight talking.

'Oh, I know,' Suse said. 'Office politics is oblique but I've no time for that. I can tell you don't agree with my outlook – you're a bit too bleeding heart liberal. Whereas I'm more hard headed, practical.' She sipped her over-hot coffee and the two women stole sideways looks at each other, measuring up. 'So, the fact that you've come to me, well, that is interesting, isn't it? What's Slater gone and done now?'

'I think it's partly my fault.' Emma took a deep breath. She was about to cross a line. 'Listen, can I trust you?'

'Let me guess, you're still in touch with Rob Haines? Our disgraced ex-leader who's hiding from a corruption charge by staying on medical leave?'

'That's a bit harsh. And is it that obvious?'

'Yeah. I mean, you are the type who would be loyal to your friends even against your boss's instructions.' Emma was momentarily stunned that she was so transparent. 'It's not you, I make it a point to know who I'm working with. I intend to get on in this job and that won't happen if I get blindsided by something.' She softened and attempted to look conciliatory. 'What's Rob done now? I wouldn't worry about trashing his reputation – I think that ship has sailed. And I know how to keep my mouth shut.'

'You sure?'

'Oh for God's sake, Emma! You wanted to talk to me away from the office, either tell me or we can both go back to work and carry on bashing our heads against the wall that is this case.'

'Okay. Well, you know Rob was briefly attached to the case but had his access rights removed?' Suse nodded. 'That's not quite the whole story. Rob made some written notes on the case which he kept. He's still been working on them and he's found something that we've missed. Could be just what we need to crack the case.'

Suse chuckled softly. It was the first time Emma had seen her even vaguely cheerful. 'And you went to Slater with this? Oh, I wish I'd been there to see his face. I know it makes sense bringing in more local experience, but Slater hates it. Having to ask for help from the last person to run CID is bad enough, but the fact that he was a chief inspector as well? He outranked Slater and was everything that he wasn't – popular, unorthodox and a good thief taker. That's such a blow to his ego. He can't solve a proper case on his own, so he has to go to a bent copper for help.'

Emma opened her mouth to say that Haines wasn't bent. But she had to shut it again. 'Haines had his heart in the right place,' she said weakly.

'Oh, that much was clear,' Suse agreed. 'He was a good officer, someone I could've dealt with.'

'Anyway, he's found the pattern we've been looking for. All three crimes were reported by women who were all the same age. And they grew up in the same area and went to the same school, in the same year.'

Suse went very still. In a perfectly even voice, she asked, 'Which area exactly did they grow up in?'

'On the Seaview Estate, why?'

'Oh Christ! We have dropped the ball on this one. Give me a moment, Brian needs to hear this.' Without waiting, she got her phone out and had a hurried conversation with Brian. Then, the two women waited awkwardly. Emma knew they had little in common, so instead of making small talk, she concentrated on eating her sandwich. She could sense that something big was happening and her instincts, honed over her years in the police, were to eat now, before something big happened.

She was also curious. Suse didn't appear bothered or upset by her revelation. She actually seemed excited, as if Emma had turned up with a missing piece of the puzzle.

Finally Brian bustled into the café. As usual he looked slightly dishevelled and a bit out of place. As soon as he sat down with his food and drink, Suse said, 'Emma has the missing piece of the Seaview Theory.'

'Seaview Theory?' Emma asked.

Brian heaved a huge sigh. 'We've been working on some theories under the table. We figured that our esteemed boss, DI Slater, wasn't, how shall I put it, open to new ideas. But equally we could see that the old ideas weren't panning out. I was listening when you kept on at him about Callum Frost. You were right, it was a clue and a big one.' Emma couldn't hide her surprise. 'I'm not a bad copper,' Brian insisted. 'I know you're in thick with Rob Haines and he's no doubt told you how I'm a wife beater who's lucky to have a job and not be in prison. How close am I?'

'Yeah, something like that,' Emma said, mortified that what she'd been thinking was laid bare.

'Well, I didn't get on with Rob Haines, that's no secret. And I did get in some trouble. But I'm still police and I still want this killer caught.' There was an awkward pause. 'Back to what I was saying. I heard what you were saying and started looking at the Seaview in relation to these murders. First of all, you could walk from there to the motel in around twenty minutes. No CCTV, no car number plates, in and out. The second victim, Garner, was sofa-surfing and several of the places he stopped over were also on the Seaview.'

'And the third one was stuffing leaflets through doors on the Seaview Estate,' Emma said in a stunned voice. She was amazed. Not only were the two sergeants actively working behind Kev's back, but they also had uncovered more links between the killings. And it all pointed back to the Seaview Estate.

'What's Emma's new information then?' Brian asked.

Briefly, she repeated what she'd just told Suse, emphasising that the three witnesses would've just finished school and been on the estate at the time of Callum Frost's disappearance.

Brian and Suse looked at each other. They nodded as they reached agreement. Suse said, 'We need to action this. And fast.'

'We haven't got enough manpower,' Brian said. 'We must interview each of these three women at the same time. If they know each other, then we don't want them comparing notes. Suse, you take Emma and do one. I'll tell Andy to take young Nick along. And I'll call in a favour I'm owed and get a uniform to accompany me. This has to be done completely by the book.'

'What about the boss?' Emma asked.

'You've already tried to tell him, haven't you love?' Brian said kindly. 'And he wasn't listening. We can't let this get bogged down in his protocol and form filling. Let's find out what the link is between these three women, Callum Frost and the Seaview Estate. Then we'll go to him.'

Chapter Thirty-Eight

Soon, everything had been put in place. In order to catch everyone when they were in, and to avoid Slater finding out too much about what they were up to, early evening interviews had been planned.

Suse and Emma drove together, initially in silence, until Suse spoke. 'We're going to have to approach this carefully, you know.'

'Why? What could be the problem?'

'Well, this is a witness for one thing, so no charging in there like she's a suspect. And, while your information is very useful, we still have no idea why there is a link.'

'I did say–'

'I know what you theorised with Rob Haines. But there's no way to know if that's right or not. Usually we ask people if they have any enemies, anyone who'd be capable of this. But I don't want to tip our hand too early, I don't want them knowing that we're looking at all three of them.'

'Surely we can simply ask if they know the other two, or if they're in regular touch? Some people make friendships at school that last a lifetime.' Emma kept focused on the road ahead, but she could feel Suse turn to study her. It was no secret that Emma had few ties to her past.

'That'd be fine. But we just need to fish, ask how they're doing, see what they remember of Callum Frost, that kind of thing. And we need to make notes, to record as much as we can.'

This was really basic interview technique and Emma would normally have felt insulted and patronised. But she also knew how key these three interviews were going to be. And how nervous Suse must be. They were going behind the boss's back and this was their one chance to get the information before the three women knew that the police had made the connection. Until they knew what that link was, there was no way of preventing the killer from finding out what they knew either.

Finally, they arrived at the house in Coopers End. Where Seaview still clung on to some community spirit, Coopers End was the poor relation. Despite that, Eileen Sanders let them in and soon they were sat on a crushed velour sofa.

'We just thought we'd pop in to see how you were doing after the incident at the hotel,' Suse said.

'Did you now?' Eileen replied, her eyes sliding from one officer to the other. 'Always send out plain clothes to do that, do you? Weeks after the liaison officer has buggered off?' There was a tense silence. 'Well, if you must know, fairly awful. I couldn't work at the hotel any more. Every time I went to open a door, I had flashbacks and started shaking. The boss tried to be nice about it but,' she shrugged, 'it's tough out there. Can't live on benefits, they'd force me to go back to the hotel. Now I'm cleaning offices. The hours and pay are worse, and there's no chance of promotion.' She looked down and sullen. 'I was trying to get it together, you know. The hotel trade, you can work your way up, supervisor, housekeeper.' She stopped talking and looked mutinous. Both Emma and Suse knew that silence was the best way to keep her talking. Eventually she started again, but hesitantly as if the words were dragged out of her. 'Teachers always said I could be something, but well that didn't happen. Thought if I did well at the motel, I might just make something, finally. But now? Cleaning offices, that's a dead end. You know, what can you do?'

There was an awkward pause after the emotion from Eileen, but she was unfazed about laying her heart open. She just picked up a packet, shook out a fresh cigarette and lit it. All the time, her face was hard as she blew smoke up to the ceiling.

'Have you heard of either an Amelia Spark or a Jenny Plover?' Emma asked finally.

Again, Eileen's eyes narrowed and her shoulders tensed. 'Names don't ring a bell, what are they supposed to have done?'

'Are you sure? They would've been in your year at school,' Emma prompted. 'They grew up a few streets away from you on the Seaview. Probably went to the same pubs, hung around with the same friends.'

'The Seaview's a big estate and Bradwick High was a big school. I can't be expected to know everyone there.' Eileen looked defiant. Emma and Suse's silence meant that they weren't impressed. 'Oh wait. Did Amelia get married? Wasn't she Amelia Foyle?' She frowned and her eyes cut left and right. 'Yeah, I think she were in my class. Can't be sure though, it was a long time ago. Don't see many people from back then, if I'm honest.'

'So, you don't remember then?' Suse asked.

'Not really, we left school, went our separate ways. Didn't end up in the same pubs or jobs or whatever.'

'Did you leave school after GCSEs? Or go into further education?'

Eileen laughed, a short bark without much humour. 'Oh yes. I went and got me some fancy degree at a posh university so I could end up living here and clearing up other people's shit for a living. That was always my great life plan.' She took a drag on her cigarette, aggressively blowing smoke to the ceiling.

'So, if you left at sixteen, then that would have been around the time that Callum Frost vanished,' Emma said, picking up the thread.

'Maybe. What of it?' Eileen was suddenly focused on Emma, the muscles in her jaw bunching.

'Well, you were there,' Emma said, then stopped when she sensed the tension in the room. 'On the Seaview Estate, that's where you grew up, isn't it? What were you doing that Saturday?'

'Right, I don't know what you two are playing at but I don't have to answer your questions. I've got to get ready for work.' She stood up and pointedly opened the front door.

Suse and Emma exchanged glances before silently leaving the house.

When they were sat in the car, Emma spoke first. 'Well, that was odd. I mean, she was hiding something.'

'That much is obvious. The real question though is what exactly she is hiding.' Suse got her phone out. 'No word from the other two interviews yet. Maybe the other two witness were a bit more forthcoming. We'll head straight to the pub and wait to meet up.'

Before she could start the engine though, Eileen bustled out of the house. She was carrying a bag, obviously on her way to work. She also had her phone out. But she was scowling at it, stabbing it viciously with her finger. Finally she jammed it into her pocket and stomped off down the street and out of sight.

'Damn!' Suse said. 'What I wouldn't give to have a trace on that phone, know who she's trying to contact.'

'Oh, I think we can make a good guess. Want to bet that she can't get through because the two people on the other end are sat down being interviewed?'

'Yeah, no I wouldn't take that bet,' Suse said. 'Something does link those three women together and they'll want to talk about it.'

CHAPTER THIRTY-NINE

Soon five members of Bradwick CID were gathered around a table in a quiet pub on the seafront. Sergeant Brian Chisholm had kept all the notes but had dispensed with his friend.

At first they each gave a summary of their interviews. Emma didn't need to concentrate on all the details – it was obvious from the outset that all three interviews had gone along the same lines.

'So,' Emma said, 'it does seem that all three women are hiding something and yet we have no idea what.'

'The real problem,' Brian said, 'is that we have literally no idea what they are hiding. And all three of them are victims. What we need is a fourth person.'

'A fourth? Three are confusing enough,' Andy Stonor said.

'No, listen, they are all victims. So, there must be a fourth person, one who knows all three women and is persecuting them for some reason.'

'Well, Eileen kicked off when we mentioned Callum Frost,' Suse said.

'Yep, Amelia was the same. She said that she remembered it, but only in a general way. But both of us had the distinct feeling that she was hiding something. The tension in the room went right up, as soon as we mentioned it.'

'And the same here,' Brian confirmed.

'So, what?' Emma asked. 'If Callum Frost was killed back in the day, maybe the three witnessed it as teenagers and now the killer is trying to terrify them back into silence.'

'That doesn't make any sense though,' Suse said. 'There were posters left at all three crime scenes. Three linked murders it stands to reason that we would investigate. Surely if the killer wanted to keep things quiet, then they wouldn't want to draw our attention to the old case?'

Everyone shook their heads and muttered.

Brian tapped the table in frustration. 'What we need is a direct route to find who knew them fifteen, even twenty years ago at school. Some window into the past.'

'I think that might be possible,' Emma said. 'But we'd have to go even further off piste.'

'Of course,' Andy said. 'Plug their names into the Haines' network and see what pops out. At the very least we should be able to find out if they really knew each other or not. Was that what they were hiding?'

'Yes, it is part of the network,' Emma said. 'But I know her too. I'll have to get the number from Rob. See if she's free this evening.'

'Well, you'd better get onto that sharp then,' Suse said. 'We've stirred the hornets' nest without any real idea of what we were looking for. Someone, somewhere is ahead of us on this.'

* * *

A strange group of people gathered in one of the chain pubs that was just off the seafront in Bradwick.

Suse was sat there looking a bit awkward, in her plain work clothes. Opposite her was Rob Haines, and next to him was his Aunt Bea. She was an ex-head teacher and centre for all gossip in the area. Joining them was Emma.

'Officially, on the record, this is a meeting between Detective Sergeant Suse Berman, Detective Constable Emma Angel and yourself, Bea Mathews,' Rob Haines said. Bea's brow creased at his strange formality. 'So, I'm not really here. Except, of course, I couldn't turn down the chance to see my favourite aunt.'

'So, you've resorted to flattery,' she said warmly, 'and bribery. You said that this would all be paid for?' She waved her hand at the meals that had just arrived.

Emma nodded sadly, thinking that her and Suse would have to tighten their belts to pay for this. There was no way this would be on expenses.

'What's so important then?' Bea asked. 'I mean I don't mind seeing you, but you were insistent that it had to be tonight.'

'We've got three women who are of interest in a case,' Emma said, sliding a list of names over to Aunt Bea. 'We think they were lying when they said that they didn't know each other at all.'

'But I checked back through school records,' Rob Haines said. 'And they were all in the same year at Bradwick High. So after five years in the same school, the names at least ought to be familiar.'

Bea took the piece of paper and scanned down it. Everyone around the table saw her face blanch slightly. 'Early noughties? Probably left around, what, 2003 or 2004?' She looked at Rob for confirmation.

'Left in July 2004. I'm guessing from the fact that you know them by name that they stood out for some reason. Either really good or really bad.'

'I've met one of them,' Emma said. 'I don't think it was for academic achievement.'

Bea shot Emma a look and she knew that she'd been told off. 'Oh, don't you underestimate these girls, Emma Angel. They were all bright and could've gone far. Been a real credit to the school.'

'What happened?' Suse asked.

'Went the other way. Too bloody bright. I tell you, the year those three left, minor instances of theft and bullying dropped right off. Trouble was we could never prove a thing. We searched their lockers, tried to get statements from pupils. But there were three of them and they always backed each other up. But they were horrible.' She held her hand up as if to apologise. 'I'm sorry. As a teacher, it's ingrained in me to see the best in our pupils, but every once in a while, you come across some who, well, they're just mean and spiteful.'

'What kind of thing do you mean? How bad were they?' Emma asked.

Bea sighed and ran her hands through her hair. 'This is very tricky. As I said they were bright and there were very few official reports or sanctions. Right. This will give you an idea. There was this girl started in year seven when The Beths were in year eight.' There were confused looks around the table. 'The Beths – we did Macbeth as a play in English and some pupils started calling them the Three Witches from Macbeth. Pretty soon they became simply The Beths. Anyway, this girl lost her mobile phone and was certain that The Beths had stolen it so she reported them. The next week, her cat vanished. The whole school lit up with rumours about what they had done to the poor animal.'

'But there was no proof?' Emma said. 'I mean, cats go missing, wander off, get run over. It's not exactly evidence of a crime is it?'

'That was their twisted genius.' Bea shook her head. 'Either they were willing to kill someone's pet, which is shocking. Or they were happy to let people think that they would kill a pet. To capitalise on an unfortunate event to build their reputation.'

Rob nodded. 'I see what you mean. Rumours in a school can be so powerful. But without proof you can't actually move against them. I bet that no one made any more reports after that.'

'Exactly. I mean, the teachers were aware, unofficially. And there were several incidents in PE. We had one broken collar bone after a heavy tackle in hockey, for example.'

'And you couldn't do anything about that?' Suse asked.

'No, that was Eileen. As best we can figure out she just went in heavy for a tackle and didn't pull back. I was down there as part of the senior leadership team when the ambulance was called. Just for a second I saw a look on Eileen's face. Kind of a smirk, but not quite. As if she was satisfied with what she'd done. But again, hockey is a contact sport, she said she slipped and went into the tackle harder than she meant. Turned on the tears, showed all the signs of remorse.'

'It's so weird. We've just interviewed these women. You'd never know it now,' Suse said.

'And it's no wonder that they didn't want to admit to knowing each other back in school,' Rob said. 'Maybe they've straightened out now and are a bit embarrassed of their past?'

'I don't know about that,' Bea said. 'But they were trouble when they were in school. I don't think Eileen did well out of school, Amelia got married and I think Jenny has a good job.' She shrugged. 'It's one of the facts of the job – you do your best but often you never know how the children turn out when they leave you.'

'But you're sure about them? The three women on this list?' Emma asked, just to be clear.

Bea nodded. 'Of course it'd all be different now. They'd have the Wellbeing and Support team involved, probably integrated with social services. We'd be able to invoke child protection and safeguarding guidelines. Of course, they escaped all that, I think it came in about the same time that those girls left.'

'I'm not sure how much this helps,' Suse sounded frustrated.

'Well, first of all we know they're lying,' Emma said, ticking off the points on her fingers. 'They definitely did know each other. And we have a fair idea why they are lying too, if they were the local bullies.'

'And,' Rob said, 'we now have an idea why someone would target them.'

'Target them?' Bea asked. 'What's happened to the girls.'

The other three all looked at each other, realising that they'd been talking shop in front of Bea.

'You might as well tell her now,' Rob said, even though he didn't really have the authority. 'I have to say, in all my years in the police, nothing that I've told Aunt Bea has ever gone any further.'

'Well,' Emma started. 'These three girls, well women now, have each discovered one of the bodies in a recent string of murders.'

'Those horrible ones that have been in all the papers?'

'Yes, those,' Emma said. 'It's just too much of a coincidence that three people who all knew each other were all at the right place and time to find a staged body. That's why we're looking at them. And if they were bullies, well then maybe one of their victims might be striking back.'

'Yeah,' Rob said, 'but it'd have to be some fairly serious bullying for the victim to wait fifteen years then start killing people and use the bodies as props just to get revenge.'

Emma and Suse looked hopefully at Bea.

She picked up the unasked question. 'Those three girls didn't really have one target. It was more complicated than that. Among the girls that were the in-crowd, they were the top of the tree. Everyone wanted to be their friends, or at least to be like them. But anyone who didn't quite fit in, well, that's who they picked on. The kids who weren't good at sports, or were too academic or didn't have friends. Either to steal things to sell, or just to humiliate them, make themselves feel bigger.'

'But there wasn't any one victim?' Suse asked. 'Even if it wasn't someone they focused on, it could be someone who was more sensitive? Took it harder than those around him or her? This could be really important, it's the best chance we have of finding the killer.'

'Sensitive?' Bea said, frowning. 'Hold on there was a boy, but he wasn't one of their victims. He was a couple of years younger. But we worked out, as teachers, that if we saw him hanging around, then he was probably acting as lookout. But if we went over to where he was, he'd run off to warn the girls. Then when we got there, all we'd find would be the victim. We couldn't ever catch them at it though and with three of them, they always covered for each other with alibis.'

'What was the lad's name?' Emma asked. The excitement was building now. This could be their mysterious fourth person. 'If nothing else, he could be the next victim. We need to talk to him and make sure he's safe. If he has any routines, then we might actually catch the killer in the act.'

'Oh, it was such a long time ago. Jeremy something? He really didn't stand out. Had a couple of brothers that you'd know, Rob. The type who weren't dangerous but always stealing cars and motorbikes, drinking in public, that kind of thing. Bradford or something?'

'The Bradleys? I know them all right. Not major league but always in and out of prison for something or other. At least the older two were. I remember that there was a younger one, but I don't think he even got cautioned.'

Which is why he was happy to leave his fingerprints everywhere, Emma thought.

'That's it! Jeremy Bradley.'

Emma made a note of the name. 'You said that he was two years younger?'

'Yes, now I've heard the name, I'm sure he was two years behind them. It was an odd relationship, to say the least. Kids usually stay in their year groups. If I had to make a guess, I'd say the girls met him when they were selling stolen phones to his brothers. But it was a really odd pairing. He was quiet and sensitive, I'd have expected him to be a victim, not part of their gang.'

'Okay, that's great.' Emma was genuinely apologetic. 'I'm really sorry, I've got to go back to the station. We need to learn more about this guy.'

'I could at least finish my drink,' Rob said, reaching for another chip. 'Seeing as I'm not officially here at all.'

'And I need to go with Emma,' Suse said. 'This is the first possible suspect that we've had in this case.'

Chapter Forty

Suse and Emma were driving back to the office when Emma broached the awkward subject. 'How much does Slater know about all this?'

'I had to tell him that we were following up a new line of enquiry. But I said there was no point going into details until we saw how it was going to work out.'

'That's a good plan.'

'But now, we've got a name that's worth checking out. We'll need to come clean and make this official.'

'How official exactly? We won't win any favours with Kev Slater if you start bringing Rob Haines' name into it?'

'I was going to see how far we could go without it,' Suse said. 'I know you have some loyalty to him, but it could hold us back from finding this killer. We need all the resources available on this.'

'I do know that you're right, that the case is more important. But on the other hand Rob is owed a break. All that anyone ever sees at work is the times that he messes up. He's about to work out a deal and being seen to be helpful to us could really help him.'

There was silence as they drove on. Finally Suse said, 'How about this? We'll go back to the office now. It's getting late, it's a Thursday, chances are high that Slater will have gone home already. We can do some searches, have a bit of a poke around at this Jeremy Bradley character. See what we find.

'If he looks like a good candidate, then we go to the boss with it without mentioning Rob Haines. But, if we have anything solid, something that even Kev Slater can't deny, then we'll bring his name into it.' Emma nodded. 'How much can we get past Kev? I got the impression that you already knew his aunt, Bea?'

'Yes, I met her a while back, the old CID went round to her house for a big summer barbecue.'

'That's good. Any of us could've made the link between the witnesses who discovered the bodies. And then, you could've done the research with the school. And when we sat down with Mrs Matthews, then that was a pre-existing contact that you had.'

'And we did a proper interview,' Emma confirmed. 'Two people present and we took notes.'

'Let's just hope that he buys it,' Suse said.

Back at the office, Suse and Emma were joined by Nick Dent who'd pulled the overnight duty manning the phones.

The first thing Emma tried was the main police computer even though none of the fingerprints found had been recognised. But she did get one result – about nine months earlier, he'd notified the police of a theft from a vehicle. What had gone missing was a quantity of explosives. She copied the details over and emailed a quick query off to the army bomb disposal team who'd helped with the crime scene. She asked if the type and amount was consistent with John Garner's crime scene. But she knew that she was just covering her bases – Jeremy Bradley was looking like their man.

She was just about to start a DVLA search when Nick Dent said, 'Hold on, I've got something.'

'What you got?' Emma asked.

'He has his own LinkedIn profile. This could be the easiest job ever.'

'LinkedIn? What line of work is he in?'

'He's got his own company,' Nick Dent said slowly. 'He does special effects for TV companies as a subcontractor.'

'Suse,' Emma called out, 'Jeremy Bradley has just moved up to number one spot on our suspects list.'

'Seeing as he was the only one on it, that's not hard,' she said, moving closer so the two of them were now standing behind Nick's desk. 'What have you got?'

'You're not going to believe this,' Nick said, 'but he works in special effects for TV.'

'Bloody hell!' Suse couldn't believe it. 'So he'd have all the skills needed. Making things move, blowing things up, working out the numbers on the bridge job.'

'Yeah,' Nick said. 'Even better, his whole CV is there. He started off doing models for an architectural firm.'

'So, used to doing detailed and precise work,' Emma said. 'It's all starting to fit together.'

'He's definitely strong enough to take to Slater now,' Suse said.

'Now or in the morning?' Emma asked.

'I think it'll keep. We'll need to raid Bradley's house so we'll need to get everything sorted. First thing though, we bring this to Slater.'

In the end, DI Kev Slater was slow to totally believe Emma and Suse's story.

'So, you just came up with this link and then went round to see Mrs Mathews, the ex-head teacher of Bradwick High. Just happened to have her phone number to hand, did you Emma?'

'Yes,' she said evenly. 'I'll hold my hand up – you must know that she's Rob Haines' aunt. She holds an annual barbecue and the whole team went, just weeks before the big raid. So, I met her then and thought she'd be a useful contact to keep.'

Kev Slater narrowed his eyes. It was clear that he didn't totally believe their story. 'Well, as long as you can get that past the CPS, we should be fine,' he said before going back to his office.

As soon as he was gone, Suse turned around to the board. She clapped her hands a few times until the whole room looked at her.

'We have a suspect,' she said, turning to write on the board. 'Jeremy Bradley. Some of you will already have had the pleasure of meeting his brothers, Lee and Steve.' There were nods and murmurs around the room. 'But the youngest, Jeremy has kept under the radar, until now.' She briefly recapped the theory about the three girls and their young lookout. 'So now we need to know everything there is to know about Jeremy Bradley, most importantly where he is now.'

There was a new energy in the room as people went back to their desks to do some work that could actually lead to the case being closed.

'We need to find an address and bring him in,' Brian said. 'As soon as possible. He left plenty of evidence behind so as soon as we've fingerprinted him we'll know for sure.'

Nick Dent practically rolled his eyes. 'I don't know how they did things back in your day, sarge, but Emma just said he had a company. Let's start off by seeing what his registered address is. Smart people set it to their accountant or a PO Box, but you never know.'

'Let's just hope that he's made a mistake for once,' Emma muttered under her breath as Nick's fingers flew over the keys.

'Looks like a residential address on the Seaview Estate,' Nick said. He went to the board and wrote the address under Jeremy Bradley's name.

By this time, Kev Slater had come out of his office. 'Right. This is the first proper lead we've had in the whole case. We are not going to mess this one up. I want everyone to work this name and address today. We'll get a full workup on the place, some idea of the lay-out, background checks on our suspect. We'll go in there first thing tomorrow and surprise him.'

'I've got contacts on the Seaview,' Emma said. 'I'll go and chat them up. Make sure he's still living there. See if there's anything we need to be aware of that won't be on a computer screen.'

Kev Slater merely nodded. For someone who had a strong lead on catching a killer, he looked decidedly miserable.

Chapter Forty-One

Emma wasted no time in going round to see Margaret Watts. Luckily, she was in and glad to see her. Soon the two women were sat in her best, front room with tea and cake – rich fruit this time.

'Listen, Margaret,' Emma said nervously. 'We have a suspect in this series of murders that we're trying to solve. But it needs to be kept very quiet.'

'I'll not be spreading any gossip about the murderer, you can rest assured of that. Everyone here on the estate wants him caught. You can feel it when you go outside. Everything's changed and not for the better.'

'Well, we've got a lead, and we're not sure whether or not it is the murderer, but we'd certainly like to find out a lot more about him.'

'Well, go on then, dear, let me know the name. I'm not any kind of mind-reader, you know.'

'Okay, well, what do you have to say about Jeremy Bradley? I've got an address for him that's literally three streets from here, on Brindle Drive.'

'Brindle Drive? That's where his mother lived, all the boys did too when they were at school. She died a few years back, so I'm not sure who's there now. There's never been a For Sale sign though.'

'He has registered his business address as that house. He changed it a few years back.'

'Must have been when his mother died,' Margaret said. 'Do you know what he does for a living?'

'He does special effects for TV companies. He used to make the models for architectural companies. Why did you ask?'

'Oh, that makes sense. He does keep very much to himself on the estate but it's no secret that the garden out the back of that house has all but disappeared.'

'Disappeared?'

'Yeah, there's sheds out there. Well, I say sheds, but it's more of a huge workshop, lots of them all linked together. You know how big they made the gardens on these old properties? It's a right shame though, when the parents lived there, they had a lovely garden. All gone now.'

'So, Jeremy's likely to be there, then?'

'Like as not, if he's registered it as his business address.' There was a pause as Margaret studied Emma. The two women were separated by decades but there was a link between them. 'Are you all right, dear? You look like you've been working too hard.'

'I'm fine. It's just this case. We've all been working so hard on it. You tend to put other things aside when you've got a killer to catch.'

'Well, don't you put off looking after yourself forever, will you? I know I'm old-fashioned, but you need to find yourself a man. Make time to settle down and enjoy life.' Emma looked amazed at her suggestion. 'Oh, I know I'm an interfering woman. But ask yourself, would you want to get to my age and think about how you spent so much time at your desk, about how many cases you solved. Take it from one who knows, the real prize in life is family. Give your parents some grandchildren, spend time watching them grow up.'

'I haven't spoken to my parents in nearly ten years,' Emma said, slightly sulkily.

'Well, that's something that should be your first order of business,' Margaret said firmly. 'You need your family around you. You need to cherish the ones you have and make new ones. Look at my boy Gregory. He's only in his thirties and he's already given me a lovely clutch of grandchildren.' Her eyes misted slightly as she considered her extended family. 'I mean, I won't lie, I would have preferred it if they all had the same mother and my boy was married to her. But, you know, it's the modern world. It's nothing like the one I grew up in. So, you've got to take what you're given.'

'Yes,' Emma said. This was the opening she'd been waiting for. 'What about your boys, Greg and Don? Did they ever know the Bradleys?'

'No, I wouldn't have stood for that. It's the way you bring your children up, isn't it? I knew they were headstrong, but I made sure they didn't associate with that kind of element.' She lowered her voice as she prepared to share a confidence. 'Don was the more easily led of the two. I had to make sure he didn't spend too much time with the likes of the Bradleys. They'd have made him their fall guy given half a chance. Didn't have to worry too much about Gregory though. He was always a smart lad, that one.' She looked proud. 'If he set his mind to something, then he'd do it. He saw the Bradleys for what they were and had no time for them. Look at what he's done already with his career and children.' Margaret paused and considered Emma. 'What about you, dear? Any family or plans in that direction?'

She had never even considered marriage, children or any of the traditional trappings of life. She vaguely assumed that at some point in the future she'd find The One and settle down, but hadn't given it any serious thought, hadn't made any plans.

Her parents on the other hand were a more complicated matter. It was them who had cut the cord when they learnt of the direction her life was taking. But it had been a long time, and while she hadn't changed her mind, she had to be open to the fact that maybe her parents had changed their opinion. Maybe she owed it to them to reach out, to see if they wanted to talk. She still had contacts, it could be done.

'Oh, I'm sorry. I'll never call myself old, not by any means. But I do know that I can meddle a bit. It's written all over your face – I've gone over the line a bit and stirred you up. What are you going to do about the Bradleys?'

Emma leaned forward, to betray a confidence. 'I'll have to check with my boss, but I think we'll be paying Jeremy a visit tomorrow morning, when he's least expecting it.'

'Well, he won't hear it from me. Whenever you put one of the elder Bradley sons in prison we all breathe a bit easier round here. Of course, we never thought the youngest one was any trouble. A bit odd maybe, but there's no harm in that.'

Well, we'll see about that, Emma thought.

Chapter Forty-Two

For once, there was a palpable sense of energy in the CID office. Kev Slater was at the front, taking charge. Alongside the main CID team, a stocky man in uniform was with them. He was introduced as the tactical lead that would be in charge of both securing entry and ensuring the overall safety of the team.

'Right, so we have a number one suspect, Jeremy Bradley, and I understand that we have two known addresses for him?'

'Yes, that's right,' Nick Dent said. 'He has a business address and a home address.'

'I've been and knocked on some neighbours' doors around the home address,' Brian said. 'It seems that at most he visits the house about once a week. He's likely to be living elsewhere.'

'And I went to check out the business address,' Emma added. 'My sources say that it was the mother's house until she died about three years ago.'

'Uniform have had a quiet drive by this morning,' Kev said, picking up a report. 'We've already got the DVLA records so we know that his car is parked outside the house. With luck when we turn up he'll be there and we can close this out. What else do we know about this address?'

'I have contacts in the area. Apparently there is a lot of workshop space over there. All built since he moved in.'

'Workshops?' the tactical leader asked with a frown.

'Yeah, sounds quite makeshift. Workshops and sheds, all inter-connected.' Emma couldn't help but think about the body that had been frozen, the explosives that had been primed and the mechanics of turning a body into a puppet. She wondered what exactly they would find there. How many other horrors had Jeremy managed to dream up?

'What do we think the overall threat level will be? How dangerous is this suspect?'

'He hasn't used firearms at all,' Kev said. 'He prefers a taser to incapacitate and then improvised weapons to finish his victims.'

The tactical leader nodded as he considered this. 'Stab vests will stop that. And we'll be mob handed so even if one of you gets tasered, we'll have batons out and take him down before he can reload.'

Everyone around the table looked uncomfortable at the thought of being tasered. But they could also see the logic. Over the course of three killings they'd built up a picture of someone who was ruthless and remorseless. But the level of planning involved suggested someone who thought things through, made plans. Not someone who'd rush out of their house brandishing a gun.

Curiously, during the meeting, Emma found herself thinking of the barrel that had carried the remains to be dropped onto the cars below. Jeremy Bradley had taken the time and effort to attach a stay to the bottom of the barrel. That had prevented any following cars from being hit by the falling barrel. Hopefully, that meant that he was trying to avoid casualties who weren't any part of his twisted revenge plan.

However, it was a slender hope to base any planning on. And she wasn't going to be the one to mention it in case they went in all complacent and ended up getting hurt.

She had other matters on her mind as well. She needed to do the right thing by Rob Haines. She waited until the meeting was breaking up and then caught the eye of Suse. She in turn laid a hand on Brian's arm. They were going to back her up.

'Boss,' Emma said, 'there's one more thing.'

'What is it, Emma? We've got to get on with the raid.'

'This information came from Rob Haines.' Under pressure from Kev, she'd just blurted it out.

Kev's eyes flicked from Emma to Suse and Brian. The two sergeants weren't exactly standing square behind her but they were still in the room. 'What are you two skulking there for? Did you know about this?'

They both nodded. Brian added, 'Yes, boss.'

'How safe is this? Is it proof enough for the CPS?'

'Of course, boss.' Suse managed to sound slightly offended that her professionalism was brought into question. 'Emma brought it to me and we worked it without any prejudice at all. Every single interview was carried out with two officers and notes taken. All the information is out there for anyone to find. No part of this case rests solely on information from Haines.'

'Well, that's fine then,' Kev said, sounding annoyed. 'Why did you have to bring it up at all then? We can go off and nick Jeremy Bradley and know that we'll make it stick.'

Brian took up the baton. 'He should be there, as an observer.'

Kev didn't reply, just glared at the three officers.

'It's the way it should be,' Brian explained. 'He could've just walked away from the whole job. He's off on medical, no one would be surprised if he just went to the beach with an ice cream and didn't think about the police from one day to the next. Now, I don't like the man, but I do respect that he didn't let the case drop. And without him, we'd still be pissing in the dark.'

'And you all feel this way?' Kev asked.

'More or less,' Suse said.

Emma said, 'This will be a real boost to his mental health. And his final hearing is this afternoon. They'll decide on his future so it'll look good if he's seen to be helping us.'

'Fuck's sake,' Kev muttered under his breath. He was much more a desk policeman, not used to the loyalty between active officers. 'Go on then. I'm not calling him, though. And any part of this goes tits up and I'm going straight round to his tribunal and letting him have both barrels.'

'Thanks, boss,' Emma said.

She wanted to tell Rob herself but didn't want to do it in the office so she went down to the canteen and made the call.

* * *

Rob was back on his couch, watching a James Bond film. He wasn't really watching it as his thoughts were running around the same track – the three girls, Jeremy Bradley and how they might be connected.

His mobile rang – it was Emma. He was glad that they were talking again – he'd been really low when they weren't talking. But he'd never tell her that.

He pressed the button. First of all, Emma brought him up to date on everything that they had learned about Jeremy Bradley. Rob agreed that while they didn't know his motives, he was a very strong suspect. He had all the skills and opportunity to carry out the crimes.

Rob felt a huge wave of relief. He wasn't totally washed-up. He could still do the most important part of his job – solve crimes. He had the combination of tenacity, connections and dumb luck to put the pieces together.

'Even better news, both Brian Chisholm and Suse backed me up and Slater had to agree that you could come to the raid as an observer.'

'Brian Chisholm on my side? Never thought I'd live to see the day.'

'Well, not on your side but I think he respects you. And this is the right decision – this is your break and you should see the end of it. You've earned it.'

Rob thought about going to the station. Back to the workplace he'd been at for over twenty years. More importantly, he couldn't go back and meet the people he'd worked with for twenty years. Everything he'd done relied on knowing everyone from the desk sergeant to the chief constable. The thought of going back filled him with dread.

'Rob? You still there?' Emma sounded concerned.

'Yeah, yeah. Just trying to work out if I could do that.' He thought as fast as he could but couldn't see an escape route.

'What, got a busy schedule have you?' she asked. There was a really awkward pause. 'I'm sorry, Rob, that was thoughtless of me. What do you need?'

'What do you mean? What do I need?' He didn't know how to feel about this, how to deal with it. He'd gone from the high of knowing that he could do the work back down to the low of knowing that he couldn't ever go back to the office.

'Well, how do you recognise people? What can you do? Hair, height, build?'

'Um, well, yes. I guess all of those would help, yes.' Rob could see where she was going now. Maybe he could do this. 'Slater was the one I upset at the crime scene in the woods?'

'Yeah, right. DI Kev Slater. He's taller than me, obviously, but not really tall, probably around five nine if he's lucky. He's so average – brown hair, side parted, little reading glasses that he takes on and off, neither fat nor thin. Oh, and he'll be wearing a shirt and tie, even on a raid, that I can guarantee.'

'Right, yes.' Rob might have had a bang on the head and all the consequences, but at the end of the day he was police. He was used to dealing with descriptions of suspects. He could just treat it as if he had some dodgy CCTV without faces and still needed to identify people.

He went quiet as Emma worked her way through the new shape of CID. Brian Chisholm – big guy, run to seed, curly hair going grey. Suse Berman was at least three inches taller than Emma and probably twice as wide. Nick Dent was the smallest bloke and looked like a blond sixth former. He already knew Andy Stonor, he just had to focus on his mannerisms and voice and he'd have him down.

When she was done, he made his excuses and hung up. He restarted the film but soon he put his head back and closed his eyes. He'd seen it before and let the soundtrack wash over him.

Chapter Forty-Three

Soon, the whole team was lined up on a quiet road in the Seaview Estate. It was a nice early morning with clouds scudding over a blue sky. Emma was hot and bulky in her stab vest. With her were a couple of uniforms who were holding a ram to open the front door. The rest of CID were there too, Brian and Suse looking hopeful. Nick looked even more uncomfortable in his vest than Emma. Kev Slater had actually brought a clipboard to the party. She caught Rob's eye – he was standing at the back looking like a gate-crasher, studying everyone with a frown. She gave him a brief thumbs up and watched as his eyes darted from one person to another. Luckily for Rob, they had to be quiet and everyone was nervous, so there was little small talk.

One of the uniforms went to the front door, everything ready to put it in. He put a hand to it, ready to start breaking it down. And the door swung open on its hinges.

Emma and Suse looked at each other and back to Kev. 'Go on then,' he said. 'We've got a warrant and the door's open.'

They walked up the path and opened the door fully. There were no lights on and the interior was dark, all the curtains drawn.

'Ever feel like you're expected?' Emma said darkly. Suse didn't reply.

They stepped over the threshold.

Emma recognised the layout was similar to the other houses on the estate. It reminded her of Margaret Watt's house. There was a corridor leading away from them, with doors opening off to either side. It was obvious that the place had been well looked after at one time, but then not maintained. Obviously when Jeremy had moved in, he hadn't bothered with redecorating. There was a nice carpet which matched the wallpaper but both were faded and worn.

Emma gently pushed open the door on the left. In Margaret's house this led to the front room, kept for best, where Emma had been entertained. However, this room was dark, with the curtains not only drawn, but nailed down around the edges. Both Suse and Emma had torches in their left hands and batons drawn.

They both jumped as a light flicked on automatically. It was single spot lamp which illuminated a model on a table in the middle of the room. Suse impatiently flicked her torch around the room – it was bare apart from the model on the table.

'It's empty, he's not in here,' Suse said. 'This is a distraction, move on.'

'Wait a minute, haven't you seen the model?'

'It's an architectural model, our suspect used to build them for a living. It means we have the right house.' She shrugged and turned to leave.

'No, look at it. It's the station.' Both women looked more closely at the model. It was indeed a street scene, with the Bradwick Police Station right in the centre. 'Look at the detail. Think about the hooks and wires in the hotel room. Tell me that the same hand didn't make both. It's the same attention to detail.'

'I already said it meant we had the right house,' Suse said, but she sounded less certain now.

But as they both looked closely at the whole scene – the trees and the little people outside the buildings, they instinctively leant back. They could smell smoke. In the light, a thin wisp of smoke started creeping out of an upper window. Soon there was a yellow flickering, and flames started licking out of a window.

Slowly the two women backed out of the room.

'You don't think that means?' Emma asked nervously.

'No, it's just a model. All that voodoo rubbish isn't real.' But Suse looked worried all the same. Tucking her torch under her arm, she pressed the button on her Airwave. 'It's DS Berman, can we have someone with a fire extinguisher in here, please. First door on the left.' She paused slightly, then pressed the button again. 'And can you get in touch with the station?'

'Will do. What do you need from the station?'

'Nothing,' she said sheepishly. 'I just need to check that everything's okay back there.'

While they were waiting, they continued down the corridor. The next room was obviously used as a bedroom and equally obviously never cleaned. They heard someone come in behind them and the hiss of a fire extinguisher.

'Nothing happening at the station. What were you expecting?'

'Nothing, really,' Suse said uncomfortably. 'Thanks for checking though.'

'Kitchen ahead,' Emma said, gesturing to the obscure glass door ahead of them. She wondered what waited for them ahead. She could hear another team moving around to check the upstairs rooms.

She pushed the door open with her baton. The room was well lit. Both women entered and stood to either side. With a whirring, a pair of small toy cars ran across the room in front of them, each with a pinkish white rubber glove glued to its back. They gasped as they realised that it was a pair of human hands. The fingers wobbled slightly as they drove in circles.

Emma flicked her baton and flipped one on its side. But it kept running and scrubbed its way around in circles, looking more like a dead fish than it did before. 'Oh, for fuck's sake,' Emma said, getting more frustrated. She saw a battery compartment as it spun and the next time it went round, she brought her baton down sharply. There was a crack, batteries rolled out and the horrible thing was finally still. Suse took the cue and did the same thing to the other vehicle.

'Do you think...?' Suse asked.

'...they were real hands?' Emma finished. 'Given who we're looking for, I'd say it's likely to be. He's killed three people we know of. Maybe he killed more for practice? Scene of crimes will have a field day here.'

Now they were not focusing on the floor, they looked up and around at the rest of the room.

'Weren't all the cupboards closed when we came in?' Suse asked.

'They were,' Emma replied slowly. She was staring at the bread bin. In a loaf of bread, two bloody eyes were staring back at her. There were red marks and smears on the loaf.

Suse pointed dumbly at a cupboard where a stack of plates were topped with a foot. Like the previous room, everything was perfectly lit.

'You know, both of us are better than this,' Emma said. 'We've seen his crime scenes and we know what he does.' Deliberately not looking at the horrors on display, she pushed open a half glazed door that should've led to the garden. Instead, there was a kind of lean-to shed. But she didn't go through – she swept her torch left and right across the doorway in front of her. 'There. Can you see it catch the light? He's upgraded from simple tripwires to infrared beams. That over there is the sender, an IR bulb. And here is a mirror. Once we walk through them, it's like tripping a wire.'

'We have no idea what they're connected to, but he could easily know exactly where we are in this place.'

Together they stepped carefully over the beam. Emma started to feel a bit better. Now they wouldn't be controlled and led through the maze like lab rats. They would be able to choose their route and hopefully come across Jeremy Bradley unawares.

They passed through another doorway, this time having to duck under one beam and over another. They edged through a shed with several boxes lined up on a workbench.

'I am so glad we didn't trigger that one,' Emma said. She was not paid enough to go through and see what bizarre specimens were in the boxes. She was sure that if she'd tripped the wire then they would've opened like gruesome jack-in-the-boxes.

At the end of the next corridor though, something made them both stop short. There was a faint but clearly audible scratching noise.

Emma thumbed her Airwave and leant down to her shoulder to speak. 'Anyone following in, be aware that there could be tripwires or light beams anywhere. Check every corridor and doorway before proceeding.'

Suse and Emma looked at each other anxiously. 'What do we know about this joker?' Suse asked nervously.

'To be honest, I think we've gone past what we could reasonably anticipate. We need to open this door and arrest Bradley.' Emma reached for the door handle with the end of her baton.

'Are you sure it's safe?' Suse asked.

In response, Emma moved close to the door and stopped for a second.

'What the hell are you doing?' Suse asked.

'Listening. Whatever's the other side of that door is an animal of some kind. It'll know we're here and it obviously wants to get out of there.' She paused for a second. 'I can't hear any growling or barking, so we can rule out a guard dog.'

Even so, they both held their batons a bit tighter as Emma eased the door handle downwards and hooked the door open.

A white furry shape hurtled straight between the two officers and disappeared behind them. 'A bloody cat,' Emma said. 'Of all the things that had us all wound up. Poor thing must've been fed up with being cooped up in there.'

'And,' Suse said darkly, 'that beast is going to trigger half the tripwires between here and the front door.'

'Let's get on with it then, I'm getting fed up with all this nonsense.'

Suse stopped for a moment. 'Fed up? You're not worried? Scared? We have no idea what this guy is able to do.'

'Actually, I have a fairly good idea of what he's capable of. If he'd wanted us dead, he'd have found a way to get one of us alone and tasered us and then overpowered us. That's his method.' She turned around slightly to gesture behind her. 'All this, it's his trade. It might be called special effects but basically he just makes illusions. He is paid to fool people into being scared, but there's nothing behind them. It's all smoke and mirrors. Even against his victims, he wanted them to see disturbing things. He didn't want to hurt them.'

'So, you think there's no danger?'

'You know that body that was dropped onto the car? He secured the barrel so it didn't fall into the traffic.'

Suse stopped a minute and thought. 'So he avoided collateral damage?'

'Yeah, I should've seen it earlier. He was only targeting those three women.'

'It always easier with hindsight,' Suse said. 'What about the explosives then? We might be heading for a makeshift bomb?'

'There's not much chance. I got a reply back from the army. The amount he reported as missing would be enough to blow up the body plus a couple of test runs. Likelihood is that he hasn't got a lot of it left.' After she'd said this, Emma strode off down the makeshift corridor. At the next doorway, she checked for tripwires and beams and then stepped in carefully. Suse was at her heels.

It was the workshop. On the walls were racks of tools, each in its place, neatly outlined in marker pen. A workbench was covered in steel, hardly a scratch on its surface. Along the edge of the bench were a range of vices, in varying sizes. All around were wall-mounted sets of plastic drawers. Most disturbing however was a chest freezer against the wall opposite.

'I'm guessing it's not full of chickens and ready meals,' Emma said, pointing to the freezer.

'I don't really want to know what's in there.'

'But the rest of this place,' Emma said. 'It shows that we have the right man. Everything from the tiny hooks to the bracket for the head could've been made here. Probably the bomb in the body too.'

'You're right though,' Suse conceded. 'I mean, we don't know what would've triggered if we'd just blundered in, but there's no threat. Just a sad little man playing make-believe.'

'There can't be many more rooms,' Emma said, looking at the door.

Once she was through, with the usual precautions, she saw that the room was small and hexagonal – obviously originally a summer house. The floor had been carpeted in white and the only furniture was a large white globe mounted on a large white round foot. With a start, Emma realised it was a chair from the sixties and it was turned away from her.

Nothing happened. Emma and Suse looked at each other nervously. Emma cleared her throat, and as she did so, the chair spun around. Sitting in it was a man, thin and scrawny, with a neat goatee beard and glasses.

'I'm afraid we've already let Mr Bigglesworth escape,' Emma said with a half-smile.

Jeremy Bradley frowned from his chair. 'You know what I was going for,' he said testily. 'And it wasn't Austin Powers.'

'I got that,' Emma replied. 'But Blofeld's cat was never named.' She could tell that Jeremy Bradley was impressed, so she decided to press home the advantage she'd gained over all those afternoons watching films with Rob Haines. 'Although Ernst Stavro Blofeld appeared in over half a dozen films, his cat was never named. So I went with the most obvious parody.'

Bradley looked put out. 'I must admit that it isn't going the way I expected. It's not what I planned out at all. You're meant to arrest me, not banter film trivia.'

'I must admit, I agree with our suspect,' Suse said. 'Although this is much more civilised. I'm used to chasing and tackling them.' She took a deep breath and formally arrested Jeremy Bradley on suspicion of at least three murders. As he stood up to have the cuffs put on, Emma was struck by how unimpressive he was. He was short in stature – certainly no Telly Savalas or Donald Pleasance. The sort of person you'd never notice in the street.

Emma saw the outline of another door and went over to it. It was bolted from the inside and opened easily to a passage up the side of the garden.

Soon enough Jeremy Bradley was loaded into the back of a police car. Various uniformed and technical officers were already starting a room by room search of the whole property.

Emma looked around nervously. A small crowd had gathered – not coherent but a few groups of people standing around with their phones out. Emma could feel the mood was restive. Someone called out that they should be sorting out the drug problem, not spending all their time harassing residents of the estate.

'You coming back to the station to help with the interview?' Suse asked. 'This is a proper result, you should be proud.'

'Yeah, I'll be along in a minute. I'm just going to give Rob the edited highlights of what happened. Then I want to go and talk to one of my contacts.'

'Don't take too long, you'll miss all the action.'

'Seriously, I'll only be a couple of minutes. Margaret only lives three streets away. If I tell her what happened here, she's got contacts on the estate and should be able to calm things down a bit. The last thing we need is everything kicking off around here.'

Suse looked at the groups of people and nodded. 'If you think you can help, you should do it.'

Chapter Forty-Four

Emma decided to leave her car at Bradley's house and walk over to Margaret's. As she moved away from the crime scene, she saw that there was no one about. She approached the traditional green gate, with her head full of what she'd just been through in the house. The emotion of the last few hours had left her hollowed out. On the one hand she desperately wanted to put all the pieces together. She was sure there was a link that existed somewhere between Gregory Watts and Jeremy Bradley, even if his mother couldn't see it. And if Emma could prove that, then it'd be a short route from there to linking Watts to Callum Frost.

On the other hand, she knew that she was already on thin ice with her private investigations into Gregory Watts. She was only here to let Margaret know what had happened and to try to calm tensions. But she wasn't at a stage yet where she wanted Watts to know that she was talking to his mother. She was one step away from a formal complaint as it was.

Her reverie was broken when she heard a door open. She knew that it was Margaret Watt's door immediately. The immaculate form of Gregory Watts was turning from his mother who was holding the door open.

'It was lovely to see you, Gregory.' The words floated over to Emma across the still air. 'It's so good of you to come over every week.'

'Really, Mum, it's no bother at all. It's family and that's important. You're important to me. I'll give you a call in a couple of days, see if I can get Kaycie to bring Jayden over and I'll definitely see you next Saturday.'

He turned and started up the path. His mother closed the door behind him without noticing her other visitor. Emma took to opportunity to observe Watts while he thought no one was looking. He looked smug and content – everything in his world was right. Then he caught Emma watching and his entire face darkened. He stopped mid stride and stalked off to the side of the house.

Emma stood there for a moment, indecisive. One hand was still resting on the gate. Should she go after Gregory Watts? Or continue with her original plan to visit Margaret? Or simply call off the whole idea and go back to her car and get to the station to start interviewing Jeremy Bradley?

'Are you still here? You can't be here, you're not allowed.' Gregory Watts was back, his voice tight with barely suppressed anger.

Something in Emma reacted to Gregory's antagonism. She was a constable who was at work with a job to do. She forgot for a moment that she was just going to see a friend, a simple mission to calm tensions on the estate. Instead, she saw a man interfering with her life.

Her anger reached a deeper level. She was a woman and here was a man who would tell her where she could and could not to go.

'I am a police officer and going about my business. It's not up to you to tell me where I can and cannot go.' Despite her annoyance, she kept her voice level. Long experience had taught her that calmness was the best way to defuse a situation.

'But this is my family. You can't be involved with my family. I forbid you to speak to my mother.' He glared at her hand, still resting on the garden gate.

'I can investigate where I want to, when I want to. You may not have noticed but the world is changing. Women have had enough of men telling them what to do.' She pushed the gate open with her hand.

He moved to block her way. 'Don't make me do this. I have to protect my mother. If you pass that gate then I won't be responsible for my actions.'

The earnestness in his voice gave her cause for a momentary pause. Should she call for help? She didn't like the way that Watts was getting into her space and she didn't want to be alone with him.

She reached for her radio and unclipped it – she didn't want to be leaning her head down to talk which would make herself vulnerable. But as soon as she had hold of it, he slapped her hand and the radio flew upwards. In any other situation it would've been comical, the sort of thing that starts a fight between children. But here they were deadly serious. Slapping at each other's hands, they fought for control of the radio, until it slipped from her fingers and he batted it to one side, where it landed on the lawn. Firmly inside the territory of the Watts family.

Right, Emma thought, that's it. A line had been crossed. A line marked assaulting a police officer. It might be a slap on the hand but in law that was as much an assault as a punch or a kick.

'That's enough. Not only are you impeding an officer in the course of their duty but you've just committed assault.'

'Assault! You are deluded. I barely touched you – there's no mark. And it's all your fault. You came here to disturb my family. If you'd done what I'd said, left me alone, none of this would've happened.'

For just a second he sounded so reasonable. She had been relentless in her pursuit of him and had driven him into this corner. Unable to find any evidence she'd gone after his family and pushed him over the edge.

Then common sense reasserted itself. Gregory Watts was bad, from his grooming of schoolgirls through to stopping her doing her job.

'Give me back my radio, right now, and we can stop this before it goes any further.' While Emma was talking, her left hand crept towards her pocket, towards her mobile phone. But she didn't take her eyes off Gregory Watts.

'I won't be doing that,' he said with a flat voice.

'Well then, I'm arresting you for assaulting a police officer.' Her left hand curled around her mobile phone.

'I told you that wasn't assault!' Gregory shouted.

She brought her phone out to call for backup. In her peripheral vision she saw him bend down to retrieve something from the side of the path.

She looked at her phone, about to unlock it but her hand stung and the phone flew out of her hand. At the last moment, she managed to tilt her hand and her phone went behind her and onto the road.

He held a short length of pipe in his hand and had a smug look on his face. Without thinking, she took one step back, setting her feet into a fighting stance.

Realising now that it was about survival, not technicality and making arrests, she unclipped her baton. In one smooth movement, she swept it upwards and connected with his hand. The pipe was knocked clear and landed soundlessly on the grass.

'You fucking bitch! You hit me! How dare you?' Gregory Watts crumpled down to a crouch. 'Fuck. I think you've broken my wrist! I'll sue you for this. You'll never work again.' He was cradling his wrist in his other hand.

Emma breathed out and relaxed. She put her baton away and reached around for her handcuffs as she approached. His wrist was already swelling so she'd have to consider how to cuff him safely.

She got to him and said, 'Gregory Watts, I am arresting you for–'

He sprang up like a jack-in-the-box, launching himself at her. She was taken off guard and staggered back through the gate.

There was a sharp pain, just above her right hip, followed by a deeper ache that signalled something wrong. Gregory was still close to her, holding something that had stabbed her. Her clothes were lifted as he leant forward, using his weight to drive the blade in. She could feel her stab vest being tugged. Emma didn't know what she'd been stabbed with but he had managed to get it up and under the edge of her protective vest.

Gregory Watts stepped back at the same time she took a step back. She caught the edge of the kerb and staggered slightly. He brandished a long screwdriver at her, held in his left hand. Its shaft was black and glistening with her blood. It must've been up his left sleeve and the whole broken wrist act was just a feint.

She wobbled slightly and her vision blurred. Her side was now burning and tears were coursing down her face. Everything was getting more distant, less important to her now. Vaguely she saw Gregory drop the screwdriver and grab his wrist in the other hand.

Dizziness swept over her in another wave. She had to get back to her car, retrieve her phone, find a radio, something. Gregory Watts was watching her. His expression was fascinated, exactly the same look that a small boy has after pulling the wings off a fly and waiting for it to die.

She could feel the blood running from the wound. It tickled and was warm. Strangely intimate, it followed the contours of her hip and thigh, tracing its way ever downward. When it reached her sock and started pooling in her shoe, she realised how much trouble she was in.

The pain was there, a constant companion, throbbing in time with her heart. With each beat more blood, more life, left her body.

She turned to go, not caring that she'd expose her back to the enemy. She had to leave now, while she still could. As soon as she shifted her weight to start the turn, her legs buckled. With effort of will, she lowered herself to the floor, struggling to stay in control but still falling the last few feet to the pavement. Lying on her side was better, and she took a deep breath.

She blinked and cleared her vision. She was cheered because she now had a view of Watts' shoes. He had built-up heels to make him appear taller. His weakness, and now she knew it. Next to his heel was the green metal post that secured the gate, sunk into concrete. She could also see the first bush in the hedge. She was happy with this vision. Her head swam and she felt sick, still with the constant background pain in her side. Why was she happy that she could see the gatepost? Her head cleared for a moment, and she realised why.

With infinite slowness, battling the waves of tiredness that threatened to overwhelm her, she reached for her cuffs where they had dropped. Her fingers touched them. The leather and metal were reassuring in her hands. She dragged them closer, then closed her fist around them. So many times, in training, she had snapped them open and secured them one handed. Now, she had to rely on that muscle memory. This time it was vitally important.

With a deep breath, she reached out. Snap, one link around his ankle. Snap, the other cuff around the gatepost. She placed her hand flat on the ground and put in the biggest effort she'd ever called on her body to give.

Like a dying fish, she flopped over, just as Gregory Watts lashed out with a foot but couldn't reach her.

'You cunt! You fucking cunt! Do you have any fucking idea who I am? Unlock me right fucking now!' He was literally screaming at her, spittle flying from his mouth. 'Ha! No, you can't, can you? Because I fucking killed you! That'll show you! You can't fuck with me! I'll just watch you die, in your own blood, like a fucking dog in the street!'

Emma watched the clouds float above her. She let her head flop to one side, so she wouldn't die looking at Gregory Watts. A small crowd had gathered on the other side of the street to watch the spectacle.

A thin child, maybe eleven or twelve, right on the cusp of adolescence tugged at her mother's sleeve, pointed to something on the floor. In complete clarity, Emma saw the emotions pass over the mother's face. She looked at Gregory Watts with disgust, finally understanding what he was really like. Anger and disappointment also chased across her face. Then the woman's eyes showed deep pity and empathy when they dropped to look at Emma lying on the floor.

Emma looked straight at the unknown mother. Mouthed, 'Help me, please,' the words were little more than a croak. She had no idea if the other woman had heard her.

The mother leant down and whispered something to her daughter. The girl skipped across the tarmac and bent to retrieve something.

Then she approached Emma, carefully, as she would a wounded animal.

She laid her mobile next to her head. On speakerphone, a tinny voice drifted to her. 'Emergency, which service do you require?'

'Ambulance and police. Officer Angel, number ten forty-nine, injured. Wingfield Road, Seaview, Bradwick.'

Emma breathed out. She had done it. All the energy she'd expended was worth it. She could feel the cold and the dark encroaching. But that didn't matter because she had climbed her mountain. Gregory Watts was immobilised and she was out of his reach. Help was on its way and now she could rest. She closed her eyes and struggled for another breath. Maybe a nap would be all right. Just until help arrived. She drifted off as she waited for whatever end to her pain would come.

Chapter Forty-Five

Everyone was gathered back at the station. Jeremy Bradley was being held in the cells while a strategy was hastily assembled.

'What have you got on fingerprints?' Rob Haines asked.

'You shouldn't even be here,' Kev Slater said stiffly. 'Seeing as I can't get rid of you, you'd do well to remember that you're here on sufferance and as an observer only. So observe.'

Rob smirked to himself but wisely kept quiet.

'We've lifted good quality prints from each crime scene,' Nick Dent said, earning a sharp look from Kev. 'It's hardly a state secret. We have prints from specific items at each of the crime scenes, that we knew the killer brought with him. Those prints have already been cleaned up and entered onto the system. They'll print Bradley when he's arrested and then try to match those with his. As they're not doing a long search, it shouldn't take more than a few minutes to get a preliminary match. Of course, on a case this important, we'll need to get an expert to carry out a final inspection of both prints, so that we're one hundred per cent sure.'

'It'll do him good to stew for a bit,' Suse said enthusiastically. 'And it'll do us good to have all our ducks in a row before we start the interview. There's nothing like conducting an interview when you already know that the bastard's guilty.'

'We still need to know why though,' Haines said grimly. 'Don't get too cocky and mess it up.' Kev Slater glowered at Rob Haines, but he wasn't fazed. Instead his brow furrowed as he had a thought. 'Where's DC Emma Angel? I'd have thought that she would want to be in at the end.'

'She wanted to go and talk to a contact she has,' Kev Slater said, an edge of pride in his voice. 'She wanted to get our message out early and calm tensions on the estate.' He looked at his watch and now he frowned as well. 'But she is late. Nick, get onto the radio and see if you can track her down.'

Just then three different desk phones rang at once.

Nick ran to pick up one of them, and Suse and Brian sat down to get the other two.

For one awkward moment, Rob and Kev stood listening to the sounds of the office.

'Yes, yes I understand.'

'Okay, thanks, that's brilliant news.'

'Yep, thank you.'

All three phones were put down within a few seconds of each other and the officers stood up and looked at Kev, the DI, for direction.

'Brian, you first. What's the news?'

'The news, boss, is very good,' Brian said. 'That was the head of the search team at Bradley's house. All the remains so far are, on preliminary examination, human. That's enough right there to confirm that we got the right man.'

'Oh, that's absolutely definite,' Suse said. 'That was the fingerprint expert. Not only has the computer made the match, but they've got a human to look over them. All three prints, from all three crime scenes. There is no doubt, Jeremy Bradley was present at all three murders.'

There were muted words of thanks and congratulation around the room. Kev Slater nodded to himself and then noticed Rob Haines stood with him. Haines waited for the other man to say something. None of them would be here without his insight. If he hadn't seen the link then Jeremy Bradley wouldn't even have been on their radar. He raised his eyebrows to see if Kev Slater would say anything or even give a nod of thanks. Instead, Kev turned away and went to have some words with Suse.

Haines could've just walked out at that moment. But he knew he was on thin ice. He should be on medical leave at home not in the office. And it was still a couple of hours before his tribunal so he had nowhere else to go. He bit his tongue, determined to see the case through to the end.

Slowly though, the mood of the room changed. People remembered that there had been three phone calls and that Nick Dent, the most junior of the team was standing off to one side looking awkward. When all eyes were on him, he spoke.

'That was the nine nine nine control room. They've just received a request for assistance from an officer down. DC Emma Angel.'

'Do we know what happened yet?' Kev asked urgently.

'No, but she should be all right. We had paramedics standing by for the search and there were also uniforms there to guard the scene. So help got there within minutes of the call.'

'What else do we know?' Kev asked.

'Nothing else. That was the dispatcher. All she got from Emma was her name and number, location and request for police and ambulance.'

'There must be more. Surely they kept her on the phone?'

'They did but couldn't get a response.'

Again the room fell silent. No one knew what was happening across town at the Seaview Estate. They did know that once paramedics and police officers arrived they would be totally focused on helping Emma and not on updating the station with their progress.

A stunned silence fell over the room. It was left to Suse to pick up the pieces. 'One of us has been attacked. We can't do anything about that until we know more, until the reports come in. But what we can do is finish the job that Emma started.' She looked straight at Kev. 'Boss, let's do the interview. Hit Bradley with everything we've just learned and nail the bastard properly. Give Emma something to smile about.'

Kev nodded slowly. 'Uniform and ambulance can deal with Emma. She's called for help so we know she's okay. Suse is right, and she should take the lead on the interview. You were the one who uncovered this trail with Emma. I'll take the other chair. The rest of you can watch from the video room.'

Soon they were all crowded into the video room, focused on the monitor that showed Jeremy Bradley sat at his table, faced with Suse and Kev. Even sitting still he had an intensity about him.

Once they'd gone through the whole process of reminding him of his rights and making sure that he really didn't want a solicitor present, Suse opened the questioning.

'So, Jeremy, why don't we start at the beginning? What's your relationship with Oliver Fairthorpe?'

'Oliver who? I have no idea who that is.'

Suse was stopped short. She looked sideways to Kev Slater, realising that he was out of his depth as well. She decided to go straight in with the evidence.

'Oliver Fairthorpe,' she repeated. 'Financial advisor, family man, left a wife and two children behind? Not ringing any bells?'

'Nope. Sorry, not a clue.'

'You have no idea who he is? Well, could you explain how we found your fingerprints in his hotel room? Not only that, but on the bracket used to attach his severed head to the wall?'

'Hotel room?' Jeremy slammed his hand on the table. 'Why didn't you say? Oliver whatever was hotel man? Yes, he was a prop I set up for Eileen. I find it much easier if I don't know their names. Don't really need to, if I'm honest. It took me weeks to figure out which floor she cleaned, what her rota was. That was the hard part. After that it was easy to find someone on the right floor who was travelling alone and staying one night.'

Suse processed everything that he had just said and homed in on the important part. 'So, you admit to killing Oliver Fairthorpe at the motel?'

'Oh no. I'm not going to go there yet. You're asking the wrong questions. We need to do everything in order, go back to the beginning.'

Kev hastily scribbled on a pad of paper and slid it across in front of Suse. "Don't let him dictate the interview." Suse knew this, it was basic strategy, drummed into both new recruits and seasoned officers on refresher courses. An interview was by its very nature an unequal affair – the police knew everything and held all the cards.

'So, Jeremy, where did it all begin?' Suse asked, with deep misgivings.

Kev stabbed his message on the paper with his pen leaving not just marks but holes in the sheet. Suse scribbled on the paper, "We need to get him talking". Kev frowned at the paper and looked uncomfortable. Finally he shook his head.

Jeremy Bradley sat back and practically rolled his eyes. 'I still don't think that's quite the right question.'

'Interview suspended at ten oh seven,' Suse said in a clipped voice before they both left the room.

As soon as they were in the corridor, Kev Slater had a face like thunder. 'What the fuck was that? It looked like amateur hour in there!'

'I knew precisely what I was doing,' Suse said, her voice tight with fury. 'You're right, he knew what he wanted to say. But if we let him say it, then he'll think he's in control. But we're recording the interview. He'll mess up sooner or later and we can go over the details and trip him up.'

Kev said, 'Bradley has been running rings around us since we found the first body in the hotel room. He's shown us what he wants us to see. It's time to break his control, tell him that we're running this show.'

'Can I say something here?' Rob asked, trying to sound contrite.

Kev glared at him for a moment, then nodded.

'The only thing we can pressure him with is if we show our hand on the forensics. I'm with Suse on this one. Let's give him his head.

Ask him the questions he wants. Then he'll relax and feel like he's in control. That's when he'll make mistakes.' He paused to check that Slater was listening. 'If we push him and he goes "no comment" on us, then we can probably push it through CPS with the evidence. I've no doubt that the full search results on his house will mean that he's looking at a life sentence no matter how the interview turns out. But from what we've seen so far, this might not even make it to trial. If he gets a sniff of a solicitor, he'll be having a psychiatric assessment and off to the funny farm before we can blink.

'But there is one place we can make a difference. If we let him talk then maybe we can get some answers for the relatives left behind.' And, he thought, maybe we'll find out why he did what he did and properly close this case.

Kev pinched his nose between thumb and finger. Finally he gave his answer. 'We know that Jeremy is calculating – look at the way he set up his crime scenes. That indicates planning and forethought. We don't know if he is planning to bring in a solicitor at a later point. I would be uncomfortable about showing too much of our hand too early and giving him ammunition.' He was pleased with himself – he'd taken Rob's words and made them his own ideas. 'So, Suse, give him enough rope. If he wants to talk, let him. But this isn't a fishing expedition. Let's keep him focused on the three murders and the three women who were his real targets. If he strays off that track, bring him back. Are we all clear?'

There were nods around the group. Suse and Kev went back to the interview.

Once they were through the formalities of restarting the interview, Suse asked, 'So, Jeremy, what can you tell us about your relationship with Eileen Sanders?'

'Oh, now that's a good question. Maybe you should've started with that one. I can't think about Eileen without also thinking about Jenny and Amelia too. That's how they were. The three of them came together as a package. A nasty little package. The Beths. They were two years ahead of me so by the time I went into year seven they were already year nine and their reign of terror was well established. I never really understood it, I should've been their number one target. My family never had much money so I had these awful NHS glasses and I've never been a big guy. Even back then I was interested in film so, you know, just a walking victim really.'

'So what happened?' Suse asked.

'They did pick on me, at first. Just the usual things like hiding my stuff, pushing me over or pinching me. But then there was a change, I think they argued and then they started being nice to me. I really didn't trust them at first, but you know, free cigarettes, so I hung around. They started using me as a lookout.' He paused and looked confused. 'And there was... well, other...'

'What?' Suse asked. 'This isn't going to work if you hold stuff back. We have to know all of it. No editing.'

He took a deep breath and let it out as a sigh. 'I suppose now it'd all be different. But back then, you know, I was the boy and they were the girls. So, you know, now it'd be looked at as if I was the victim but back then, I'd have been in so much trouble.'

'Are you saying there was a sexual element to your relationship with Eileen?'

'Yeah, I suppose so. All three of them really. Not, you know, sex as such. But kind of messing around like kids. Show me yours and I'll show you mine. That kind of thing.'

An awkward silence fell across the room. Suse knew the importance of keeping the pace moving. 'Why didn't you report this? A younger boy being abused by three older girls? Safeguarding and all that.'

'Do you know my surname? Bradley? My brothers are both used to sitting in interview rooms. We don't talk to the police. We don't go to teachers. We keep our heads down.' He paused and thought for a moment. 'I know you said all that guff about safeguarding but I started school at the beginning of the noughties. The teachers were pretty much just trying to get through the day without any pupils stabbing each other. It was more containment than safeguarding.'

Suse had an idea of where this was going and how the whole case was shaping up. 'Can you tell us about the last time that you met Eileen, Amelia and Jenny?'

'Ah, yes. You are good, aren't you? Well, it was the first weekend in July 2004. It was one of those hot sunny days. The girls had finished their GCSEs and were free. I was just about to start the run up for my own GCSEs so I was keen to enjoy the summer holidays. We were all hanging around the estate but it was boring. Too many adults, people our parents knew, so no chance to have a smoke or a drink. As soon as we could we slipped off towards the beach, cos we had our own secret den up there. You know where the canal runs down into the river and then the river goes onto the beach and the sea? Well, there's a bridge down there and under the bridge is a room set into the side by the canal. It looks locked but we had managed to rig it so we could open it and no one would know. Hundreds of people must've walked past that and never even noticed there was a door there.' A hint of pride crept into his voice. 'Anyway, that's where we used to hang out. We stashed bottles of vodka and packs of cigarettes down there. Made it a place of our own.'

He paused, so Suse pressed, 'What happened on that day, Jeremy?'

'We were walking down there, just like normal, when we noticed this boy following us on his bike. It was a hot day and we just wanted to get into the den, where it was cooler. We'd already turned up onto the canal path, so our only choice was to follow it past the door, away from the beach, then come back up further into the Seaview and loop back around and try to lose Callum before coming back.' Suse tensed at the mention of the name. 'But we were tired and hot and just wanted to get there. It was Jenny who first said it. "Why don't we ask him to play with us?" We all knew what she meant. My stomach churned up because I knew what would happen next. They'd find some new way to torment him, and I'd be forced to watch. The number of people I'd seen slapped, punched, pinched and even once cigarette burned.' He shook his head. 'So they invited him into the den. All the usual stuff followed, except somehow there was an edge. All three of them were kind of crazy, knowing that they were free from school and could escape. Then he said the words, "I'll tell my dad on you." I think they worked out Callum wasn't like me. He would tell and complain. We'd lose our den, lose everything. So they started trying to pour the vodka down his throat and blow smoke at him. Thought that if they could get him drunk and smelling of fags then no one would believe him.' He stopped again.

'What happened to Callum Frost?'

'They started struggling over the bottle and he wanted to get to the door. I don't know which one of the girls said it first. "Put him in The Pit." At the back of the den was this corridor. It led back to this shaft that went straight down, over twenty feet. I guess it must've been some old flood defence system or other. But we never saw any water down there or anything. We'd brought torches and had a look but it just ended in a small chamber, with a pipe leading in and out.

'They kind of bundled and wrestled him to the edge and then there was an awful sickening thud. And silence. We just looked at each other. Then we left the whole place. Didn't say anything, just walked away. When we got back to the estate we all went back to our own houses. I haven't talked to any of the three since. I don't know whether the girls have kept in touch, but I doubt it.'

In the silence, Suse had only one question. 'We need to know where that den is, Jeremy.'

'I'm not going back there. Never. I won't even walk down that canal path.'

'But think about Callum's parents. They need to know.' She had a thought and without saying anything she got up and went to the door. 'Can we get a map in here please? Large scale, showing the Seaview, Coopers End and the beach.'

After an awkward five-minute wait, a uniformed officer passed a map in. Jeremy leant over it and traced roads with his fingers. Finally, he stabbed at the map with his finger. 'There. It's that bridge. Sure of it. But I'm not going back. You'll need something like a tent peg to jimmy the door. We used to keep one in the grass by the path.'

Suse suspended the interview and then went out to give the map to the team so they could set the search teams off. It was vital they get to the scene before the girls found out that they knew. Then it was back to the point of the interview.

'Now that we've got that out of the way, we have other business,' Suse said. 'Did you kill Oliver Fairthorpe to get revenge on Eileen Sanders?'

'I did. All on my own. And that down-and-out in the woods, I did for Amelia. I killed him too. And the guy with the leaflets. He came round at the just the right time. I did him too. He was hard to chop up, but I think it was worth it. About time those girls got to see things they can't forget.' He paused as if considering what to reveal next. 'There was a tramp in Bristol. Early on when I was planning. I tried to do it with special effects first, but then I got hold of my first body and I realised that you can't beat the real thing.' He nodded to himself. 'Special effects are one thing, but having the real bodies lifts the whole thing to another level.'

Back in the video room, all the officers silently looked at each other. This was a once in a lifetime moment. A killer confessing to four murders as calmly as if he was ordering his shopping.

Chapter Forty-Six

Emma Angel tried to open her gummy eyes and failed. She was so tired and so thirsty. And in pain. Her right side was on fire. Awareness gradually seeped in. She knew that smell. There was the squeak of shoe on vinyl floor, counterpointed with the steady beep of machines and the low hum of conversation.

Bugger. She was in hospital.

She knew that, of course. From the steadily growing burn in her side, the painkillers were starting to wear off. Together with the increasing pain, awareness was coming in. Her memory of the past few hours was patchy. Time in her memory was elastic. She thought she'd spent hours, maybe days in the ambulance. The rocking of the drive, every speed bump feeling like she'd been stabbed again. Paramedics discussing saline solution and blood pressure.

Her memory went further back. She'd had a confrontation with Greg Watts and stripped away all his pretence. In return, he'd plunged a sharpened screwdriver into her side. With skilful precision he'd slid it under the edge of her stab vest and cruelly twisted it upwards.

The transfer from ambulance to A&E to this room was all hazy. She had seen a thousand ceiling tiles, interspersed with lights and concerned faces. With a flash of panic she remembered all her clothes being cut off with surgical scissors. She breathed again when she realised that she was wearing something – probably a hospital gown.

All her memories were hazy with painkillers. She remembered the drip being inserted, she had been lifted into a bed and moved around, hands had checked her. But there were large blank spots. She had woken up with an ultrasound wand being moved over her side but the pain had made her black out again. When she came to, she was in this room.

Shit. She'd been stabbed. Her thoughts were like sludge, slowly moving from subject to subject at random. Was she paralysed? Experimentally, she tried to wiggle her toes and fingers. They didn't move much but she could definitely feel them and everything in between. A wave of relief of swept over her.

Time to open the eyes. Everything was blurry and slowly swam into focus. There was a windowsill and a section of wall. The glass was black, reflecting the room. If it was dark, she must've been drifting in and out for far longer than she realised.

'Angel? Are you awake?'

Damn. She recognised that voice, even if she hadn't heard it for nearly ten years. That was her father. Badger. Badger Stardust to give him his full name. How bad was her injury if they'd called him in? And how long had she been drifting in and out if he'd got here? As if to answer, her side gave a weird spasm and sent pain shooting down to her knee and up to her armpit. She gasped.

'Drink,' she said. Even her voice was croaky.

Her father reached forward and held a glass of water to her lips. Like a child, she slurped a little water and dribbled some down her chin. She hadn't seen him since she, well she hadn't left home. He'd headed off on one of his tours around the country, attending various festivals and meetings and, after a vicious row, she'd stayed behind to go to school. By the time her parents got back, she had left.

He didn't look too bad, given all the years that had passed. He had gained weight, his face filling out. His hair was thinner and grey at the temples, but still curling over his collar. He was still doing the faux-gypsy thing – work shirt, black waistcoat and a red check bandanna.

Her neck was stiff so she experimentally rolled her head to from side to side. And immediately felt worse. Sat on the other side of the bed, silently observing her and her father, was Rob Haines.

She laid her head back onto the pillow and closed her eyes. Why had the stab wound not killed her? It might have been easier to bear than sharing a room with her ex-boss and her estranged father.

'Angel, are you okay?' Badger asked, concern in his voice.

'Emma? Are you still awake?' Rob Haines asked at the same time.

She didn't reply but half closed her eyes as she observed the two men.

'Why did you just call her Angel? Aren't you her father?'

'Because,' Badger said slowly as if Haines was stupid, 'that's her name. It's the name we gave her when she was born.'

'I know that. Emma Angel. I just thought a father would call his own daughter Emma.'

'Oh, Angel, are you still pretending? I thought you just did that in a fit of teenage pique. I honestly thought you'd be gone for a few months, blow all the rebellion out of your system and then, you know go back to being yourself.' There was a dangerous pause. 'Are you going to tell your boss your real name then, Angel?'

She found the energy to shake her head. She shut her eyes and tried to sink back into the bed. With luck she'd be able to sink through the bed, through the floor and out of the room all together. But, no matter how much she hoped, that didn't happen.

'Detective Chief Inspector Rob Haines,' Badger said with exaggerated politeness, 'allow me to introduce my daughter, Angel Rainbow Stardust.'

To his credit, Rob didn't laugh. There wasn't even a suppressed snigger or a smirk. On the other hand, her life in the police was now over. This was a seam of gold for station banter.

'My wife and I changed our names before Angel was born,' Badger explained, answering the unasked question. 'Did you know that after the big bang, elements clumped together to form stars and those were like factories that churned out new, heavier elements. Those then coalesced together until they made the universe that we know now. So, we literally are all made of stardust.' There was a slight pause before he added. 'And of course, there's the David Bowie connection.'

Emma sneaked her eyes open a crack. She could see that the words were flowing over Rob, but he wasn't really understanding what was being said. She felt a rush of warmth and affection. Conversations with her father always involved leaping around subjects. Linking astrophysics with seventies pop stars was quite normal to her.

'Well, I've always known her as Emma Angel,' Rob said evenly. 'And that's what it says on her warrant card.'

She had to intervene. With all her energy, she opened her eyes and turned to her father. 'Sorry, Dad, but if I was going to get anywhere in the police I had to leave the past behind. I got my name changed, all my documents updated, the whole lot.' She paused for breath. 'Mum's sister, Aunty Belle, is down as my next of kin.'

'I know. She called us. Your mother's here too but she went back to the hotel to rest. I texted her as soon as you started to wake up. She'll be here soon.'

'Oh good, a proper family reunion,' Rob said with heavy sarcasm.

Emma took a deep breath. 'I should explain why my dad, well, I'm surprised he's sat in the same room as you,' she said to Rob.

'I did notice that he hasn't warmed to my charm,' Rob said, still being sarcastic.

'Dad, show Rob your forearm, please.'

Badger rolled up his sleeve. Tattooed on his forearm in ink that had faded from black to blue were the words "18th June 1984", then "NEVER FORGET" and under that, "1st June 1985".

'And?' Rob asked.

'Battle of Orgreave.' He tapped the first date. 'And the Battle of the Beanfield.'

'Were you there?' Rob asked quietly.

'Beanfield, I was. Part of the Stonehenge free festival convoy. Herded into a field and attacked by riot police. Unarmed civilians.

Orgreave, I knew folk. I wasn't directly involved with the miner's strike, but people in the community talked about it. I know what happened. I know what the police do, what they are.'

'What some of the police did a long time ago,' Rob corrected.

'Hmph.' Badger stared him down. 'Things haven't changed that much.'

Rob stood and looked out of the window. With his back to the room, he spoke to the glass. 'Yes, I was one of those, a corrupt cop.' He paused to gather his strength. 'I mean, I was never into breaking heads, nothing like what went on with South Yorkshire. I did take money that I shouldn't have and a few other irregularities. But your daughter, whether she is called Emma or Angel, well she wouldn't be corrupted, wouldn't join.'

'What the hell!' Badger moved instinctively towards Rob, hands balling into fists. 'Listen, Angel joining the other side, the filth, was too much. But you were her boss. If you're not one of the good ones, what hope does she have?'

'You're not listening. Emma, Angel, whatever, is one of the good ones. In fact, it was her who shopped me, the whole team, to Professional Standards. She did a lot of good for this town. Wouldn't be swayed by any argument. Good old-fashioned copper.'

Badger nodded slowly, taking in the compliment and what it said about both his daughter and her ex-boss. Slowly, his hands relaxed and opened.

Emma for her part was stunned. Yes, she had saved Rob's life but she had also shopped him to Professional Standards. She had stopped any possible return to the force, although thankfully for her guilt his head injury made that impossible. She still couldn't feel completely guilt free though – she wished she could've moved faster, saved a life and prevented Rob's injury.

But she was amazed that Rob had forgiven her – he even sounded proud of her and the choices she'd made. She must still be foggy with what she assumed were strong painkillers. 'So, what happened then, boss? I guess I missed your final interview?'

'Yeah, no that went okay. I've retired from the police on medical grounds, full pension rights. And I've been assured that the CPS have closed my case, no further action.' He paused for a moment. 'All I need now is a country pub with roses around the door.'

The room went quiet, the tension palpable. Badger obviously wasn't comfortable with all the police talk.

'Angel! My darling! Are you okay? Are they looking after you properly?' A woman burst into the room, all flowing skirts, jangling bracelets and a cloud of incense-like perfume.

'Mum!' Emma burst out. 'You're here!'

The tension diffused. Rob leant against the windowsill and studied Emma's family. Jenny Stardust was clearly in her mid to late forties, with laughter lines around her eyes. Straggling blonde hair fell to her shoulders, dyed in lighter and darker shades. What impressed him most was that she was full of energy. In the muted tones of the hospital room, she brought in colour and life.

'Of course! You think I'd leave my baby girl in a hospital all alone. Besides, we have friends in Taunton, and outside Bristol. We can stay in the area. We'll be here as long as you need us.' She gently laid her hands on Emma's shoulders and looked at her square in the face. 'You don't look too bad. Your aura's got some holes in it though, and it's obviously depleted but that's only to be expected. What exactly happened, love?'

Emma took a deep breath. Both Rob and Badger drifted closer, but kept the bed between them. 'There's this bloke, Gregory Watts. I've been aware of him for ages. Has an interest in schoolgirls but up till now he managed to keep it legal.' Rob nodded. 'I've got friendly with his mum. I went round there today after the raid as I knew there'd be lots of gossip on the estate and I wanted to get our message out first.' She paused for breath. 'Anyway, Watts was there and he didn't appreciate me talking to his family. I was really stupid. He pretended I'd broken his right hand when I smacked it with my baton.'

'No pretending, you did break it,' Rob said with pride.

'But he had a screwdriver, hidden up his left sleeve. Bastard knew exactly what he was doing. He went low and stabbed up and into my hip. Managed to get it right under the edge of the stab vest.' She could see the wide-eyed concern of her family.

'Did they operate?' her mother asked in a hushed voice.

'No, they've been monitoring my fluid levels and blood loss. They think, based on ultrasound, that there's minor trauma to my liver, but no point in operating.'

'And it was a screwdriver?' Jenny said. 'Blood metal, that's what the fairies call it. Iron is never good.'

Rob bit his tongue. He wanted to ask if Emma would be in better shape if she'd been stabbed by sharpened bamboo. But he knew he'd be treated with scorn and then told that the tree spirit would help the healing process, so he kept quiet.

'What happened to the man, Gregory, did you say, who did this?' Badger asked, his voice tight with suppressed anger. 'Have they caught him yet?'

'I'll say so,' Rob said, obvious pride in his voice. 'Young Emma here only managed to handcuff his ankle to a gatepost while she was bleeding out. By the time the uniforms got there to arrest him, he was like a rabid dog. Took three goes with the taser before he could be cuffed.' He chuckled to himself. 'Of course, we had a sharpened screwdriver with his fingerprints and your blood on it, plus you can give a statement when you're recovered. I doubt it'll even get to court. Attempted murder on a police officer means he won't be out for a long time.'

'Still, you were very lucky, Angel,' Jenny said. 'It just shows the kind of risks you're taking.'

'Mum, this is not the time or the place,' Emma said. 'I'm exhausted. I need to get better from this, get my fitness back.' She paused to make sure that her mother was listening. 'But I have to warn you that I'm already working out how to get back to work.' She paused again to take a deep breath and gather her strength. 'I make a difference here. I may have been stabbed but Gregory Watts is currently in a cell. That's one more bad person off the streets. I'm helping. Didn't you say I should be the difference I want to see in the world?'

'It was Eleanor Roosevelt,' Jenny said sulkily. 'Damn it! I raised you, we raised you, to be strong and independent and above all do your best to show compassion.' She shook her head and went to take Badger's hand. 'We wanted Angel to grow up into a headstrong woman and she has.'

Rob, feeling more and more uncomfortable, said gruffly, 'This looks like family time. And it's only two visitors.' He slid out of the door, hardly noticed.

'Wait,' Emma said weakly. 'What happened with Jeremy Bradley?' She was exhausted but still wanted to know exactly what had happened in the interview. Letting Rob speak would give her a time to recover her strength.

Rob looked nervously at Badger and Jenny. 'I'm about to tell Emma things that should stay out of the public domain. Jeremy will be charged soon and that's when the papers will have to stop reporting.'

Badger held up a hand. 'Say no more, we'll get a coffee. Great to see you awake, love, and we'll be back in fifteen minutes.'

When they were alone, Rob ran through the result of the interview and the revelations Bradley had shared.

When he finished, Emma asked, 'So the Callum Frost case?'

'As soon as he highlighted his den on the map, we dispatched a specialised search team because we wanted to get there before any of the women knew we were onto them.'

'And?'

'And we got there first. No one had been in that place for the last fifteen years. There was the vodka bottle with bits of blood on it from where they split his lip. Most importantly they found the shaft with the remains of Callum Frost. We're not sure yet but the evidence should put the four of them there at the same time as Callum.' He stopped and looked shifty.

'What? What aren't you telling me?'

'Well, it looks like Bradley did us a favour. The three women are now so upset by what they've seen that we're going to keep pressuring them. I'm guessing that fairly soon one of them will crack and tell us what we need to know. We'll keep telling them that we've found the den, we have his remains, we have their fingerprints in the same place.'

Emma took a deep breath. She needed to stay awake. 'But the parents. They know.'

'Yes. I mean, it's not the answer they wanted but it is an answer.'

Emma lapsed into silence as she struggled to process this new information. She was saved from dozing off in front of her boss when a nurse bustled into the room.

'Right, time for meds and obs,' she said brightly. 'Good to see that you're looking a bit brighter.' She peered closely at Emma. 'But these visitors have tired you out.'

'And that's my cue to leave,' Rob said.

As she went about her job, the nurse chattered. 'That's a nice bloke you got there.' Seeing the look of confusion on Emma's face, she continued. 'No, not those two. Don't you remember? The painkillers and shock can do that. No, I meant your boyfriend. Brought up a bag with a few bits and pieces. Clothes and the like. Mind you, if he's like most men it'll be stuff you never wear, perfume you hate and nothing useful. But it's a nice thought.'

'Pete was here?' Emma asked.

'Yes. But as soon as the others turned up he left. Don't think he quite wanted to meet the parents, just yet.' Deftly the nurse laid out a small pot of pills and a glass of water.

'It's complicated,' Emma said. How could she explain that she'd just met her parents for the first time in years? Instead she swallowed her pills, then let her eyes close so she could gently doze off.

WOOTENSHIRE

The Wrong Victims is the second Angel & Haines novel and is set in the fictional county of Wootenshire which is in the UK, just south of Bristol and north of Somerset. It is the first instance of a new concept in writing - a Shared Word where many authors can write stories in different genres but all set in the same world.

Please visit www.wootenshire.co.uk for more details.

Please also note that Wootenshire and the associated logos are trademarks.

Learn more about Graham H Miller's books and get a free copy of The List by signing up for my mailing list at:

GrahamHMiller.com

Printed in Great Britain
by Amazon

63894220R00163